MENDED CROWN

MICE AND MEN BOOK 4 (THE WAR OF ROSES UNIVERSE)

LANA SKY

Mended Crown

Mended Crown By Lana Sky

Copyright © 2021 by Lana Sky
All rights reserved.

This is a work of fiction. Names, characters, businesses, places, events and incidents are either the products of the author's imagination or used in a fictitious manner. Any resemblance to actual persons, living or dead, or actual events is purely coincidental.

Cover Design and Interior Formatting by Charity Chimni
Editing by Charity Chimni

ACKNOWLEDGMENTS

Thanks so much to everyone who supported this draft along the way, including the many beta readers who provided encouragement! Please keep in mind that this story includes dark, graphic, and explicit content matter that is not suitable for readers under the age of 18—or for readers who are uncomfortable with the following subject matter: age gap relationships, explicit sex, mentions of sexual abuse, and graphic depictions of violence.

WILLOW

I understand just how fragile the world is. So delicate, in fact, that even a simple drop of blood can tip the scales.

It's happened before. Seven years ago, blood ties were the catalyst to what turned my life on its head. I lost everything, and in the aftermath, became someone else. These recent events are merely history repeating itself—though, laughably, this time based solely on a mistake.

I'm sure of that, despite what everyone else thinks.

Why waste any energy getting upset over a lie?

Mischa did. Anger was his initial reaction, and he shouted in a voice so booming it reached the furthest wings of the manor. I had no idea what he might do. Ironically, a silence fell afterward, so thick that not even the children seemed willing to break it. For days, that suffocating quiet lingered.

I was sure it would last forever.

Finally, a giddy sense of denial broke through. It's like some internal switch was flipped within everyone, and they all woke up determined to ignore and forget. The past few weeks could have been written off as a crazed, shared nightmare—if it weren't for the injuries Ellen and Eli still sport.

And the subtle tension looming over everything like a sharpened knife, waiting to descend at a moment's notice.

Even so, I should be the most eager to play along with the shared denial. Ignore and smile and clamor for breakfast like nothing has happened.

Live on as though Donatello Vanici isn't lurking somewhere beyond these walls.

But he is.

So, I don't leave my room. Not to eat. Not to mingle with the others. I just sit in a corner by the window and read the same series of crumbled pages over and over. They've become worn beneath my fingertips, creased so badly in places the slightest pressure could tear them apart.

I've come to know each passage by heart, anyway. They're my only tie to reality, reinforcing the darkness lurking beyond these walls. Greedily, I scan the gnarled handwriting and sniff the cologne faintly clinging to the paper.

I tell myself that the pain I feel stabbing through my chest with every breath is just a necessary evil in a quest to know more. The truth? Some sick part of me has grown addicted to the agony aroused by anything connected to him.

Masochism alone explains why I keep re-reading these letters more than anything else. The fact is, despite days of study, I still haven't deciphered their meaning in full. At the same time, they remain my only clue to the past, and what really served as the catalyst to the downfall of Donatello Vanici.

I used to think my memories held the answers, but I was wrong. This stack of crumpled letters does, because Olivia, Donatello's wife, wrote them to another man—my biological father, Gino Mangenello. They lack the emotional passion of her letters to her husband. They're blunter, more honest, conveying stark desperation that strikes me to my core.

I parse through the potential explanations, ignoring the obvious answer. Maybe she was lonely and desperate enough to seek out the companionship of her husband's closest ally? Perhaps Donatello disapproved of their friendship?

Or she betrayed him by sleeping with his righthand man behind his back.

I keep picturing her, that beautiful face and hazel eyes. I can't ever recall seeing deception in them. Just sadness. A sadness so heavy a child could never comprehend it.

Years later, I'm only getting a mere taste of that despair. It's emptiness. A hollow agony you can only feel after loving someone so much it desolates you by the end. Then, to top it off, you watch them throw that love away. Throw *you* away as if you never mattered. In the grand scheme, you were worth nothing.

And you'd do anything in the world to fill the gaping wound left behind. Anything. Even tell yourself that you hated him from the very start. If you have to turn that man into a monster, you will. No matter how you distort the past to believe it, you do until it becomes the only truth.

Until the pain can diminish to the point that you can breathe again and even dream of saying his name without screaming.

He's already taken so much from me, and yet it feels like this is his final, cruelest game played at my expense. Take from Mischa something he can never, ever erase and rub his nose in their twisted feud.

I want to believe that. Over the past few days, I've convinced myself that it might be true. Revenge is all that drives him. That and hate. He hates me…

Then I remember that Donatello wasn't who pushed our relationship past that invisible boundary.

I did.

In this instance, he isn't the monster.

I am. Only my victims are far more numerous, and unlike Donatello, I didn't have the decency of leaving them behind. Every day, I serve as a living reminder of the damage I've caused, and nothing assuages the guilt.

"Willow?" A tiny knock on the door heralds the presence of the only person more persistent than Ellen in striving to visit me every day. He sounds winded as if he ran here, forsaking playtime with the others. Still, I hear the thud of him resolutely claiming his place in the hall, most likely sitting cross-legged with a puzzle or book to pass the time.

For a moment, he's as silent as always. Then he sighs.

"Willow… Are you sick? Is that why you're going to a hospital?"

A hospital. I haven't heard of such a trip directly, and I can't ignore a sense of dread prickling down my spine.

"I hope you feel better soon," he adds. "But I don't want you to go away. Okay?"

I don't move to reassure him. Deep down, I can't ignore the small voice in my head warning that my going away might be the best option for everyone involved.

The only option.

"*W*illow?" A stern series of knocks rattles my door.

I must have drifted off, because at some point, Eli was replaced by a taller figure who isn't content to hold their vigil in silence.

"Willow?" The doorknob is tested once more before the door itself opens from the outside, revealing Ellen, framed in the doorway.

I barely manage to shove the letters under my bed before standing to take her in. This isn't a regular visit. She looks tired. Her hair is loosely piled atop her head, her plain blue dress overbearing amid the gray daylight filtering in from outside. With a sigh, she wipes her hands on her skirt and enters the room, closing the door behind her.

I stiffen. She isn't one to barge into a situation unannounced. For days, she's let me hold my silent vigil, respecting the unspoken boundary of a closed door.

One look at her face, and I know that whatever drove her to break that truce is serious. Serious enough that her forced, thin smile doesn't even reach her eyes.

"You haven't been eating," she says tiredly, glancing at the plate left on my bedside table. The untouched oatmeal looks ice-cold now, flanked by a bowl of sad-looking fruit and deflated toast.

"Willow…" With a sigh, Ellen turns the full brunt of her gaze to me. Her lips part, only to purse before parting again. Finally, she swallows as if gathering up the nerve to speak. "Tomorrow, we've arranged an appointment with a doctor," she says softly.

I don't know how to process that—though at least Eli's statements make sense. It seems he's been eavesdropping again, though at least he felt fit to tell me. Apart from knocking on my door throughout each day, neither Mischa nor Ellen has spoken more than a handful of words to me directly.

Not that I can blame them. I've buried myself in old love letters and silence—but they can't escape reality so easily. My heart pangs as I meet Ellen's gaze and examine her delicate features in full.

It kills me to see the hurt in her eyes. At the same time… I can't feel anything. It's like I'm numb, an observer unconnected to unfolding events. I merely watch.

"I know that this isn't a comfortable conversation, but it's one we need to have," Ellen continues. "Whatever decision… We should get confirmation."

There is no mention of whether Donatello will be there.

Because, even if invited, he wouldn't come.

2

DON

"You look like hell," a voice declares, startling me awake. "Don't tell me you've slept here all night, Don."

If the speaker is referring to the hard as hell leather chair I'm slumped in currently, they're right. Groaning, I open my eyes to a dimly lit room where a scowling figure watches me from beyond an open door. "Fabio? You decided the first fucking thing you wanted to do at the ass crack of dawn was visit me?"

Apparently so, not that this is shaping up to be a pleasant visit. He's standing with his arms crossed, that judgmental look on his face. The same one he's been sporting for the past two weeks, in fact—not that I can blame him.

The truth is, I'm lucky he hasn't cut me off completely.

Still, I bristle at his arrival, feeling like a child on the verge of a scolding.

"Why are you here? Let me guess. Mischa's decided to launch another attack on my life? Let's hope he doesn't go after Vin at least."

I'm only half joking.

Thankfully, Fabio doesn't seem like someone desperate to prevent an assassination attempt. If anything, he looks more like a man dragged here against his will.

"There have been some developments," he says, utilizing the stern tone he prefers to deliver bad news in. "Gregori Saleri is dead. Best to get the good news out of the way before giving the bad."

"Good news," I say, swiping at my eyes as I sit upright. My brain sluggishly processes the bombshell. Unlike Fab, I don't consider it good news at all.

"What happened? It seems too much of a coincidence if the old man dropped dead of a heart attack."

"It happened last night, apparently," Fabio says grimly. "There aren't too many details out now. The only bit of information we can be sure of is that Mateo is now solely in charge."

"That is bad fucking news." I brace my hands over the desk before me, scrambling to get my bearings. As Fabio insinuated, I fell asleep here—again. If sleep is even the right word for maybe an hour of unconsciousness. "You're only this morbid when you're stressed. Even if he was working with our enemy, I don't see how his death is a good thing. Especially for the girl—" I jerk my chin in the vague direction of the room where Kisa Salvatore is sleeping. First her father, now Gregori.

"Good news is relative," Fabio says with a shrug. "In comparison to the bad, at least. Keep in mind, Don, that I'm not telling you this because you deserve to know," he adds to preface this unannounced worse news than the death of my enemy. "Call me naïve, but I still think you should have a heads-up…"

To heighten the drama, he sighs before pursing his lips in disapproval.

"Any minute, Fabio," I snap.

"Word is the Stepanovs have booked a private appointment at the hospital for some time this week—"

"When?" I'm on my feet as my brain jumps to the obvious conclusion as to what that private appointment could mean. Son of a bitch, I was hoping even Mischa wouldn't go that route. "What time? Tell me!"

Fabio sighs again. "I'm not telling you when. Not even which day."

"But you know?"

He raises an eyebrow. "Could be tomorrow. Could be ten days from now. It doesn't really matter. Don't get the wrong idea, Donatello. This isn't a heads-up so you can intervene. If anything, I want you to show restraint. This is just so that you can prepare yourself in case…"

His low tone alludes to an outcome even he has the tact not to voice.

"In case they terminate the pregnancy." Saying it out loud guts me. Could Mischa really be that cynical? Though, hell, if I had a daughter, would I encourage her to do any different?

"Don…" Fab frowns, wringing his hands together. He's wearing a suit as usual, but the tie is crooked. He probably rushed here to make sure I heard it from him first. "I honestly don't know the details. We're lucky that one of my contacts at the hospital thought to notify me. But if it is to… At least this way, it won't come as a shock."

"A shock?" I hiss and slam a fist against the desk, so hard pain shoots through my knuckles. So much for restraint. "Do you even hear yourself?"

"Do you?" Fabio counters, crossing his arms. "I'm trusting you to handle this maturely. Barging into the hospital will only result in you having some startled nurse alert the authorities. This is for the best, Don."

The best.

God and Fabio must share the same sick fucking sense of humor—because that's all this is. A twisted joke at my expense, and Mischa gets the last laugh.

Ha ha.

But it's not one damn bit funny. No…

The potential consequences of this mess are too twisted to explore in full. It *must* be a joke. If only I could get ahold of Mischa or his lying daughter, confirm the ruse, and put this all to rest.

Fuck.

"If I could just be there," I muse out loud—but I'm not thinking of the hospital. Instead, I picture Stepanov Manor and its intricate layout. "Mischa's security is good, but no structure on earth is impenetrable…"

"Not this again. You need to slow down," Fabio warns, surging forward. "Listen to me, Donatello. Plotting and scheming won't help anyone—"

"Don't tell me what the hell I should or shouldn't do."

Fabio winces at the fury in my tone, but so do I. Anger toward him is unwarranted, but I can't fucking help it. "Not after your 'advice' got me into this fucking mess in the first place. I think I'm done listening to you—"

"Are you saying that this is my fault?" He inclines his head, his eyes narrowed to slits. Somewhere at the back of my mind, an alarm bell goes off. I've pushed him to an emotional state the man rarely reaches. Enraged. But, like always, his true emotions are hidden behind such a carefully crafted veneer that it's hard to tell what he's thinking at all.

My own expressions aren't so fucking polished. In the reflection cast over the blade of a small knife resting in front of me. It's hers—who knows why I've kept it all this time. I grab the hilt to see myself more clearly, and goddamn what a poor son of a bitch I make. My eyes are bloodshot. I haven't really slept in… I can't remember. My hair is a mess, but it's the look in my eyes that I find the most unfamiliar. The most unsettling.

I don't recognize this pathetic son of a bitch. Deep down, this man knows exactly what Fabio's been hinting at.

This is my fault. And hell, I deserve it after all the shit I've done. My punishment.

Absently, I stow the blade in my pocket, running my thumb over the sharpened edge.

"You need to think clearly," Fabio insists, coming to stand before me. He braces his hands over the desk, his expression contorted into a forced imitation of his usual calm. But he isn't calm now. A blind man could see that. "Plotting a way into Stepanov Manor isn't going to fix anything," he insists. "What we need to be focused on is Vincenzo. Getting him out of the hospital, for one. According to his doctors, he's ready to be discharged as long as we arrange for daily visits from a nurse. Have you even been to see him lately? He asked about you…"

Fabio's gotten his wish. Instead of Willow Stepanova, someone else just as important takes center focus. Guilt is a gnawing parasite feeding off what little sanity I have left. Since that bombshell about the blood test broke, I haven't set foot in the hospital, not even to visit Vin.

I'm too much of a coward to face him.

"Don?" Fabio waves his hand in front of me. "Did you hear me?"

I stopped listening. Not even my old friend has the answer to the problems facing me now. Still, I'm driven to ask, "How can I even look at him?"

"Don…" Fabio blinks, baffled by the question. In truth, there's no good answer.

After seven years of believing the worst—thanks to my lies—he finally has his Safy back. Only now I've gone and…

"I'll tell you how." Fabio slams his hand over the desk, sending a nearby pen rolling off the edge. "You focus only on what you can change. Getting Vincenzo somewhere safe? That's fully in your control. As for the rest? You put it out of your mind. You have to, Donatello. You'll drive yourself mad if you don't. One thing at a time, and only what's within your control."

But he's forgetting that Safy… Willow—she is fully in my control. If I can reach her, I can demand an answer either way.

What will she do if she really is pregnant? End it?

"You want me to focus? Then I need to know the truth. I'll ask you one more time to get me an audience with Mischa. Nicely," I add, meeting his gaze. "If you want me to do this your way, then you owe me that. If not, I'll do it on my own, and I don't think you'll find my methods very diplomatic."

He raises an eyebrow. "You think that this is the time to be giving out ultimatums?" His polished mask cracks further. "Seriously? I know that deflection is one of your primary tactics, but I don't understand how you can even turn this on me."

"How?" I incline my head sharply, eyeing him up and down. "You insisted I work with Mischa one on one. *You* agreed I should marry her—"

"And you promised me that you wouldn't touch her," Fabio counters. "Don't turn away one of the few allies you have left, Don. I know that self-sabotage is another one of your defining traits. Frankly, I'm not in the mood to have you go on a downward spiral. You want to play with ultimatums? How about I set one of my own? You owe it to me to do what I say. Stay out of this. You let Mischa and anyone associated with him come to you, but you don't go looking for a fight. Not in this instance, because I can tell you, Don, that you don't have a leg to stand on anymore. If this was what you wanted all along, then congratulations, you've truly made Mischa pay for what he did to Vincenzo. At least you didn't kill anyone."

His face is red, the veins in his neck distended. I've never seen him this riled, not even during my lowest trips to rock bottom. It figures. Even high on heroin and drunk out of my mind, I still showed better judgment than sleeping with Willow Stepanova.

"I'm sorry, Fab," I say. "But if it's true? If she really is…" I force myself to grate the word through gritted teeth. "If she really is pregnant?"

Fabio looks away rather than answer. He knows what will happen. If it's true, I couldn't just ignore it. I can't stay away and wait for Mischa to stew and plot his next round of revenge.

I couldn't ignore her, either. If Fabio thinks I've won this war, then she's gone and crowned herself the grand champion of it. She got exactly what she wanted all along —revenge.

She may not have my life in her hands, but it's damn close. Would she be cruel enough to lord that control over me?

Could I even blame her if she did?

Fabio's right, though even he has enough tact not to state it outright. This is my fault. I fucked up, and in this scenario, there is no easy way out. Not for me and not for her. No one wins at the end of this game, and neither Mischa nor I have a damn say in it.

Just her. Willow Stepanova.

Her choice controls everything hanging in the balance, and for the life of me, I have no idea what that means.

But I know exactly what it is that I want.

Badly enough that even Fabio and his logic can't derail me.

I need to face her. I need to see her.

And for what it's worth, I need to state my case.

If not for myself, then for *them*—an unborn child brought into existence through no fault of its own.

To do that, I'll flaunt whatever norms I have to.

I'll fight Mischa Stepanov himself.

3

EVGENI

"It's like this motherfucker doesn't exist," Mischa snarls, slamming his hands over the surface before him—a desk overburdened with tax documents and property listings, all stemming from the attack on the harbor.

In the span of time since, we've come no closer to unearthing the figure at the heart of it all. In a sense, Mischa is right. Whoever this mystery figure is, he's damn near invisible, on paper at least. The only clue we have to go on is a name. Jonathan.

That, and the secrets held by a woman who seems determined not to reveal them.

"There hasn't been any sign for weeks," I point out, frowning at the prospect of what that could mean. "There's always the possibility he's gone underground."

"Or, he's planning something," Mischa says. "I've kept eyes on the Saleris, and they've been far too quiet lately. Word is

Gregori has gone silent to his allies. We need to know why. I want you on it. You haven't gotten anything from *her?*" His disgusted tone alludes to exactly who he's referring to.

"No," I say stiffly. I can't resist casting a glance toward the corner of the manor Briar Winthorp has claimed as her own. "It could be that she doesn't know. Or…"

"She's been playing us from the start." Head cocked, Mischa eyes the materials scattered before him as if they might contain the answer. Abruptly, he looks up, fixing me with a probing stare. "You still want to handle this your way?"

My way being sans torture or more brutal methods. Turning my gaze to the ceiling, I mull over the answer. "I think using violence would only give her more of a reason to lie. She seems like the type who won't break easily."

"Fine. Then you find a way to make her cooperate," he growls. "I don't trust anyone else around that witch."

His voice booms to the furthest corners of the study, but the Winthorp woman is the source of just a fraction of the rage simmering within him.

The main culprit is a topic I know better than to broach without tact. To stave off the inevitable, I bite my lip hard enough to sting—but even the taste of blood doesn't serve as a big enough deterrent. Finally, I ask, "And what about Willow and Vanici?"

He doesn't answer, but what can he say?

With a swipe of his hand, he clears the desk instead, sending an array of documents and pens to the floor. The resulting thuds serve as a symbolic representation of the bellowed insults he doesn't voice. Amid the chaos, he strolls to the window overlooking this half of the property.

"We can't afford to be caught off guard again," he says with his back to me. His voice is eerily level, but I feel myself tense, unnerved by the display of calm. "I trust you to handle the Winthorp whore—but I need you to find out what she's hiding. By any means necessary, short of killing her. You have my permission to do whatever it takes. In the meantime, I will handle Vanici."

That statement rings far more ominous than it should. Mainly because I doubt he'll be under the same restrictions I am.

I can't kill Briar Winthorp.

But when it comes to the mess Donatello Vanici may have caused, who knows what Mischa will determine to be adequate punishment.

Something tells me that even death won't be good enough.

The potential consequences of another cold war weigh on my mind as I leave the study and turn aimlessly down another hall.

I nearly run into a figure racing from the opposite direction.

"Sir." A man in black fatigues skids to a stop paces away—but his sheepish expression warns me that he isn't here on official business. "Your guest wanted me to tell you—"

"My guest?" Damn it. Mischa apparently wasn't kidding about the level of control I'd have over a certain unwelcome visitor. As far as the rest of the manor is concerned, she is *my* responsibility. "What does she want?"

"Uh… Tea," the man says. His lips twitch, contorting his mouth into a pained grimace. Though, I suspect his discomfort stems from holding back laughter more than anything else.

"I'll get it," I say, heading for the kitchens.

With Mischa's vague permission of "any means necessary," to go off of, I contemplate if poison would be a sanctioned method.

***

I always hated the saying "when shit hits the fan." It seemed like a lazy summation when a simpler expression would suffice.

Until now. The only terms that come remotely close to describing the mess that has become the relationship between the Stepanovs and Donatello Vanici is a comparison to literal shit flying in every which direction. Never in my worst estimations of how bad things could get did I ever calculate something like this.

At least now I can finally grasp a fraction of the irrational anger Mischa must have felt all this time. To have a danger so close to the very family you'd do anything to protect. Any man with a soul would give in to that rage.

And only God knows what Mischa might be driven to do now. I should be by his side to minimize the risk—not here, on the opposite end of the manor, playing babysitter to a woman who serves as just as big a threat as Vanici.

If not bigger.

My steps slow as I round the deserted wing Mischa ensconced her in. I smell her before I even reach the room. Her presence is like a fucking viper's or some other insidious creature meant to ensnare and poison.

She is poison. Even her voice, seeping through the door as I approach, has corrosive properties.

"Did you bring my tea?" The door opens before I can knock, revealing her leaning against the doorframe, her eyes narrowed, blond hair piled loosely on her head.

The disheveled appearance takes a back seat to another glaring detail—she must have been in the bath, the most likely explanation for the towel slung across her hips—leaving the rest of her bare. Water drips from her body onto the polished floor beneath her feet. She must be freezing, and a quick glance at her breasts reveals hardened nipples alluding to that very fact.

With an exaggerated sigh, she extends her hand toward me without attempting to cover herself. "I hope this time you didn't forget the honey or the sugar."

"You still owe me answers," I point out, keeping my gaze focused on her face. For the past two weeks, that void has loomed between us, not that she seems inclined to fill it.

With Mischa preoccupied, she's been able to go unnoticed, keeping her secrets close to the vest. But who knows when he'll come to his senses and recall the thorn nestled in the heart of his family?

Or decide to destroy her completely.

"You're grumpy today." She reaches for the mug, but I step past her, forcing my way inside.

For all her bravado, she's barely made herself comfortable here despite the passing weeks. Apart from the water dripping over the floor, the rest of the room looks untouched, the bed neatly made. Remove the woman from view, and this room could be as abandoned as the rest of the wing.

But judging from her ripe, slow grin, she's right at home in the Stepanov mansion. It's her mystery that confuses more than anything else. She hides her secrets well behind those glinting blue eyes, but I'm tired of waiting.

I slam the door behind me and cross over to a wooden table positioned near a row of windows overlooking a part of the east lawn. There, I set the mug of tea down.

"Forget the honey," I say to her, claiming a nearby chair. "I would much prefer honesty. You've had days to lurk in the shadows, avoiding any direct questions, but time's up. I want to know everything about your little friend. And I won't accept the excuse that you're still healing. In fact." I grab her tea before she can reach for it, taking a sip of it myself. "If you don't start talking, I'll inflict an injury of my own."

She laughs, slinking into my line of sight. At a glance, no one would be able to discern the wound on her thigh from this angle. But lurking behind those glittering eyes is a shadow that grows more prevalent the closer she comes. With a sigh, her smile falls, revealing a glimpse of the real woman beneath the poise and smirks. Instead of mocking and secretive, this woman?

She's terrified.

But not of me. Her eyes dart to the windows, and I imagine her picturing whatever she believes lies beyond these walls. Perhaps another sniper waiting to silence her forever.

"You're safe here," I say grudgingly, though, in reality, I should want her scared and skittish. It might prompt her to open her mouth a little faster than she seems inclined to. "But if you want to test your luck on the outside, then I suggest you continue not to give Mischa a reason to keep you around."

Her upper lip quirks, reviving that cat-like grin. "He seems to have plenty of reasons not to remember little old me at the moment," she murmurs, toying with the edge of her towel.

Damn. I risk taking my gaze from her face to watch her twisting fingers, envisioning just how many messes she's had her hands in. The more I've mulled over her connection to the violence plaguing Hell's Gambit, the more convinced I am that she's played a much larger role than she's alluded to.

The only question is how.

"Have a seat."

"Give me my tea." She stalks forward, swaying her hips to jostle the positioning of the towel. Deliberately, I suspect. Whenever she's threatened, resorting to her sexuality seems to be her one tried and true trick. Running is the other tactic she loves to employ.

I focus on her eyes again, unsure of which method she'll fall back on now. Heavy-lidded. Her gaze sweeps over me, lingering on any potential spots I may be concealing a weapon. Even while feigning poise, she's still on guard. As expected, her sexuality is her chosen crutch. She runs her fingers across the length of her towel, drawing attention to the pale legs exposed from the knees down.

Gritting my teeth, I don't take my eyes off of her face, ignoring anything lower. Like the pale throat jerking around a hard swallow...

With bold, sure steps, she approaches me and wraps her fingers around the handle of the mug, easing it from my grasp.

I let her take it, noting everything from the way she takes a furtive sip down to the fact that her eyes keep drifting to the door.

"Run if you want," I tell her, leaning back into my chair. "I'm sure Mischa will remember your presence if you come traipsing past his children's nursery half naked and dripping wet."

She laughs, spinning to face me as she continues to sip from her tea. "If I'm dripping wet, I can assure you that it wouldn't be for his *children's* benefit. Just yours."

My eyes narrow before I remember to school my expression. Damn her. I've known women like her before, at least in their beauty and confidence. I've just never met anyone so damn bold in flaunting it. If she thought that by stripping herself naked, she could manipulate me into doing her bidding, I have no doubt that she would.

Honestly, I should probably be alarmed that she hasn't. She must think I'm above such a display, which means she has a different ploy up her sleeve. Luckily for her, I have my own in mind.

Bluntness is the only option worth trying.

"Tell me the truth now or so help me God, I'll drag you from the manor myself and see who comes to claim you."

"Ah, but you don't believe in God," she remarks innocently before taking another sip. Her blue eyes sparkle with mischief. "After all, how could an omnipotent being be so cruel as to put you through the life you've endured? Tsk,

tsk, Evgeni. What a life it's been. No wonder you're so mistrustful and, dare I call it jaded?"

I bristle at the reminder that she knows more of my past than I'd like. In fact, I don't even know how much she's aware of. Which brings up another important factor weighing against her continued presence here.

"You seem to have a close association with the sorts of men who know about my past. Men, I might add, who I wouldn't consider allies of Mischa. Another mark against you in the friend or foe column, and I'll give you a hint— I'm not leaning toward friend."

"So, what are you leaning toward?" She sets her mug down, arching her waist to strain the state of her towel a little further. "Should I inform you that two weeks is more than enough time to wreak havoc if I wanted to? And yet all is well." She gestures around us with a wave of her hand. "No more explosions. No attacks. No kidnapped daughters or injured little boys. While I've been around, everything has been safe and sound."

Which is exactly what I'm afraid of. The fact that she's taken care to point it out, only alludes to how strange this momentary peace has been. It feels less idyllic and more unsettling—like the calm before the storm.

And something tells me that the woman before me is the equivalent of a dark cloud, heralding the first drops of rain.

"I want you to tell me what you're after. What you want. Why you're here. Considering you've barely left this room, I don't think you're inclined to spark much of a family reunion, either. So, if you aren't planning to 'wreak havoc' and you've changed your mind about supposedly wanting an audience with Mischa, then why are you here?"

Her eyes flit away from me, and an answer springs to the forefront of my mind.

"You're hiding."

She laughs, but her smile isn't quite so wide anymore. "You certainly do love to play detective—"

"I do," I say over her. "In fact, I've done my fair share of research on you these past few days." Utilizing Louie, one of the men she pumped for intel on me, in fact. "I've learned that you haven't left much of a paper trail since your initial disappearance over seven years ago. There is no record of a marriage. In fact, there seems to be no record that you've had a son at all. Can you tell me what kind of woman would lie about something like that?"

Though if I did have any doubts about that last part, the way her lip quirks into a frown gives me reason not to. She's a good actress, but not that good. The boy wasn't a lie, which means she's been off the grid since before he was even born. Why go to such lengths? I don't think the fear of Mischa alone explains it.

"If you think I'm such a liar, then why am I still here?" She extends her hands and shrugs. "It seems like you must need me for something, Mr. Evgeni. I think I should be the one asking you to explain your motives."

"My interest is in *information*," I snap. "Tell me everything you know. Unless… That's been your plan from the start. To stall and obscure."

She smiles wider. "Now, why would I want to do a thing like that?" Her tone alone would be enough to confirm my hunch—that's been her game from the start. But no… There's something in her eyes…

And the real answer comes to mind as if planted there.

"You're afraid. You don't know what he's planning, and you can't anticipate his next move. Staying here isn't your ideal course of action, but you don't have a better idea, and you're too afraid to confront him directly or try to weasel your way back into his inner circle. That's the real truth, isn't it?"

She's still smirking, but a glimpse of emotion flashes in those blue eyes, and I feel confident enough to name it this time. *Fear.*

"You're as much in the dark as we are, and, even worse, you aren't sure which tidbits of intel you know could prove your case as an ally, or damage you further. I don't think you're half as innocent in this as you pretend to be. My guess is that you never planned on sticking around this long, and now you're in a bind. A smart man would call your bluff and attempt to glean from you whatever he could; however, he could."

"Is that an allusion to torture, Evgeni?" She crosses her arms, her head inclined. "I wouldn't be surprised if it were.

It's only natural for a man such as yourself to revert to his old ways when challenged."

My spine goes rigid. She got the rise out of me that she wanted, and it's too late to disguise it. Damn her.

"However, I will spare you the dramatic descent into your old naughty habits," she scolds mockingly. "Perhaps you're right, and I've depleted my bag of tricks, forcing me to rely on the kindness of Mischa Stepanov—" She laughs, her serious expression cracking. "Does that even sound likely to you?"

"No, but then again, nothing you've done seems to square with anything most women would be 'likely' to do. Most women would never presumably leave their young son in the hands of a monster, for example."

"I suggest you leave your opinions on women and your expectations for them to yourself," she replies dryly. "I don't think you're in any position to judge anyone—"

"So then tell me the truth, and there will be nothing to judge. What are you after? Why stay here and not try to leave? Not even to find your son, if you're so afraid of this man. This Jonathan."

If I'm not mistaken, she cringes at the name. "I think the question you should be asking is, what kind of man would inspire so much fear in a woman that she wouldn't seek out her own child? That she would rather hide behind Mischa Stepanov, the man who is responsible for the deaths of her own father and brother."

"If I had a child of my own, no one would keep me from them. No one."

She frowns at that, turning her back to me. I've spoiled her game. Deep down, I think she's been dancing around the truth—there's no grand master plan to explain her presence. She's merely a coward.

"I'm going to approach Mischa directly and see what he wants to do with you." I brace my hands against the table and stand. It irritates me to realize that if her aim has been to hide and stall, I've done more than a little to assist her in that effort. I convinced Mischa to take her in and give her a room that isn't a jail cell. I've submitted to be her errand boy.

No more. There are far more important things to deal with, other than Briar Winthorp. Willow, for one. With a sigh, I head for the door—and nearly run into the woman who darts to block my path.

"Wait!" She places her hand on my chest, and I swear I can sense her pulse through the trembling fingers. For once, she doesn't attempt to disguise her nervous energy—it seeps from her, and her expression openly displays one overriding emotion—terror. "You want to hear me beg, is that it? Fine. You send me away, and he'll kill me. Want me to tell you the real reason why I've allowed myself to hide out here like some goddamn criminal? It's because I don't know what he's planning next. I don't!" Her voice breaks, rising in pitch.

No one is this good of an actress.

"Then what are you so damn afraid of?" I demand, pushing against her until she lets her hand fall away.

Her bottom lip trembles, but she fights to keep her expression blank. "I… I'm afraid that I'm next on his list of things to blow up. He has no reason to hurt Ali, but frankly, I've been waiting for him to storm this place since the day you brought me here. The fact that he hasn't isn't a comfort, and especially not after this long. The truth is that I don't have a damn clue what he might be up to. And I can assure you, Evgeni, that's not a good thing. Whatever happened at the hospital must have forced him to change course—"

"Stop speaking in riddles!" I grab her arm, dragging her closer.

Unlike our past encounters, she doesn't pull a knife out of her ass. She gasps instead, her eyes widening.

"You are going to tell me everything you do know," I warn her. "Starting from the beginning."

"Oh, I am?" That smirk returns, igniting a fire in those blue eyes. For a second, she appears as bold and confident as the first day I met her in Mrs. Stepanova's hospital ward.

And that smugness lasts the entirety of five seconds until I palm the back of her skull. A shudder runs through her, and I briefly consider how easy it would be to press too hard. To squeeze this delicate structure between both hands.

I've never killed someone in this way, but some detached part of me isn't unwilling to try. She would make for a tempting target.

"Tell me, or I'll—"

"He contacted me a year ago." The confession spills from her lips as that smug grin falls.

I step back, letting her go, and she scrambles to compose herself, wrenching her towel up to cover her torso.

"My life didn't end up like my darling younger sister's. I wasn't lucky enough to find myself a husband capable of funding the lavish lifestyle I'd grown up accustomed to. After what that monster did to my family, I was lucky to escape with pennies to my name."

"But you were married at some point," I say, hazarding a guess.

Her eyes gleam as she turns to the window, gazing at the impassive fields below.

"Married," she says dryly. "I found someone I thought I loved. I stayed with him. Lived with him. But, as it turns out, I don't know much about love after all."

"You left him," I say, another guess, but she shakes her head.

"No. He died… But the world kept spinning." Her brows furrow as if the concept is one she can't comprehend. "I thought everything was supposed to come to a crashing halt or something. That grief would consume me, and I wouldn't be able to go on. That I'd turn myself into a martyr and end my life in a nice, hot bath." She sighs and shrugs. "But I didn't. I felt nothing, and there were bills to pay and a life to lead. No time for tears or worry. No chance for heartbreak."

"But you had a son."

She nods. "I didn't expect him, mind you. In all honesty, my first impulse wasn't perhaps the most maternal. I never saw myself as the motherly type."

There's a blunt note of honesty in her voice I wouldn't expect. It's blatant and raw, with none of her usual bravado slathered over every word. It's brutal.

"What changed your mind?"

She shrugs again, her head tilted thoughtfully. "I had nothing left to lose, did I? No one else, and I'll admit to you, soldier—I may not understand love, but I'm not meant to be alone."

I raise an eyebrow. Is loneliness what drove her to a man who supposedly stole her child and sent her on the run for her life? Her expression is unreadable from here, and as if aware of me watching, she tilts her face further away.

"I can practically smell you judging me, such a noble man like yourself. But I have to wonder if my little niece, Willow, might be wondering the same things I was at that point in my life. A child brings so much change with them. And yet, sometimes the alternative seems just as daunting."

"Don't bring her into this," I warn, hating the anger leeching into my voice. She knows she hit a sore point, and like any worthy opponent, she's bound to dig in to inflict the deepest wound.

"Why should I? In fact, I think I know far better what she might be going through than you. Though, to be fair, I never had a child with a madman crime lord, merely an ex-Stepanov guard, if you were curious."

"We aren't talking about Willow," I warn. "We're talking about you."

"Yes." She nods. "And you want to hear all the nitty, gritty details, don't you? Well, I had Alexander, and I didn't turn into Mother Teresa overnight. Children are harder than they look. I knew early on that I wasn't cut out for it. I lacked my sister's nurturing instinct, you see. Perhaps I carried resentment toward my own neglectful mother? Who knows, but I found it hard."

"And so, you gave him away to the first man who came asking for him?"

She turns to face me slowly, and I realize that the brief glimpses of anger I've seen from her until now were part of her carefully crafted façade. Real rage on Briar Winthorp is volatile and ugly. Her eyes narrow, her upper lip pulls back from her teeth. Just as quickly, she banishes all emotion beneath a thin smile.

"Why, of course, I did. You've cracked the code, dear Evgeni, and figured me out, motives and all. What use is there for me to explain any further?" She throws her hands into the air and saunters past me for the door. "Our conversation is over, apparently—" She wrenches on the doorknob, revealing the empty hallway beyond. "Now get out—"

"I want to hear," I admit, hissing the admission through clenched teeth. "Or are you just afraid that the full truth will make you sound even worse than you already do?"

"Because you know everything." She laughs, inspecting me with a cold, raking glance. "You've birthed a child alone in a foreign hospital where only the janitor spoke broken English and helped you translate the stacks of paperwork the doctors dumped on you without explanation? You went through labor alone, with only the ashes of someone who gave a damn about you to keep you company? Then yes. You know exactly what that feels like."

The pain in her voice is evident, displacing the charm and leaving it harsh in the aftermath. This is the real Briar Winthorp. A woman left bitter and scarred by life, too cold to see past her own pain.

"Have you?" she prods.

"No. But I'd like to think that I wouldn't abandon any child of mine, no matter the circumstances."

"Oh?" She juts her chin defiantly. "Even if you had no love for the mother? My own dearest mother certainly felt that way when it came to me. She was forced to marry my father for survival, you see. I was just a casualty of that. But my sister? Did you ever hear the tragic story of sweet Ellen's conception?"

She laughs again, but it's a harsher sound. As the seconds tick by, it's as if she's shedding more of her carefree persona, exposing the simmering fury beneath.

"I'll skip the dramatics and give you the short version. My mother had an affair with one of my father's sworn enemies and birthed his child in secret. The catch? She actually loved him, and begged to keep her precious illegitimate child, no matter the cost. I think she convinced herself that I never knew."

She returns to the window, bracing her hands on the sill. As if in a choreographed motion, her hair uncoils from the mass atop her head, falling down her shoulders. Instantly, she resembles more of the disheveled woman lurking beneath the haughty act.

"She thought I never realized that I was always an afterthought to her. That her real daughter lurked in the basement, and while she treated me with care and affection, I never really had her love."

"Is that your justification for everything you've done?"

"Perhaps," she snaps. "Maybe I just like hearing how it sounds out loud? My poor little rich girl story."

"How does this tie into your relationship with this man you're so afraid of?"

"Because I learned that parents show their affection via money," she says coldly. "I have none. Had none. Perhaps the only way I knew to be a good mother was to give my son the only semblance of security and affection I understood."

"So, this man promised you money. Security. The Winthorp fortune?"

"I thought my mother was the only one to stray from her marriage," Briar continues as if I never spoke. "As it turns out, my father might have done the same long before she did. A man approached me when I was at my lowest, with a child I could barely care for on my own. He offered me a way to get Ali everything he was rightfully owed and more. I had no idea the price I would eventually have to pay."

"And what price is that?" I advance on her slowly, expecting her to dart out of reach—but she stays, her back rigid, eyes on the field.

"My soul," she says simply. "As it turns out, I had one left after all."

"So, this man, he claims to be a missing Winthorp heir?"

She exhales slowly and shrugs. "I have no definitive proof. He only showed me a birth certificate, but it seemed real enough. My father never legally recognized him, so he couldn't claim anything on his own."

Suddenly, one piece of this twisted puzzle makes sense. "He'd need a proxy if he hoped to get near the inheritance. Like your son, or Eli."

She nods. "Children from two known and registered Winthorp heirs. He could make a claim to the fortune and wrestle it away from Mischa Stepanov's grimy hands."

A decent plan—yet it sounds too damn simple, all things considered.

"What is it you aren't telling me?"

She spins to face me, but we're too close. Her breath grazes my lips as her eyes find mine, steely and impenetrable.

"I thought I knew what I was in for. That anything was worth securing Ali his future."

"And let me guess." I lower my mouth near her ear. "You had a miraculous change of heart and realized that you'd made a grave mistake."

"No," she says without an ounce of emotion. "I went along with whatever he wanted. I all but shoved my son into his hands, and I waited for the peace I think I was meant to feel. But do you know what happened instead? I looked upon my son one day, and love wasn't what I saw in his eyes. I saw myself staring back at me, and then I had a miraculous change of heart."

She is a damn good liar when she needs to be. I can't decide now if she's telling the truth. Maybe it's a little of both. She's still concealing something, dancing around a larger issue, and I'm tempted to wrap my hands around her throat and wring from her what I can. Anything.

But then she steps into me, pressing her body against the contours of mine.

"If you were a simpler man, this would be the part where I offer my body to you in the hopes that you'd take pity on me and bend yourself to my will. I could distract you…" She trails her fingers along my shoulder, down my chest. "Lure you into bed to dislodge everything I've said from your memory."

I shrug her off, and she chuckles, stumbling back a step. "But I forgot. You are Evgeni Volkov, the stone-cold soldier, loyal only to Mischa Stepanov and his family. So, I would need to devise a Plan B when it comes to dealing with someone such as yourself."

"And what is that?" Too late do I realize I've stepped right into the trap she's set.

Sure enough, a slow, ripe grin unfurls over that pink mouth. "Jonathan's plans extend beyond Mischa, and even me. He has his sights set on the Saleris for now, but I suspect within these past few weeks, both sides have worn out their welcome."

I frown. "I've had my men watching Mateo, but they've spotted nothing unusual."

"Because they aren't stupid enough to operate out in the open," she quips, her head cocked knowingly. "You'd need to look a little deeper to unearth anything they might be hiding. Underground perhaps."

"That hunch you had with the docks proved false. They've been abandoned, and there's been no sign of any activity whatsoever."

"On the surface," she murmurs. "But I suspect they're more active than you think."

And suddenly, I have a suspicion as to why she's hidden out here for so long. "You're waiting for a signal, aren't you? But it hasn't come. That's the real reason why you're cowering beneath the roof of a sister you resent. You're afraid he's written you off completely, and you have no other backup plan. You've been cut off."

"Oh, you make it sound so devious. But it's a good thing you initiated your interrogation when you did." She crosses to the bed and crouches, reaching beneath it. "I was just about to seek out my own answers, but I'd much prefer your company."

I try to hide my shock when I see just what she has—a rolled object that looks like a sleeping bag, dark enough to blend in with the shadows and initially go unnoticed. She unravels it from one end, exposing an array of equipment that seems eerily similar to the various items Mischa's detail are issued.

A flashlight, batteries, a dark jacket most likely stolen from one of the men, sturdy boots, and one object that draws my notice in particular—a knife.

"It seems like a strange tactic for a thief to divulge their stolen goods before one of the people they stole from," I point out.

Her smile resembles that of a cat toying with a baby bird. "If I believed you were willing to do anything about it, I wouldn't have shown you in the first place. But perhaps you aren't as rigid and chained to your rules as I thought. You came here, without your master, for a reason, and if you want answers, you'll come with me."

This woman… It's disarming how hard it is to predict her, and yet she somehow manages to act in a way that isn't the least bit surprising. Selfishness seems to be her one true motive, but—at least on the surface—her current proposal doesn't make any damn sense.

"Why wouldn't I have you tied down and beat the answers from you myself?"

"Oh," she purrs, rising to her feet. "I might have thought you were that sort of man once, but now I've changed my mind. It seems that you might be more…unorthodox than I gave you credit for. You were willing to torture me, after all. That is the kind of initiative needed to outsmart a man like Jonathan."

"You keep speaking in riddles."

She scoffs in exasperation, and once again, a hint of the real woman beneath the bravado peeks through. "Because you aren't listening. If you want answers, then come with me and find them. Otherwise, you can pretend to lock me up and throw away the key, but you know I'll find a way out. Somehow. Someway. Think of this offer as a truce, and believe me when I say that I won't extend this chance twice. Come with me."

"And what was your plan?" I demand, eyeing the items she stole. Among them is a packet of crackers. "Hide out in the woods and hope he forgets your existence?"

"No." She looks up at me, teeth bared, expression fierce. "My plan was to look past the maudlin Stepanov family drama and try to make up lost ground. He's planning something. I know Mischa has his own little plans in motion, but he doesn't know Jonathan the way I do. If you want to find out as well, then come with me."

"Why?" I'm genuinely curious—and on guard. "So you can lead me into a trap?"

Her smile widens. "No. Because, as you pointed out, I'm desperate, and the more silence comes from his end, the more uneasy I become. Something isn't right."

"If I come with you, it will be on my terms," I warn. "Not yours."

She grimaces, and I wonder if she truly thought I'd follow her lead with no questions. Then her resigned sigh gives me an answer—she was hoping I wouldn't.

"Fine. Tell Mischa so he can send out the hounds and make it painfully obvious that we're suspicious. That will surely lead to answers and totally won't drive Jonathan further underground."

"I said I'd go with you on my terms," I say. "But I never said I'd call in reinforcements. You've gotten your wish. I'll babysit you myself, though I think a smarter move would be to act on my previous suggestion to strap you down."

Her throat twitches, and I know that I hit the mark. Still, she expertly conceals any fear beneath another brazen grin.

"That would only slow us down," she says slyly. "I have a much better idea. We go see firsthand what Mateo Saleri and his papa are up to and garner answers. I have enough sense not to take silence as a good omen. So, are you with me or not?"

If I value my sanity, I should lock her in this room and mount my own search. But I can't deny that her intel hasn't proven false so far. I'm sure she has another motive up her sleeve. I'd be a fool not to take her hunch seriously.

Besides, Mischa's orders were crystal clear—any means necessary.

"Get dressed," I say, though she's already shimmying from her towel. "We'll leave within the hour."

"I knew you'd see reason," she simpers, now stark naked.

Internally I'm questioning everything she told me about her so-called past. As much as I want to ignore her completely, I can't escape the feeling that some sliver of truth was lumped within a few carefully crafted lies.

The hard part is to decipher which were which…

Without getting myself killed in the process.

4

DON

I love Vincenzo with all my fucking heart—literally. There shouldn't be room for anyone else in that shriveled, beaten shell. For a long damn time, I believed there wasn't.

Lo and behold, the chaos with the Stepanovs opened up a new space after all. Within that neglected crevice grows something I never in a million years would have expected to feel again. It's so fragile and alien I don't even know what to name it.

Hope? That's too strong a term. Maybe just a chance. A chance for something different, something new.

And now that "chance" lies at the foot of Mischa Stepanov himself. Son of a bitch, no one could have planned this better—but I have no choice but to face this mess head-on. Only, considering my usual methods of conflict resolution, I can't brandish a fist at this problem or kidnap its daughter. Once again, Fabio and his unrelenting logic has a point.

There is no easy way around this other than confronting it directly…

Willow Stepanova is pregnant, and it's mine.

It's a dangerous statement to admit, even inside my own skull, but there it is.

Fabio, to his credit, hasn't been nearly as disgusted with me as he should be. If he punched me in the face, it wouldn't be punishment enough. A good man would cut the cord and leave me out to dry for this.

And there is no telling what Vin will think.

I can't worry about that now. The only thing that matters is getting answers. I spent all morning convincing myself that I would handle this as Fabio suggested and avoid the hospital. Maybe even make a diplomatic appeal to Mischa directly? By sunset, I finally settle on a course of action…

And I wind up in the car.

The hospital is my only lead, but I know before I even put the key in the ignition that it's a waste of time without a definitive date to go off of. I'm heading there for nothing, which means there is no reason at all to alert Fabio. The man isn't my babysitter, and—in this instance, at least—he has no say.

This is my battle to fight. My mistake to salvage.

My future on the line.

I've had seven long years to bury any hope of a legacy beyond Vincenzo. That prospect died with Olivia, and I never regretted that. I never once tried to seek out a different outcome with another woman.

I didn't deserve a second chance at a family, so, on its face, this present reality is too cruel to be true—it has to be a lie.

No one could blame me for wanting confirmation, not even Fabio.

With one last glance at the house, I start driving. Predictably, I've barely left the driveway when my cell phone starts ringing. My first impulse is to ignore it. Keep going. The less he knows of this, the better.

Still, maybe guilt is what finally makes me wrestle the device from my pocket and answer.

"Another scolding for today, Fab?"

"Where are you going, Donatello?" His voice is carefully restrained, falling into that calm cadence. I'm not fooled.

"You're spying on me now, Fab?"

He doesn't even try to deny it as he usually would.

"I know that you wouldn't be heading for the hospital," he says tightly. "Because causing more trouble is the last thing you need right now."

"Of course not," I say, matching his tone. "But this is one issue that doesn't concern you. We tried it your way, and now I suggest you stay out of it."

"Doesn't concern me?" Anger breaks through the pleasant façade. Usually, I'd take it as a warning not to push him further.

But right now, he can just get in line.

"Donatello, I hope you do realize how hard I've busted my ass to keep you out of the frying pan thus far—and that you are dangerously close to worming your way into a situation that pretty words and fast-talking can't get you out of. I think you should turn around right now, get back to the house and wait for me there—"

"Have a good night, Fab." I toss the phone aside and consider throwing it from the car altogether.

Though I can't deny that he's right. There is no turning back from this, but that's been the lesson learned from the very minute Safiya Mangenello came back into my life.

We're tethered together whether we like it or not.

I can blame Fab all I want, but I'm the one who touched her, who kissed her. Who took from her something that I didn't have the fucking right to.

I started this mess.

And I know that nothing I could ever say or do would make this right again. The options are limited in this situation, and some would claim I don't deserve a say in anything.

I don't.

At the same time…

I can't slink into the shadows and watch from a distance. Not this time. I can't wait seven damn years for the consequences to catch up. I can't pretend like this isn't fucking happening.

It's happening.

Even if I don't have the balls to admit it outside of my own head.

Alone in this moment, I try to, only to wind up laughing at the insanity of it all. The cruelty of it all…

My life ended seven years ago. I'm not entitled to more.

And now…

God, it's like the universe is mocking me.

I swerve to the side of the road and slam my foot on the brake, parsing the jumble of thoughts and emotions tumbling through my skull. Impulse is the overriding force, urging me to storm Mischa's manor and confront him directly. Mow down the front gate if I have to. Make my case. Shout. Threaten. Demand.

It's harder to push all of that aside and listen to the small sliver of Fabio I've internalized. Maybe it's my actual conscience? That faint voice warning me to slow down, that this situation is far too tenuous to risk relying on rage now.

Rage started this mess, blinding me to everything but the need to salvage my own pain. But looking back, I can say that I was never alone in this. I was never the sole victim fucked up by the hands of fate.

I hurt her first. I opened the initial wound that she had to suffer and let fester for seven damn years.

And this time, I can't use Mischa as a scapegoat.

Barging onto the Stepanov property would indulge a part of me desperate to react, but in the long run, it would only cause more damage. More fucking chaos.

I can't avoid reality either. No longer can I shun my responsibility.

So what's left? The sad part is I don't know how to even begin to answer that question. For so damn long, I've relied solely on fighting for Vin—either out of vengeance or trying to protect his future.

But when my own future needs protection, I don't feel that same fire. I've drowned myself in alcohol and drugs to ignore the pathetic creature I see whenever I look in the mirror. I've clung to my past as a monster and reflected only on that aspect of who I was.

But *Il Monstro* was a fraction of who Donatello Vanici is at his core. Another version of me existed once. A man who was willing to trust those he cared enough about. A man who dreamt of a family, and cherished his wife more than his own life.

I thought that man was dead and buried—and I preferred it that way.

Resurrecting him is an agonizing process. Hell, it's almost impossible to think back to that mindset, and picture what someone might do if his entire reality wasn't consumed by violence and anger.

When I met Liv, my tenure with the *famiglia* was still in its infancy. I was just a few years in, the youngest recruit to climb the ranks as quickly as I did. She was so damn beautiful. In the midst of running a job, I stopped dead in my tracks, spying her leaving some building downtown. She wore a tiny yellow dress, her hair spilling down her shoulders. Damn, no one else could draw me in the way she could with just a fucking smile.

Our first date was more like an extended car ride where we drove around for hours just talking.

I sink into the memories as I put the car into drive, heading for the city. In those days, it was just as looming, a concrete jungle of skyscrapers. The restaurant we used to eat at. The park we walked through. The hospital…

I can see it towering in the distance, but it isn't the building I find myself parked in front of.

The sprawling cathedral seems untouched by time as imposing as ever. Being here could be a sign from my subconscious, driving me to repent. Or it could be a nudge toward the only damn solution left to me regarding Willow Stepanova.

Ironically, I think back to that night when I first entered the Stepanov Manor feeling some small shred of hope, willing to put my own pride aside for the chance of forging a lasting connection. What had I done then?

I brought myself, unarmed and unguarded.

I brought a gift, wrapped with a white fucking bow, and I told myself that was enough to impress the mysterious Willow Stepanova.

No gift can even begin to heal this rift now…

But it's the only method I have left to try.

And it's the only way she might hear me.

EVGENI

Discover the woman's secrets, Mischa commanded—a task easier said than done.

These days, the world outside of Stepanov Manor is a parallel universe where tension and mystery meld into a gnawing sense of paranoia I can't shake no matter how hard I try. The presence of a viper in the passenger's seat doesn't help any.

I've never seen anyone handle their nervous energy the way she does. Her careful mask conceals her anxiety expertly—from the outside looking in, she's the picture of stoic calm. It's the nuance that gives her away. Her silence. The stiff way she holds herself, straining that debutant posture. Mainly, it's evident in the way her eyes keep darting from the windows to me, as though she isn't sure which factor terrifies her more.

Me? Or whatever might lurk beyond this van?

I'm willing to suggest it's the former.

"So, you want to stake out the Saleris," I say, breaking the silence that's lasted since we left the manor. It's dark enough to obscure most of her expression, and I'm rendered blind as to how she processes those words. For all I know, she could be leading me into a trap. I wouldn't be surprised—I think I'm counting on it. "Why them? And how do I know you won't turn around and present me to Gregori or Mateo on a silver platter?"

"You don't." She's damn good at feigning confidence. Her eyes glitter in the darkness as she cuts her gaze toward me. "For all you know, I could be planning to kill you. Ah! Maybe right at this moment."

I'm watching her, already primed the second she extends her hand my way. The fact that she isn't holding a weapon is the only reason I allow the contact.

Her fingers shake, twitching as if waiting for the second I'll recoil. Or attack.

I find her reaction more amusing than her audacity. This woman seems to be nothing more than illusions and contrast. Bold one minute. Fearful the next. Poised with confidence, and then snarling with anger a heartbeat later. I don't think I've ever met anyone quite so volatile.

"Word of advice. You want to kill me, then you do it now. No fanfare. No hesitation. It's the only shot you'll ever have."

"You sound like you're speaking from experience."

I recognize the probing lilt to her voice. She's not making a low jab at my expense. She's curious.

"And if I am? You were the one who claimed to have done your research on me," I say. "I'm sure you've heard all of the gory details."

"I did," she admits. "But considering how skewed your image of me is based on hearsay and gossip alone, I'm curious as to your side of things. Perhaps you see yourself as the tormented hero of your story and not as how you appear to the rest of us."

I can't resist taking her obvious bait. "And how do I appear, exactly?"

She inclines an eyebrow. "Like the monster. I don't think you can blame anyone, either. Most would hear 'man kills innocent young girl in cold blood' and come to the same conclusion—"

"And most would hear 'woman abandons her son to a supposed long-lost brother she barely knows,' and come to a different conclusion."

"You do that a lot," she points out softly, leaning back against her seat. The shadows obscure her enough to disguise her expression, but her voice is cold. "Deflect when you think I'm getting too close to the topics you deem too personal to talk about. This time, I won't let you deter me so easily. I want to know."

"Know what?" I scoff, hazarding a guess as to her true intentions. "If I'm capable of murder?"

"I want to know if, deep down beneath that self-righteous, pompous exterior is a man who might truly know a thing or two about regret and desperation. What could drive someone to commit an act they can never outrun. That is what I want to know, but I think I'm leaning more toward you being just a pompous ass."

Her laughter adds a musical flair to the sting of her insults. A part of me is impressed.

"Rarely does someone make such a scathing assessment of me outright. Bravo."

"Well, if you aren't capable of killing a woman, you certainly do seem to enjoy mocking one. Fine. I'll let you keep your secrets, Evgeni Volkov. You'll have to prove yourself to me in another way."

"Prove myself?"

Fuck. I slam on the brake, skidding to a stop in the middle of the road. Luckily, this section of the highway is deserted enough that the nearest cars are just blips of color on the horizon.

"I'm getting the sense that we aren't on some secret jaunt to merely spy on the Saleris."

Her reply is soft. "And if we aren't?"

I swerve onto the shoulder and park, aware of the city blinking up ahead, a mismatched array of glimmering lights.

"If you aren't…" Any threat dies in my throat, and I'm startled by the laugh that erupts instead. "It serves me right for believing a goddamn thing you would say—"

"I want you to help me kill him."

The casualness of her speech catches me off guard, and my brain belatedly processes those words seconds after she's gone silent. Kill him. Mischa is my first guess—the man she's proclaimed more than once to have no love for.

Because the more obvious answer is far too reckless, even for her.

"You want me to help you kill the man you've spent days hyping up the intelligence and cunning of? The man who blew up part of the city for seemingly no reason. The figure you claim to be terrified of to the point that you sought refuge with your estranged sister, and her family, whom you hate. I don't know what's more insane? That you think I'd go along with it so easily, or that you'd think I would consent to doing a damn thing with you."

The anger in my voice is partly for show, considering I've already agreed to her plan—we're here, after all. And as dangerous as this man is, death may be the only feasible way of ending the threat he presents for good.

"Well, when you put it that way, the self-righteousness really shines through," she says dryly. Then she lunges for the door on her end, shoving it open.

I don't move to stop her. "What are you doing?"

"I'll take my chances getting struck by the next passing semi and put myself out of my misery," she says. "I thought dealing with a madman was hard enough, but a condescending murderer? That takes the cake."

For all her bravado, she doesn't move, just allowing the night air and sounds of bustling traffic to flood the space between us.

Sensing yet another trap, I decide to tread carefully. "What do you really want?"

"Do you think you can stomach hearing it, in your perfect, heroic brain?"

"You're afraid of him," I reiterate, ignoring her jabs. "But not because of what he might do. You don't like being out of his loop. You're afraid he's already written you off as a lost cause."

"Which means I'm not of any use to you anymore, lucky me—"

"No," I reply. "It means that you're worried that even Mischa's protection won't be enough. I'm sure you'd run if you could, so the fact that you haven't yet means that you feel your options are dwindling. Your last, desperate action is to go on the offensive; consequences be damned. It seems, Briar Winthorp, that you believe you have nothing left to lose."

The door on her end slams shut, but with her still inside, breathing out harshly. It seems I've hit a nerve.

"So then, if you know everything, tell me that you also know that it's better to nip a threat before it can strike rather than let it bloom."

"But if you thought you could strike on your own, you would have done so already. You wouldn't need a babysitter, and you certainly wouldn't need me."

"Ah, but therein lies the catch. I've never killed anyone before."

It's not the truth. Her face is what gives her away, in the dark.

"I almost believed that," I admit.

"Not intentionally, at least." She smiles wickedly, brandishing her teeth. "So, it wasn't completely a lie."

"Luckily for you, I'm not curious as to the real answer." I grip the steering wheel and turn back onto the road—only to cut across two lanes and swerve into a U-turn.

"What are you doing?"

"I'm taking you back to the manor. I'm done with your games—"

"Mischa is merely a stepping-stone," she blurts in a rush. "His real end-goal is much bigger, involving way more pieces. The fact that he hasn't acted yet means that he's cutting out the middleman and going straight for the jugular. All of that to say, if we follow the Saleris, they'll lead us straight to him."

"And what else?" I demand, sensing more.

Her grudging hiss reveals that suspicion to be spot on. "Fine. I think the bastard's changed course, and I need to know how. I know you don't trust me. Hell, I don't expect you to. But I do expect you to care about your Mischa and his precious family. If not them, then yourself. You've made yourself quite the target. It's only a matter of time before he comes at you directly."

"Is this your way of convincing me to help you?"

"Yes, but that's not the part that will convince you. This will —I think my son is in the city, and I need your help to find him."

I process the request for only a second. Then I laugh so loud, I drown out the honking of a car that speeds past. I've been idling down the middle lane, giving that distant traffic plenty of time to catch up.

Still laughing, I slam on the gas, picking up speed. Internally, I'm kicking myself for even trusting her this far. Of course, there's another tale to be spun. Another lie to be woven when the first falls flat.

She's nothing if not predictable.

But, fuck, I'm the idiot who fell for it.

"When we get back, I think I'll try my hand at that dungeon and torture scenario. You think I'm a murderer now? You have no fucking idea—"

"My, my, you almost sound like the kind of man who would mean a threat like that." She laughs me off, but her voice shakes. From the corner of my eye, I see her grasp the door handle, but she doesn't force it open. Yet. "If you truly didn't believe me, you wouldn't bother to take me back," she points out. "You would throw me on the side of the road and drive off without a second glance. The fact that you listened at all tells me that, not only do you believe me, you want to help me—"

"Do I?" I toy with the idea of following through on her suggestion. Leaving her behind would be the best option for everyone.

Especially if she were always a spy. She would crawl back to her master, having failed with nothing useful gained.

But if she is telling the truth…

He'd kill her. He's already tried to more than once, and I don't believe that attempt was faked.

So, fuck it.

"Give me a reason. Lie, and I'll throw you out. Tell me what you're really after."

"Alexander was always better off without me," she says bluntly. "So, I'll spare you the maternal waterworks. I left him willingly, and up until recently, I didn't second guess it. Everything I've done has been for him. For his future—"

"Even teaming up with a man you fear?"

She chokes out a scathing laugh of her own. "And how would you explain your relationship with Mischa? Don't tell me that you work for him because you admire his rousing people skills. No. Someone as high and mighty as you must believe that he's somehow working toward a larger goal. You're doing it for a reason beyond the money, don't lie and pretend like you aren't."

"So, you admit that you're a terrible mother, and now I'm to believe that you've suddenly grown a heart and transformed into a caring one?"

"If he's bringing Ali into the country, he'll do so using the Saleri contacts. He'll want it under wraps, secret from everyone. The Saleris probably don't even know what they'll be transporting, but they own enough land to safely land a private jet, I'm sure."

"Why would he even go through the trouble? Why now?"

She hisses in exasperation. "Because Alexander is integral to his end game. If I am right, and he's bringing him into the country now, it means that he's ready to make a final move. Even if you don't believe me fully, you can't deny that it feels suspicious. I bet you'll find your way to the Saleri properties anyway, with or without my assistance.

But I can assure you that I know both men far better than you do."

I raise an eyebrow at that. "You sound confident. So, what is your hunch? What do you plan to do? Storm onto a Saleri tarmac and kidnap a child from under their noses? That sounds far too reckless for a caring mother."

"No," she says softly. "That's not what I intend at all to do. We will skip the guessing game and get answers straight from the source."

I feel my eyes narrow, and driving is the only distraction I have from either shouting, or strangling her with my bare hands.

"You want to kidnap and interrogate one of the Saleris?"

Her silence conveys a rare amount of modesty on her end. I don't trust it one damn bit.

"Are you insane?"

"No. I'm desperate, as you so kindly pointed out," she snarls. "And I'm tired of sitting and waiting around. He's up to something, and I intend to beat him at his own game."

"So where do I factor in? As your muscle?"

"Don't be so hard on yourself, Evgeni." She chuckles. "But if the shoe fits..."

"And if I refuse to be used as your pawn?"

"You won't," she says confidently. "Because no matter how hard you deny it, you can't resist the chance to play the hero. And you know that I'm not lying. I would conjure a much better sob story to pique your bleeding heart if I were. So, turn around."

"Fine—" Another U-turn sets us back on course for the city. "But we do this my way."

Impatient, I ignore the speed limit, heedless of the consequences—but our destination isn't one of the many residential properties the Saleris own. Instead, we arrive at the heart of their operation—the club from which they conduct the more salacious of their business ventures.

This time of day, the place is dead. Only a single bouncer guards the front, scanning anyone who comes within view of the gilded building.

"They won't be here," Briar scoffs against my ear. "I didn't think you were stupid as well as righteous—"

"Gregori and Mateo aren't my focus right now," I hiss back. "We're here only by coincidence."

I claim a spot in a parking lot across from the club, unnoticed by the sentry. Luckily, my real destination is a block down, out of his line of sight.

"What the hell do you mean?" the woman snarls.

I shrug. "You want to go barging into a guarded fortress without intel, but that simply isn't my style."

"So, we skulk around a dead club and hope that someone just tells us what we want to know?"

"No—" I exit the van, keys in hand. "We do this my way."

"Wait!" She scrambles out as well, racing to my side. "What the hell are you planning? To waltz in there where they most likely aren't."

"No." I withdraw my cell phone and watch her eyes narrow. "I get intel. You remember our good friend Louie? Well, you should know his haunt is a bar not too far from here. He'll be able to get us more info on what the hell the Saleris may or may not be up to. *Then* we make a move. Understood?"

She's smart enough to see the benefit of that plan. Still, her expression can be politely described as skeptical. "Why bring me?"

Because I don't dare leave her at Stepanov Manor alone.

"Because he'll be resistant to telling me a damn thing without payment," I lie. "I'm sure you'll be able to use your Winthorp charm to convince him otherwise."

She doesn't seem to buy that explanation. "Oh?"

"You're collateral," I admit. "I'm sure the bastard will try to play both sides. You're the tempting carrot he needs to reach out to our enemies—and we'll be waiting."

"Sneaky, sneaky," she taunts. "I wouldn't think you'd have it in you."

She sounds impressed, even.

Which makes me feel dirty rather than amused.

"Let's go," I say, heading for the main street.

Just beyond my reach, she slinks into step behind me.

*T*he second we enter the bar, the bastard tries to run. I have to corner him in a backroom while the woman blocks the door.

Admittedly, Louie is a sneaky son of a bitch in the best of times—but this is unusual, even for him. He's spooked.

"That isn't a very nice way to greet friends," I hiss, grappling with the collar of his stained gray shirt. The bastard reeks of alcohol, and this struggle feels less like I'm fighting to keep him here, and more like I'm helping him stand at all.

"Word on the street is you've been poking very big hornets' nests, Ev," he chokes out, his bloodshot eyes comically wide. "The people in your crosshairs seem to wind up dead. Even more so than usual."

"What do you mean?"

"Gregori fucking Saleri is what I mean. He's dead."

"What?" I couldn't hide my shock if I tried. Glancing over my shoulder, I note that Briar Winthorp, however, doesn't look surprised in the slightest. Suddenly her "hunch" regarding the Saleris isn't so farfetched.

"Yeah," Louie croaks. "Gutted like a fish in his own fucking club. Word on the street is that Mateo did it himself. The motherfucker's gone crazy—"

"Mateo…" Whatever happened sounds like far more than the average family squabble. "When?"

"Last night? I don't fucking know. The point is, who the hell is next?"

"And that's all you know regarding the Saleris?"

His eyes dart to the woman. "I know they're taking their marching orders from an outsider. And I know that *she* turned back up around the same time he did. This shit reeks, Ev. I'd get rid of her if you can."

"And that's it?" I release him, stepping back.

He sways on his feet, pointing a trembling finger in my direction. "I've been too busy trying to get the fuck out of here!" He pushes me off, tugging at his collar. "Now, can I drink in peace?"

He staggers for the doorway, and the woman standing there comes to my side.

"Au Revoir," she murmurs, blowing him a kiss.

But her eyes are on me, unmistakably smug.

When we return to the manor, I regret ever leaving in the first place.

"You know more than you're saying," I snarl while driving up to the gates. "I should shove you in the darkest, deepest room possible and demand real answers. Enough games. Enough lies."

She laughs, but her eyes blaze. I suspect that she's only revealing a fraction of what truly has her so on edge. Regardless, I shouldn't give a damn. If she wants to play coy with the answers, one of my men can drag them out of her.

Slowly and painfully.

Surprisingly she's silent as we near the front of the manor.

"It looks like the darling family is refusing a visitor," she finally remarks, sitting forward.

I follow her gaze, instantly on edge. Another car bars our path, but I don't recognize it as belonging to the estate. The door to the front seat hangs open, and I assume the driver is the same man standing nearby, his back to me.

"Son of bitch!"

There is no mistaking that posture, nor that characteristic bulk.

I lunge from the van, grasping for my gun.

"I'm not here for a fight," the man says, turning to face me. "I'm just here to give this to her. Only her. Please."

Confusion goes to war with the adrenaline surging through me, demanding I fight. Instead, I settle for pointing out the obvious. "You don't have the right to even show your face here—"

"So don't let me in the house," Donatello Vanici says tiredly. "But let her have the choice to accept these or not."

I crane my neck to view the items in his arms. Both are surprisingly innocent, but I'm not fooled. His true intent is far more sinister than delivering some harmless flowers. He wants to pressure Willow and play more sick mind games at her expense.

After all, I have an expert in manipulation behind me.

Ironically, her presence is why I don't feel compelled to drive my fist through this man's skull.

As much as I care about Willow, this is her fight, not mine—and it would be wrong to play the role as a pawn for either side.

The only right course of action is what I should have done in all matters concerning Briar Winthorp in the first place.

Stay out of it.

"I'll have my men search whatever you've brought for explosives," I suggest, but the man doesn't flinch.

"Do whatever the fuck you have to. Just give her the option of whether to accept them or not."

"Then leave them," I say, jerking my chin toward the pavement between us. "And go before I change my mind. But realize that I can't guarantee they won't burn them. As they should."

"Fine," he concedes. "I'm not asking for anything more than that."

Seconds later, he drives off.

"Strange," Briar murmurs in my ear.

I jump, having almost forgotten her presence. "What is?"

Her cold laughter rings hollow. "That you trust a madman more easily than you trust me."

WILLOW

I've never realized how heavy silence can feel when it's stretched over days. Weeks. And when a sound finally breaks that quiet, it rings out louder than a gunshot.

Alarmed, I jolt to awareness, lifting my gaze from the crumpled page in my grasp. My room is bathed in shadow, and I race to the windows to find the sky beyond is a hazy twilight with only hints of the setting sun peeking through. The guards out patrolling don't seem on alert, though, strolling at a leisurely pace. The booming noise could have been thunder.

But then it echoes again, far louder. A few distinctive, piercing notes betray the sound for what it really is. Voices, coming from below.

Shouting.

My first instinct is to ignore it, even as my heart races. It feels safer to lurk within these four walls and disregard the world beyond. I try to, seeking out the same handwritten scrawl I've come to memorize, desperate to find meaning in it.

I don't love you, I don't. I don't know what this is. But when I'm with you, at least I'm not invisible for once...

"She deserves to know." That gentle murmur easily transcends the commotion of voices, despite being the softest. *Ellen.* "If she wants to burn them, she can, but it should be her choice."

"None of this was *her* choice," a man growls in response. Mischa. "You don't even know what the hell that monster might have sent to her. Or what he's written in that fucking note—"

"She's an adult, Mischa. We have to trust her to tell us—"

"Fine. If you want to let that bastard continue to fuck with her head, be my guest. But what happens next will be on you."

"This isn't our fight," Ellen warns, her tone unwaveringly gentle in the face of her husband's rage. "All we can do is be there to support whatever *Willow* decides. Please. You've handled this better than I thought you would so far. It means a lot."

Better than she thought? Perhaps that explains why Mischa's visits to my room haven't been nearly as frequent as hers. He's been restraining himself. From saying what, exactly?

If he replies to his wife, I don't hear it. Just soft footsteps, advancing toward my room, ignoring the invisible boundary I've set. Without a knock this time, the door opens, revealing Ellen, her expression constricted.

"I know you want to be alone," she says softly. "But these came for you, and I thought you might want to know. If you want to refuse them, you can."

From her position, I can't see what she holds. Not until she enters the room fully with an apologetic frown. "Just leave them outside the door, and I'll have them taken away."

Them, being a vase of roses propped against her hip, nearly large enough to dwarf her in comparison. I gape, thrown off by the beauty of them. Red, white, and pink blooms in various sizes spill from a glass container shaped like a teardrop.

It's an extravagant gift, all things considered, but I puzzle over her hesitation.

Then the answer hits me like a slap—they aren't from her or Mischa. Without admitting as much out loud, she approaches a table in the corner of my room and sets them down, along with a small white box wrapped with a matching bow.

Both catch the snippets of lighting filtering in from the hallway, tinging their pristine white. They look so sinister sitting there, deceptively lovely. Considering who sent them, the intention behind the delicate blooms could be more dangerous than a simple gift.

"We didn't open anything," Ellen warns—judging from the shouting, it was her who insisted on that. "I want to believe there's nothing nefarious in it—" She seems to bite off the rest. "If you need anything, I won't be far."

She switches on the overhead light and leaves. As the door closes behind her, I warily approach the table. The floral scent floods my nostrils before I even reach them, betraying a beautiful quality. After everything that's transpired, they almost seem surreal, and I can't place the building dread that has my fingers shaking before I reach for a small white card affixed to one of the stems.

I would be a fool to think that this alone could change the way you feel about me, reads the first line. The stern, sloping script might appear beautiful if I wasn't already well versed in pages of similar writing. I know the author's signature stroke, and how the darker ink betrays how tightly he pressed the nip of his pen to the page.

I know this scent too, mingling faintly beneath the aroma of roses.

He wrote this, every word.

Shock knocks me back, and I trip over my own feet. Suddenly the beautiful colors conjure a more menacing imagery. The red resembles blood, the white unblemished skin ripe for abuse. I wonder if this is his way of mocking me—a parting gift, meant to add salt to the wound.

I can't explain what drives me closer regardless. Perhaps a morbid curiosity to see the rest of his message—especially when his past notes are still fresh in my mind. His old letters have become engrained on my psyche, every word. Every last punctuation mark.

His gritty composition haunts my nightmares, and some masochistic part of me can't resist consuming this newer dose of poison.

I steel myself for more vague rejection and callous disregard. Or maybe he'll refer to the glaring reality that has turned me into a leper in my own home.

But, like always, whenever I hope for clarity from Donatello Vanici, all I'm given is more doubt and confusion. More pain.

We should talk. In person, alone. No threats. No ultimatums. I need to see you. Come to the café we met in before. I'll be there all day tomorrow. I'll wait for you.

Damn him.

I'm on my knees beside the table, the card in my grasp. I don't know how many times I read those words, branding them into my brain much like I've memorized the stack of letters from the past. He's written in this tone before, pleading and demanding in the same breath—when he urged Olivia to open up to him.

Trust him.

And then she died.

Of all the responses, this is the least one I would have expected, but I'm not comforted in the slightest. I'm uneasy.

He's planning something. Plotting something. Men like Donatello Vanici don't beg, not without a reason.

And I can think of several why he would want to meet with me now, alone.

Would I put it past him to make a demand or an ultimatum? Or worse, would he dare to use me against Mischa to further his own selfish aims? Yes.

After all, I've only ever been a tool to him.

That's what this really is about—using me. He can't truly expect me to come to him, even if Mischa would allow it. No, true to his self-deprecating nature, he'll relish the rejection as an excuse to see himself as the victim. It's been his aim from the very start—going back seven years ago. Even now, he has yet to tell me the whole truth of what happened then, but I can guess. A variation of what has become his life story, in a sense.

Donatello got overwhelmed.

He got angry and vengeful.

And then, when the consequences set in, he got regretful. Unable to accept responsibility for his actions, he blamed me, turning the little girl he abandoned into both a martyr and an albatross around his neck. He told Vin I was dead and used my memory as a shield.

But when I came back, what did he do? Act as though I were the enemy—anything other than accept responsibility.

I should take a page out of his book and do the same, hurt him as he hurt me. Lie. Deny. Ignore him. Erase Donatello Vanici from my history.

Our history…

I suck in a breath as everything that's happened recently comes rushing back. It's all too much. So, I shove the most terrifying issues aside and fixate on what little I have control over now.

Donatello wants a meeting, if only to use a refusal against me. But I'm done being his punching bag. He wants to see me? He will, but not on his terms.

Mine.

A shocking sense of calm washes over me. I can think clearly, at least in this limited capacity. Taking a deep breath, I even manage to stand, still facing the table—but then my gaze falls over the box, and I lose what little resolve I had.

It would be one thing if I could write it off as some careless gift he had Fabio purchase and wrap. Something without any of his input. In that case, it would be obvious, with telltale signs of perfection, to give it away.

But the wrapping is…sloppy in places. One side of the box is crooked as if the person who prepared it misjudged how much paper they'd need. In vain, they attempted to hide their mistake with more tape, and they even tied the bow off-center.

Seven years ago, I used to receive birthday presents wrapped in the same haphazard but thoughtful manner. Tears sting my eyes, burning and acrid, too many to blink back. They spill unbidden, landing over the open card and smearing the ink scrawled across it.

I lash at the gift with both hands, nails drawn, ripping through the ivory casing to the object resting beneath. There is nothing he could ever give me that would change my opinion of him.

Nothing but this.

I drop it, watching it hit the floor with an ominous thud. My first thought is that he meant it as a joke. A mocking way to taunt me with the one method of communication we managed to forge over my last few days at Havienna. Yes, it must be. A cruel joke. His way of proving that the only things remaining between us are meaningless words and crisp parchment.

I'm sinking to my knees anyway, reaching for the wooden box with a clear glass lid. Visible beneath it is a swath of stationary and a golden pen.

I would have preferred something worthless. Or priceless. An expensive necklace or trinket that would mean nothing to me.

This gift is too tailored to ignore, and I lift it carefully, bringing it to the bed.

He's gotten his wish. I'll acknowledge him, but in my own way. This time, I'll make it easy for him to hate me.

I'll make him face me.

The following morning unfolds almost too normally for the current circumstances. Even with the added visit to the hospital, the day itself could be described as boring at best. If it weren't for the fact that no less than ten men make up the guard accompanying Ellen and me from the manor.

And the fact that Mischa is nowhere in sight to send us off. Eli and the other children aren't milling about either, and I assume he's entertaining them in another part of the manor.

Ellen smiles despite the circumstances, treating this trip as though it's a usual occurrence.

"We can get tea after," she suggests. "There is a place not far from the hospital. If you don't mind the escorts."

Said escorts remain vigilant even when we reach the hospital, lurking outside the exam room. Their shadows loom beyond the doorway, creating an ominous contrast to the sterile white walls and scurrying nurses.

The doctor is a smiling woman who enters the room chatting aimlessly about the weather before sternly detailing the parameters of the exam. Still smiling, she draws a vial of blood and cheerfully attempts a conversation even on her way out. Only when she returns, the smile has vanished.

"Is something wrong?" Ellen's voice is strained, but the doctor shakes her head.

"The HCG levels are in the right range, but the lower end."

"What does that mean?" Ellen asks. "Is… Is there no pregnancy?"

I flinch at the word.

"Not quite. It's a bit unusual, but potentially nothing serious," the woman explains. "Still, I think it would be best to have another appointment soon."

Her tone doesn't convey the same hope as her forced smile, but I can't focus enough to follow the conversation. Unusual. That word could contain so many things, but that numbness prevails. Nothing breaks it but one persistent thought.

Donatello.

I need to find him.

"Another visit in a week is all that's necessary," the doctor declares. "Then we can make more definitive decisions. In the meantime, here is some documentation."

We leave, documents in tow, returning to the car, flanked by the retinue of soldiers.

"I know I promised tea after, but…" Ellen sighs, her smile gone. Looking at her stirs that unease again. That desperate feeling to avoid anything beyond the numbness. "Maybe we should head back?"

No. I grab her hand, shaking my head.

"It would be good to get some fresh air," she says warily.

The café is small, near the heart of downtown, eerily close to where Donatello wanted to meet. Does she know that?

I can't tell looking at her blank expression. She's worried, though, but it's a full second before I realize that Donatello has nothing to do with it.

"Are you okay?" she asks, catching me staring.

I nod, but she has a faraway look as if the answer only disturbs her more. By the time we leave the car and approach the café, she's frowning. In silence, we enter the luxurious dining room where plush burgundy carpet inspires a calm, cozy aura. Within seconds, a grinning waitress shows us to a table and reappears with steaming cups of tea.

As Ellen samples her drink, I finally gather up the nerve to move, lifting both hands.

"Bathroom?" Ellen asks as I sign.

Nodding, I stand, aware of the soldiers posted around the room.

The bathroom is near an exit door, and I don't think before entering a stall, withdrawing a paper and pen from my coat pocket.

The note I compose is short and pathetic in retrospect, nothing like the detailed missives of Donatello.

Knowing him, this meeting won't last long, and I might be back before she even notices.

84

7

DON

The hospital isn't my destination today. Fabio should be proud of my restraint—but I've never felt like a bigger fool. Or, in this case, a sitting duck.

It doesn't help that I'm sweating like hell. I can't remember the last time I've been this nervous—stretching back to my early days working for the *famiglia*. Serves me fucking right.

I came alone, without backup or even Fabio. It could be a trap, but I'm here despite the risk. If this is the only way to get some ounce of fucking clarity, then so be it.

I'll wait out in the open and take whatever comes my way, be it a bullet or answers. Hopefully, it's the latter.

Though how I can face either is another question. Any other time, I wouldn't dream of confronting this shit without a bottle of vodka and a cigar. Devoid of both, all I can do is try my best to process it all one step at a time.

Doubt is paramount for the most part.

She won't come. Could I even blame her?

Hell no.

The other possibility is that Mischa shows up instead, unwilling to compromise. Were I in his place, I don't know what I would do. Not that letting me see her will make much of a difference. Some goddamn flowers can't fix a damn thing. I know that.

But dwelling on the mess won't solve anything either.

So, I wait, eyeing the street beyond the café, unsurprised as the minutes tick by without the sign of a Stepanov cavalcade.

More doubt feeds on the dread building in the pit of my stomach. How the hell could I have been so damn stupid? Not even with just her. With Vin, and even Olivia. Over and over, I've failed to protect anyone who means anything to me. Over and over, I had to watch them be injured or die.

And yet, I'm the one who remains unscarred.

The right thing to do would be to fall back, like Fabio said. Let her live her life, whatever choice she decides to make, in peace. Sink into the shadows and turn my focus onto Vincenzo. His is the only fate within my control. The merciful thing I could do when it comes to Willow Stepanova is to let her go.

Like hell, I will.

The dark impulses I've fought so hard to smother break through, and I form a fist, slamming it against the narrow table. Already a million other options unfurl in my skull, threatening to push out that fragile desire for peace.

I tried diplomacy already.

The next obvious step is something a little more direct. Like returning to Mischa's manor and driving straight through the gates like I originally planned. Then I'd demand that she talk to me. Even for a fucking second. If only to…

What?

My mind goes blank. It's easier to fantasize about an impulsive course of action and run with it. If she won't see me, then I'd find a way to see her.

I *will* find a way.

Determined, I brace my hands against the table and prepare to stand. Mid-rise, I smell it. Roses. The faint scent hits my nostrils at full force, inexplicably fresh despite the lack of any such bloom in sight. Instead, a flash of gold draws my notice to the front of the café.

Damn.

If Mischa chose her outfit, the bastard has a cruel streak. Though why would he? No… *She* picked this dress, a delicate shade of yellow with lace trim visible beneath a dark coat. Her hair hangs loosely. Overall, she looks the same way she did the day she left Havienna.

Fucking perfect.

Warily, I scan her face, unsure of what I'll find. If I were honest with myself, I'd expect her eyes to be bloodshot, her mouth twisted in an expression of abject horror. Maybe then I'd be able to meet her gaze like the coward I am and face the damage I've wrought?

Instead, her eyes blaze, like burning coals incinerating whatever expectations I had of this meeting to ash.

So, this isn't a friendly reunion, then.

Swallowing hard, I tear my gaze away from her, expecting to find an army of Stepanov guards waiting to descend. All I see is the street behind her and the average pedestrian mingling on the sidewalk.

Only the lone proprietor of the café serves as the buffer between us, quietly bringing a pitcher of water to our table.

There is no Fabio. No Mischa. Not even a smiling Vincenzo to siphon off the tension.

In short? I have no one to hide behind.

"Here." I lurch to my feet and wrench out the empty chair across from me, nearly knocking it over. "You can sit."

She doesn't move. I can see now that while she came into this building alone, she doesn't trust me a fraction. Not even enough to go beyond the safety of a quick exit.

It's odd, but some sick part of me finds that comforting. Her hesitation shortens this meeting. There's no time for small talk or awkwardness. Just getting to the heart of the matter.

If only I knew what the fuck to say.

"You… You look good," I croak, hating myself the second the words leave my throat.

I might as well have voiced an insult. She flinches, her eyes more guarded than ever, concealing any hint of what she might be thinking. I can't stop myself from eyeing her waist, flat beneath the fall of her dress. Though it would be, wouldn't it? It's only been two weeks. It would take longer for anything to become more apparent.

If she didn't choose another option in the meantime.

For all I know, she could have, and my chest constricts at the thought. I've spent days avoiding that outcome, but now it's all I can think about. Would she have done that without even telling me first? Why wouldn't she?

Fabio all but hinted that he thought it would be the better option. For all I know, he conspired with Mischa to make the decision without my input. He'd deem it was for the greater good.

Do I have a better idea?

As the seconds tick by, I can't even bring myself to say a damn thing, let alone offer up a solution. The million different lines and explanations I came up with before now scatter like dust.

I owe her something. I need to say something.

"I… Uh, do you want something to drink?" I gesture helplessly to the water.

Her blank expression doesn't waver.

"Are… Are you okay?" It startles me just how much I crave even a hint of what's going on inside that head. Something. That she hates me? She'll always fucking hate me.

I deserve it.

Another heartbeat passes without a move on her end. So much for handling this on my own. If Fab were here, he would know what to say. He was always good at this shit.

I, on the other hand, just clear my throat and force myself to meet her gaze directly.

Facing her again is like tearing open a festering wound and letting the puss drain out. There is no hiding from it. The disgust. The pain.

She hides it all for as long as she can—but those eyes always give her away. They blaze, glimmering too brightly, and I stiffen at the threat of tears. Damn it…

"I'm sorry." The words slip out, pathetic and hoarse, but there they are. It's all I can say, over and over again. "I'm sorry."

I collapse onto the nearest chair, unable to even look at her. Groaning, I dig my fingers into my temples, questioning whether this really is a setup and Mischa will come storming through the door. I almost wish that were the case.

I know how to handle violence. I know how to defend myself, even against an armed man, and I know the ins and outs of the political scene of Hell's Gambit.

But this…

I can't even compare this moment to the day Liv came to me, tears in her eyes, and told me I would be a father. That was meant to be. Olivia signed up to share her life with me, and her future should have been spent with five more kids —however many she wanted—in a house she loved with only grandkids and peace to look forward to.

Liv made her choice. It wasn't forced on her.

My own sister wasn't so lucky, getting pregnant by some punk who abandoned her in the end. She loved Vin in her own way, but motherhood didn't bring her the same joy Liv craved. It overwhelmed her, driving her deeper down a rabbit hole of vice and decay. She died high on God knows what, slumped in an alleyway while I was the one left to mix up the formula and fill Vin's bottles. Caring for him was the last fucking thing in the world I wanted.

And it turned my whole life on its head.

I couldn't ask someone to take on the same responsibility.

"I didn't want this. Do you realize that?"

I hear her breathing out, every exhale ragged and unsteady. Surprisingly, the distorted soundtrack helps me gather my thoughts. Each negative, twisted realization I should have admitted from the start.

"I didn't want this. I… I didn't. Fuck, I don't even… You went to the hospital. Did Mischa—"

What? I can't even say it. Did he do what most fathers would demand in this instance? Deep down, some part of me insists that would be the best thing for everyone involved.

A larger part of me, on the other hand, can't even consider the thought. It's driving me mad not to know. Fuck...

Or hell, I'm already insane, I must be—crazy enough to imagine the warm touch ghosting the side of my jaw. I glance up, just in time to catch a small, pale hand rear back and land palm first against my cheek. I've barely registered the attacker's identity—the only other person in the room —by the time they rear back for another blow.

I lurch to my feet, grabbing her wrist out of reflex, only to immediately let her go.

"What the hell?" I demand, but one look at her face renders me silent. A slap is the least of my concerns.

She's angry. So goddamn angry, practically levitating on the tips of her toes. Without even trying, I've hurt her again.

"I'm sorry."

An apology seems to rob her of the anger—along with whatever energy she has left. She sways, and I barely manage to throw my arm around her waist before her knees buckle completely.

I shouldn't touch her, let alone hold her. Not like this.

It's harder to think clearly with her scent flooding my nostrils, her hair like silk beneath my fingertips as I cradle the back of her scalp. She's shaking, and I feel like an even bigger fool.

Why wouldn't she be angry?

"I'm sorry." I voice it directly against her ear, feeling her shiver in response. "That was a selfish thing to say. This isn't about me. This is about you."

Her face is angled away, but some of the tension leaves her body, and I'm fully supporting her weight. In her absence, I've convinced myself that it was for the best. That I didn't miss her touch. Her smell. That I didn't crave the sight of those dark fucking eyes. That I could wait until Vin fully recovered and leave Hell's Gambit, never to look back. Never to see her again.

Only now can I realize how fucking egotistical I've been. The only course of action that matters is the one she decides on. For all my scheming and planning, I never once considered asking her what *she* wanted. I didn't have the courage to.

"Tell me what you want from me." I don't make her face me, not yet. I just hold her, raking my fingers through her hair, trying to ignore any preconceived notions I may have. "It doesn't matter what I want, or Fabio, or your father. The only person whose opinion matters is you."

If she heard me, she doesn't react, her gaze presumably on the window across the shop. It overlooks a sliver of green field, and as if enacting some mocking cliché, a small family picnics there in the sun. The woman even has blond hair, the man towering over her with his hand on her lower back, and their children playing on the grass before them. It's like looking into a twisted mirror—that's what this situation should be.

Not this.

But here we are, regardless. No amount of pretending or wishing can change a damn thing.

"What I want doesn't matter," I tell her hoarsely. My jaw throbs with the effort it takes to chew out every damn word. "But I think you deserve to hear it anyway, if only so that you know where I stand."

I find myself enthralled, watching that family, seeing them interact without a care in the world. A few years ago, I was convinced that would have been the future awaiting Liv and me. Happiness. More children than we could possibly stand. Freedom. Serenity. Safety.

I wanted it all so badly I could have killed for it.

But somewhere along the way…

I found myself in my office or hunting down enemy leads instead of in my own house. My nights were spent nailing down deals rather than beside my wife. I could rationalize it if another woman had gotten my attention. Something less cliché and far more fucking enticing than chasing money and prestige. But, God, I wanted it all.

"I missed my shot once," I say, though I don't even know exactly what I'm referring to. A shot at a family? At happiness? At life?

Liv's death took so fucking much from me, that the creature left behind might as well be deemed a ghost. Beneath the drugs and the alcohol lurks a truth that I don't think either Fabio or I wanted to face—those vices merely enhanced a descent into madness I gladly welcomed. Death was my end goal, and recovery wasn't even on my radar, then. Misery was the only state powerful enough to drown the guilt.

I thought nothing could ever dig me from that despair, but for the first time, it's like the storm cloud raining down on my life has let up just enough for me to take notice of the world around me, drenched as it may be. This mindset is a new form of sobriety, and I'm not even sure if I like the feel of it.

I can think clearly again, and one solution feels so fucking obvious, the realest concept I've been able to grasp outside of hate and violence.

"I want…"

Childish laughter seeps through the walls as if taunting me with the sheer magnitude of everything I've lost. Everything I could find again. It almost feels wrong to crave that faint lifeline. I don't deserve it.

That doesn't mean I don't desire it so badly my voice breaks over the admission, "I want a future."

I feel her shiver in my arms, and I loosen my grip, waiting for her to pull away. But she doesn't. Somehow, I find the nerve to ease a finger beneath her chin, guiding her to face me.

That anger is still there, burning bright—but beneath it is a glimpse of something that resonates in me like a kick to the stomach. I don't dare name it.

"I do. You have no reason to trust me. No reason to believe me after everything I've done. Ignoring this won't fix it, and I don't want to. You came here, and I thank you for that. I have no right to ask you for more…" My throat thickens, and I tear my gaze to the window, clinging to that mocking image of family. "So, look at this more as another choice. You come with me, and we can find some way to make this work. You and I, no one else. Not Fabio. Not Mischa. This doesn't have to be a tragedy. But it's your choice, and I will respect whatever you decide, I swear on my life. But if you want another option, you come to me. Or… You could leave."

To reinforce that choice, I pull away, putting my back to her. Regardless, the thought of letting her go now triggers the paranoia constantly at the back of my mind. I could always take her to Havienna now, preempting anything Mischa might do to convince her otherwise.

But therein lies the fucking dilemma. To earn her trust, the first step is to acknowledge that I don't have control.

"I'll let you decide." With that said, I start for the door, but a flicker of movement from the corner of my eye draws my notice. I stop short with my hand inches from the doorknob, only to feel a familiar touch graze my forearm in response.

She doesn't have to say a single word to make her feelings clear—annoyance. Once again, I've aimed to have the last word with no input from her, contradicting everything I've said. Even now, I can't let her state her own case, her own thoughts.

And that was the offer I made to her, wasn't it? Before she even came here. We both know what giving her paper and a pen meant.

It meant she would have her voice.

And I would finally listen.

8

WILLOW

I'm a fool. Coming here was a mistake, and nothing has made that sink in like the sight of his retreating back for the umpteenth time. Him leaving now is a stark reminder that nothing between us could ever change. He's still determined to assert control and set the terms for whatever truce we might be able to build.

Seven years later, and he's still treating me like a little girl.

But no more.

I sense in my soul that if I let him go, I'll never see him again—but the choice won't be my own. No, Donatello Vanici will continue to do what he does best and spiral into a downfall of his own volition.

In fact, I think someone like him would crave a moment like this, only to compound his own despair and truly make himself the victim. He's so damn selfish, but I wasn't able to see it until today.

Tears of rage blur my vision, lashing down my cheeks in an unstoppable torrent. It's cruel how he does this, how easily he can turn the tables while offering the semblance of control. But to him, control is merely a word he can use to assuage his own guilt.

From day one, he's taken everything, giving nothing in return.

Until now. A strange expression breaks through the rigid mask he wears, bringing a rare hint of softness to those dark, imposing eyes.

"I'm sorry," he croaks, the only phrase he seems capable of voicing without guilt or rage. The words ring hollow, and as much as it stings, I can hear the truth in them. "I'm sorry. I… What do you need to say?"

There's too much, but, ironically, I didn't bring any more paper with me. Just his pen and the handful of documents the doctor provided.

And the letters…

Not that he'll read them. Trusting him should be impossible. How could I take anything he says at face value?

I'm too tired. Drained, I cross over to the nearest chair and sit, rocked by the reality I haven't had time to face. Or perhaps, ignored is a better word. I've ignored how my life has changed because of him.

And because of me.

That's the element of this that everyone else refuses to consider, and one that he could easily throw in my face. The prospect of him doing that very thing unnerves me more than anything else. We both know the truth.

If it were up to him, our relationship would have ended on his terms. He would use me as a pawn and nothing more. I made him cross that boundary out of some twisted sense of revenge.

I made him break his own foolish rule, but the consequences affect us both.

It's too much. The walls seem to close in, and I can't breathe. I can't think. The air is too thin in here. Too hot. I'm burning alive, suffocating…

"Look at me."

Again, he so easily asserts himself, but when I do look up, his expression is far from the stoic mask I'm used to.

Wincing, he drags his hand across his chin, drawing notice to the dark stubble there. Blinking, I take in all of the minute details I didn't have the sense of mind to notice before. The dark circles beneath his eyes. The slight unkempt appearance to his hair and the fact that his suit jacket is wrinkled, the collar crooked. I have a mental image of Fabio fussing over him, bringing him clean clothing to wear, and it hits me that he isn't here this time. Donatello is alone, devoid of his posse for once.

"If we are going to make this work, I can't read your mind," he says gruffly. "We can't keep playing with half-truths and misunderstandings. There needs to be some level of trust. Clear communication."

He makes it sound like I'm to blame for said miscommunication. Maybe he truly believes that.

I plunge my hand into my pocket without processing the action clearly. Then I feel my fingers close over the pen he sent me, and something clicks. He wants clear communication, does he?

He frowns as I withdraw the pen and rip off the lid. His eyes latch onto my trembling fingers, tracking their every movement as I reach for one of his hands.

He stiffens, curling the fingers tightly before slowly unfurling each one until his palm is bared. He must know what I intend to do as I press the nib to the calloused surface because he doesn't move, even as streaks of ink mar his flesh.

Voice gravelly, he recites each word as I form them. "You don't listen."

A grimace disrupts his pained expression. Then he sighs, leveling me with a searching glance I'm unprepared for. "You haven't exactly tried to talk to me."

His brows draw together. I've seen this look before, though not recently. It's the spark of the cunning man he used to be, unwilling to let any opportunity pass without a fight.

"We've been too busy listening to Mischa and Fabio," he continues. "Doing things their way when neither of us were ever known to be the thoughtful type. We're reckless. It's how we operate together, like with the Saleris…" His voice trails off as he recalls that day on the water, one of the few we were able to interact in relative peace. When he meets my gaze again, I swallow hard, sensing the intention lurking behind that distant expression. "We work best when we throw caution to the wind and do things in our own way. Should I tell you what I would do, Mischa or anyone else be damned?"

He has a way of sounding so damn enticing even while speaking insanity.

"I'd marry you," he confesses, raising the hand I've written on, tracing each scribbled word. "Secure the future I want. Our feelings don't matter—only the reality. I can protect you better that way."

But I'd be under his control again.

He must read that suspicion in my face because he nods. "And it would make things easier for me, but not if I offer you a lifeline. You stay with me on your own terms, and I will never deny you anything. I will never lie to you. Anything you ask of me, I will grant. I swear it on my life."

He's made this boast before, but under duress with Fabio in his ear. This time sounds different. There's a note of exasperation in his voice that I can't deny. Something raw and strained.

Warily, he approaches the table, keeping his hands in sight, his expression open. Those eyes contain a hint of the man I remember, and it stings. God, it stings like hell to see that piece of him lurking within the stranger he's become real enough to touch. Believe. Trust.

Only so I can be burned again.

There should be nothing in this world that he can offer me. Nothing.

But there is.

I reach for his hand again, brandishing the only weapon at my disposal. Surprisingly, he lets me use it, presenting the back of the hand I've already marked. Slowly, I etch each word, hating how badly my fingers shake. The lines wobble, so distorted that he wrinkles his mouth in concentration as he reads. "You want the truth."

I nod, unable to hide the desperation I can feel seep into my expression.

Answers. Answers to the questions gnawing relentlessly at the back of my psyche, demanding to be resolved. Did he know about Olivia and my father? Was their relationship as fractured as it looked on paper?

Not that it matters. I know that. The past should remain dead and buried. If I truly want to heal and focus on my future, the only logical course of action is to go home—my real home. For the first time, it strikes me how drastic the next few years could be, no matter what choice I make. Donatello's method, however, leaves no room for education, no room for music.

No identity for myself beyond my ties to him alone.

"I wish I could explain what I mean without sounding like a dumb son of a bitch," he admits with a sigh. He claims the chair across from me and sits sprawled, his head tipped back. Dark and unreadable, his eyes scan the ceiling as if hunting for an answer among the white plaster. "I was never good at this shit. I think it's a testament to my true nature that I was only married once. God knows what she saw in me. Frankly, I never wanted to venture down this road again. I didn't want this…"

It's strange to hear him admit as much out loud. If anything, some part of me craves this honesty. It's one way that differentiates him from the past. Safiya was never exposed to the real man, apart from the caring protector.

"I could deny it. Claim that it's a lie, and I never touched you. I could tell Mischa to go to hell. I could walk away. I can't lie and say I haven't considered it. I have no right to come to you and ask for you to give me anything more than I gave to you. I know that."

He frowns, his gaze so constricted. Worry lines wrinkle the planes of his face, displaying his age. We've spent so much time in the past, that it still shocks me to realize that seven years have passed. We're different people, no longer tied to who we once were.

"If I marry you, it shouldn't be like Fabio suggested. It shouldn't be carefully planned and thought out. We're not like that. With us… There is only action. Only moving forward, damn what happens after. I caused this mess. But I can't deny that… For the first fucking time in only God knows how long, I feel like myself again. Whatever that is worth. Whatever that means. If we make this work, then we make this work. No thinking it over."

I can't follow his logic. I don't want to. It's dangerous when he talks to me like this, freely without preconceived notions or hatred tainting his voice. When his tone falls into that raspy, easy murmur as if no one else is meant to understand him but me…

He inclines his head, lowering his guard, so I have another glimpse of the figure behind the hard mask he shows the rest of the world. The man beneath is exhausted and battered. He's desperate.

Whatever thought weighs on his mind is so dangerous he doesn't voice it right away. He toys with the phrasing, mulling it over, lost in thought. Absently, his tongue traces his lower lip twice before he finally croaks, "Marry me tonight."

He doesn't move. Doesn't laugh to reveal the request to be a joke—though it has to be. Stubbornly, his gaze returns to the ceiling above, eyeing the shadows painting the surface in varying shades of gray.

"There's no time to talk ourselves out of it. No going back. No more silence. It will be done, and then we move on. We make it work, and we do this the only way we both seem capable of doing anything. Recklessly. Impulsively. We do it now."

He doesn't look at me, not once, and his real motive becomes clear. He wants to scare me by voicing something so insane it can't be plausible. This must be the easiest method in his mind of turning me away. Propose something rash and watch me recoil.

Though what are the alternative options? Go home. Wait. Continue to hide and know that eventually, Donatello will find some excuse to leave.

"It wouldn't be for nothing," he adds as if reading my mind. "This way, you would be protected. I could die tomorrow, and you'd be left with something—not that you'd need it with Mischa… But I want you to have it, what little I can give to you and Vin. And the house, not that you would want it."

Again, he speaks as though he's the only one in the room. The only person whose life has been thrown into chaos. I feel my anger rising, but the second it starts to flare, he shifts.

He's watching me again, his gaze reflective, head still cocked.

"If I were to die tomorrow, I'd want you to have those things with no effort. But that's not the real reason why I'm asking for you to at least consider this."

He pivots, sitting forward, so we're eye to eye. His breath sears my cheek, and it's a nearness that churns my stomach. I shouldn't have so many different versions of him in my head to compare and contrast. The man is a chimera. Calm one minute. Raging the next. Looking at me as though I'm the only woman in the world.

And a heartbeat later, like I don't even exist.

His impression of me has shaped my life for so damn long. Would it be so bad to erase any trace of Donatello Vanici completely? The sad part is that I think it would be the best revenge against someone like him. To cease to exist for once. To be abandoned without a reason.

"I know that you have every right to hate me." He sounds like he's speaking to himself more so than me. Lost in his own world, consumed by his thoughts.

Inhaling raggedly is the only way to make him hear me and reinforce that I'm actually here. He blinks, fixating those dark eyes on my face, scanning intently for whatever he hopes to find. He's dwelling on something, I suspect, hesitating once again before finally spitting it out.

"I'm a horrible fucking husband, if you couldn't tell."

In the background, the lone proprietor rummages through mugs and glasses, returning to quietly replace our pitcher of water. It must have gotten too warm, or maybe she just feels the same instinctive need to fill the silence that I do. I fidget uneasily in my seat, triggering the wood to creak in protest.

He has that look in his eye again.

"I'm no good at love. I'm not good at any fucking thing that doesn't involve killing or money. You'd be a fool to marry someone like me, like this. But all I know is… I need to do something. You don't owe me a damn thing, but I'm willing to try. Something. Anything. Can you give me that chance?"

I flinch. It's strange to hear this note from him. Not a command or a threat, but a question.

Pleading.

My eyes narrow. I can't help the skepticism.

"You're right." Abruptly, he pushes back from the table and stands. "I should go."

Wait. I'm on my feet again, playing right into his hands. He must love how easily he can jerk me around like a puppet on strings.

But he isn't smiling.

When I reach into my pocket a second time, it's with the full knowledge that this is the last card I have left to play. My only remaining method to unnerve him.

The old note is one of the last ones Olivia ever wrote, and his eyes widen as he makes out the crumpled ridges and dried ink. A tremor seems to run through him, making him sway.

"You want to make me read those?" he demands, his voice a dangerous octave deeper. "Fine. You trust me, I'll do it. Whatever you want."

I feel the pen slip from my grasp as those three words hold the weight of so much. A twisted offer that no woman in her right mind would ever take him up on. And yet, it's the promise of the same answers he's been dangling over my head for so damn long.

And…

I'm scared.

It's the emotion I can't admit to Mischa, or even Ellen. I'm so damn scared. The level of fear that paralyzes and freezes the air in my lungs when I think about it. The kind of fear so thick that I constantly feel on the verge of tears.

I'm so sick of feeling afraid because of Donatello Vanici.

I'm so sick of the loneliness, the sleepless nights, and hating him so much it physically hurts. God, I should want to hate him. Every inch.

But for the first time in days, my brain is working again. I can think clearly. I can finally name this "problem" in my head for what it truly is.

I will potentially be forever tied to this man, whether I like it or not. Whether I acknowledge it or not. Whether I return to Mischa's home and lock myself away until I grow old.

I will never be able to escape him.

So why not finally face him on even ground? Take whatever he's willing to give. Anything and everything. Drain him dry of whatever he has left.

I don't have to love him.

I don't even have to like him.

But could I ever trust him?

The answer rings through my skull, hollow and bitter.

No, I couldn't.

I can't.

I stumble past him for the door, aware of his gaze on the back of my neck. Beyond a pane of glass, I can see the streets idling with light traffic. If I hurry, I might still be able to reach Ellen before she leaves. That family loves me. I believe that.

Though, I couldn't say the same were I in their shoes. Especially Mischa's. I've made his life so much harder. I owe him loyalty, and for that alone, I should run now never to look back.

I take another step. Then another. Another.

But I don' t leave. My jaw aches; I'm gritting my teeth so tightly when I turn to face Donatello.

He stands rigidly, his expression pained—like he understands that I'll walk right out of this door. I should.

And he'll let me, that's the confusing part. For a man so hellbent on his own relentless crusade, he'll let me go if I want to leave.

And I should.

9

———

DON

Theoretically, knocking up the daughter of a powerful rival should be low on the list of crazy shit I've done. I've faced the Hortega Cartel alone, been betrayed more times than I can count, and witnessed the death of my own wife and child. Somehow, amid all that suffering, I remained standing.

Morals aside, I have no problem admitting that this might be a new low. Apparently, rock bottom has one final layer hiding beneath it, paved with good intentions. Surprisingly, it doesn't lead to hell, but a church.

The road leading to this lone cathedral is remarkably devoid of traffic, as if the universe conspired to have all obstacles to this insanity removed. Mischa doesn't come falling out of the sky to stop this, and neither does Fabio even think to ring my cell phone. It's a brief respite from the din of arguments and outside voices. For the first time in a long damn while, the only voice I have to listen to is hers.

Figuratively, anyway.

Her speech is expressed in delicate lines of ink spider-webbing my fingers like a literal example of her hold over me. The hold she's always had.

She sits stiffly on the passenger's seat, her face tilted toward the window. I bristle at the imagery. The illusion that she's here against her will, the picture of a nineteen-year-old girl in the grasp of a madman.

Of course, that's how this appears from the outside looking in. I'm a fucking madman.

"We don't have to do this," I say thickly, though it's a lie. *We* don't have to do this—but I do. "You don't... You could still refuse if you wanted to. Leave."

In fact, her appearance without a retinue of guards in the first place should have been a warning sign. I flit my gaze to the rearview mirror, scanning the empty road as paranoia urges me to question her. Demand answers.

I bite my lip in a bid to remain silent. God, she's the only person in the world to rattle me in this way. Even around Liv, I didn't feel so fucking scattered.

Adjusting my grip on the steering wheel, I scan the street for the nearest place to park. I'll let her out. Call Mischa. Forget this insane plan and fall back. There are other matters to focus my attention on. As Fabio claimed, there's still the pressing need to find the crazy son of a bitch who plotted against me in the first place. With Gregori Saleri suddenly dead, who knows what the sick son of a bitch is planning.

So, I stop the car, still gripping the wheel. "I should have never made you come here. I shouldn't have—"

Her hand lands on my forearm gently—but with the force of a slap. I go rigid before the impact of her silent request hits me. She doesn't need a pen to make her point, at least.

Shut up.

I've selfishly made this about me. Again.

"Fuck…" I tear my hands through my hair, feeling the fingers tremble. I wish like hell assembling my thoughts could be as easy as parting the thick, unwashed strands. Logical reasoning hasn't been my strong suit for a while, but it takes twice the effort around her.

When some semblance of coherence does peek through the chaos in my skull, it's an irrational, childish fear.

Bringing her here could just confuse her further if I don't make my intentions crystal clear.

"I'm not supposed to want more from this," I rasp, watching her go rigid in my peripheral vision. "This isn't about love, but I do care about you. What will happen to you."

Out loud, the words sound more pathetic than they did inside my head. It's a confession I haven't made even to Fabio, and the real reason why my desk has seen more use than my own bed.

Every fucking night since that night in the hotel…

She's been on my mind. In my head. I can smell her. Taste her. Still feel her. Denying it all feels like trying to ignore a festering bullet wound. Sooner or later, the infection will take over.

And I lack the strength to fight it. I'm too damn tired. Too weak against the first damn thing to make me feel even an ounce of humanity after years in the dark. I don't deserve it.

But I never deserved a damn thing I've ever gotten. I've just taken it all.

"I should tell you that all I want is to do the 'right' thing and take care of you. I do… I'm not supposed to want more than that. I can't. But if you think I don't care for you in my own way. I do. God, I do. It's nowhere near enough to make up for everything you've been through, but… I've failed you so many times in the past. We aren't those people anymore, and from here on out, things can be different."

She doesn't react, but follows my gaze to the cathedral.

Ironically, I haven't set foot in this place in years. The last time was…the day I married Olivia, in fact. The memory robs me of breath.

I remember coming here with her, mounting the steps of the gothic-style building with the giddy excitement of a young boy. I held her hand in mine, sporting an idiotic grin as I envisioned her walking down the long aisle to meet me. The kiss we'd share.

The night we'd have after.

I had so much damn hope for the life we would build. Nearly a decade later, Liv is gone, but the building we forged those dreams in looks unchanged. I can't take my eyes off it, towering above like a mocking fixture of how much I've lost since my last visit.

When I finally open the door and exit the car, I'm shaking like a leaf—much like the way I was on that day. But the woman beside me then cracked a joke to lighten the mood, a naughty one about what we'd do to each other once we were finally husband and wife.

I can hear her voice so clearly. Hell, I almost expect to see her as I incline my head. I blink instead, caught off guard by the figure standing by me now. She's inches shorter than Liv, her hair a sun-kissed gold, her body even slighter. Like me, she isn't the same person she was back then. No. Maturity has transformed her features in ways I haven't noticed until now. Her lips are fuller, her chin more rounded, her jaw a firm line given how hard she has it clenched.

For once, I can't even begin to get a read on her. Perhaps I shouldn't want to. Confessions aside, this moment extends beyond our feud or even attraction. It is primarily survival. Protection. All the nuanced shit I've spent the past few years striving to secure for Vincenzo.

The future awaiting Kisa Salvatore is a fate no child carrying Vanici blood should ever have to face.

Not this unborn child. Not Vin... Though, there's no telling what he'll think of me afterward. Or how Fabio will react, let alone Mischa. For the time being, I do my best to ignore anyone else as I reach for the woman by my side.

To my shock, she curls her fingers around mine, and together we start for the cathedral.

Apart from the overcast sky, it feels so...normal. Children laugh nearby, playing tag on a field as the city around us bustles with life at the heart of the mid-morning rush hour. In an unusual twist, Hell's Gambit makes for a cheerful backdrop after the shitstorm of crime that's wracked it the past few weeks.

We enter a cathedral devoid of the tension I feel lancing up and down my spine. From the second I pass through the door, the back of my neck prickles. Something's off, but I don't know if it's paranoia or instinct.

I push it aside and approach the back of the main cathedral. It's dead silent, every footfall echoing like a gunshot. There's no telling what might happen once we leave these walls.

But for now, there's some sense of direction in my life after a long fucking time of confusion and darkness.

Even if it's wrong, I can't deny how it feels...

Better than hiding in Havienna, desperate for a drink.

10

WILLOW

The prospect of planning a life with Donatello Vanici is a cruel, sick joke. Ironic even, considering I once believed my brain was defective in my inability to envision my future the way everyone else seemed to. Sure, I could construct an idyllic one out of abstract ideas, such as performing before an audience of thousands, at one of the more prestigious concert halls scattered across the world. Perhaps in Paris, or Milan. I'd play to accompany some famous soprano, and that would be a highlight of my career.

I could visualize it all, but only a distant image, as though it were happening to someone else.

It's funny how everything came to a screeching halt after the viewing of a simple billboard. Knowing that Donatello Vanici was still in my life, and so close in proximity…

That day exposed that mental defect for what it always was —a stubborn acknowledgment that no future could ever suit me without first facing my past. The instant I admitted that to myself, all my pretty hopes and dreams burned to ash. Nothing mattered but erasing this stain on my soul. I truly thought that I had to in order to move on. Live. Return to those dreams and never have him darken my thoughts again.

But now, everywhere I look, my future only seems to have Donatello Vanici in it. Whether directly or indirectly, I will never be able to escape him or his influence.

But I'm tired of running from him.

At least in this way, he can't ignore me either.

If anyone had told me months ago that I would be contemplating elopement with any man, I would have considered them insane. And if they mentioned the name Donatello Vanici…

I would have deemed myself the insane one.

The strange part is that I've never felt more firmly rooted in my thoughts than right now. It's like a light has been turned on in the depths of my mind, exposing all the feelings I've been ignoring. The dirty little emotions I should be too mature to feel. Jealousy. Hatred. Regret. Pain.

So much pain that I've felt blinded by it. Devoid of it, I can finally face the man beside me and see only a figure who looks far too old. Exhausted. Broken. A man who might have never been worthy of my admiration in the first place.

"Two days," he says with a harsh laugh that echoes off the walls of the car's interior. "There goes our reckless plan. Two days until a priest can be secured, along with the necessary documents."

He has a habit of doing this, stating the obvious out loud. I guess it's his way of filling the silence that extends between us.

He makes the delay sound intolerable, but it could be reality's way of exposing this reckless plan for what it truly is. Even the priest seemed taken aback. The man, slightly older than Donatello, barely took his eyes from my face. I could sense the thoughts he had enough tact not to voice.

What hold does this man have over her?

She's too young.

"We won't make it ten hours before your father or Fabio come after us with knives drawn. And maybe they should." Laughing darkly, Donatello swipes a hand through his hair, his expression twisted in contemplation. He's falling back into his self-deprecating mindset. Donatello Vanici hasn't met a problem he couldn't turn onto himself. "What the hell was I even thinking?"

He drags a hand across his lower jaw, disrupting the brown stubble growing there. While doing so, he meets my gaze, and his expression transforms for a second time. "Should I take you home?"

He should. That's what every logical cell in my body is warning me to do. Let him take me home and go back to the shame and guilt, and doubt.

No. I shake my head and watch how he processes the answer. His eyes narrow, taking on that thoughtful gleam. "I thought so."

With a sigh, he sits back, bracing his hands behind his head, his gaze on the church looming above.

"I wouldn't assume that you would be willing to go back to Havienna?"

Havienna, my old home now overrun with strangers. Is the little girl, Kisa, still there? I picture her and shiver. Though, as it turns out, I don't even have to shake my head to make my feelings clear because he takes one look at me and scoffs at the notion.

"I'm in too deep, regardless," he muses. "Why not go all in and leave a paper trail for Fabio to follow. We can't hide from him forever. We'll wait for two days and then…"

He trails off, eyeing the sky for a long while before he finally moves to put the key in the ignition. Without another word, he drives off, and a part of me isn't surprised when, minutes later, we pull up to a familiar skyscraper in the heart of the city.

It's the same hotel where everything began, in a sense. A cold sweat breaks out over my neck, dripping down the back of my dress. I blink, wondering if this is a joke on his part. A mocking quip.

But when I look over, he seems just as apprehensive as I feel.

"Staying here might not flag as easily as a new hotel," he explains, a cunning scheme despite the connotations this establishment holds for us both. "Fabio will still track us down eventually, mind you, but it might buy a few hours, at least. Plenty of time for us to…talk." He frowns at the word choice, eyeing his scribbled-over hand. "I need you to hear me out. At least that way… Just hear me out, please."

Despite the plea, he's silent as we enter the building, and he reserves a room with a cheerful receptionist. Minutes later, we're in the elevators, ascending to the upper floors.

There's a grim sense of déjà vu in retracing these steps, this time without the threat of danger looming overhead. I can still recall how it felt to stand beside him, unsure of his motives—much as I am now.

And how desperate I'd been to make myself feel seen. Heard by him. Understood.

For so long, I've stopped myself from touching the memories of that night. There is no point. He even took pains to make sure I knew that it meant nothing. Nothing…

So why is the only thing on my mind now him? My chest aches in a way I'm not used to, and I nearly sigh in relief as the elevator doors finally break apart.

I scramble out first, sensing him on my heels, his silence oppressive. When we finally enter the room, one small detail I take comfort in is that it's not the same one from that day, at least. The color scheme is different, with accents of cream instead of black, and the view from this suite displays a swath of the city with the bay in the distance.

It's still beautiful—no doubt expensive—and I cringe from the thought of how most women might venture here with a lover on their arm. Not a man they've spent nearly half of their lives hating.

"I… Make yourself comfortable," Donatello says.

He moves awkwardly, crossing straight to the bar cart positioned near the door of a spacious balcony. He reaches for a bottle of liquor, only to pause with his hand inches from it. Slowly, his head roves in my direction, his eyes meeting mine. Abruptly, he withdraws his hand and sighs, raking it through his hair instead.

"I haven't even asked you." His tone is level, but I don't miss the way his eyes dart away from me, examining the view of the city. "Have you decided on a course of action? Before today."

His tone conveys exactly what he means. A course of action. An answer. A solution.

There are a million different ways I could respond to him. Slapping him is by far one of the most tempting. In the end, I merely settle for lifting my arms into the air, though I'm aware of another set of documents burning a hole in my pocket. That's right. There might be no need for any "course of action" beyond letting nature run its course—according to the doctor's vague explanation.

I can recall only snippets of what she said, and something that might be guilt pinches at my chest. Despite Donatello's newfound willingness to accept responsibility, this whole mess might be for nothing, in the end...

All I'd have to do is hand over that proof and let him process it.

But I don't.

In the resulting silence, Donatello sighs. A ball of restless energy, he fidgets with another bottle of liquor, lifting it from the cart completely, only to set it back down. Heavy footsteps carry him toward the center of the room, where he begins to pace. There is such a sharp contrast in how he holds himself compared to what I'm used to. Gone is the swagger. The bold defiance that always made him seem invincible. In this moment, his usual bravado is nothing more than a fractured shell.

Not for the first time, I get a glimpse of the real Donatello Vanici, and he is a stranger I barely recognize.

"I didn't ask," he says, whirling on his heel to face my direction. He has his head cocked, eyes narrowed cautiously. "If you even wanted this. I didn't ask you directly."

His attention sears my skin, fixed on me so intensely. There is nothing I can do that won't draw notice from him. The second I start to exhale, he tenses.

"I'm sorry for that. I…" He advances, moving slowly as if to give me the chance to avoid any contact. When I don't withdraw, he reaches out, bringing his hand within inches of my face. His fingers waver, inching closer…

Then he curls each one into a fist and turns away, storming to the other end of the room. He nears the bar cart for a third time, running his hand along the edge of it. "I don't know what to say," he admits, his back to me. "I'm sorry for that. I should know at least what to fucking say."

Shoulders rigid, he continues to pace.

That chilling sense of déjà vu grows stronger. He's done this before, withdrawing inside himself, dwelling over his own internal struggle, blinded to everything else.

I don't realize I've taken a step toward him until he stiffens, stopping mid-step. He watches me, and I think I'm just as uneasy as he is—equally confused when my hand lands against his jaw too softly to be considered a slap. I feel the rugged contours of his face beneath, vibrating with whatever words he's keeping himself from voicing.

There is something so familiar about him that, at times, it physically hurts to be this close. A part of me is still drawn to his stern features, compelled to seek out the hints of softness I know lurk beneath the stoic exterior.

I start to pull away, but then I change my mind and continue to explore the bristly stubble along his cheek. Then down around his mouth.

He watches me, his expression constricted—as though it hurts to have me touch him like this. Regardless, he doesn't resist. Doesn't slap my hand away. It's one of the few moments of power he's ever allowed me, and I extort every last second.

Internally, I mull over my reaction to him, parsing over every nuanced emotion I feel. Confusion mostly. Then remnants of old anger and primarily just…

Pain. It hurts to look at him. Judging from how his frown deepens the longer I touch him, he feels the same.

"I should have been able to face you like a man," he says, the movement of his lips disrupting the placement of my fingers. "The first time. When I saw you… I should have let you drive that knife through my chest like you planned to. None of this would have happened, and you would have… I don't fucking know. Some semblance of clarity. Closure. You could have moved on with your life for once without me holding you back." He reaches up, capturing the back of my hand against his cheek. He holds it there for so long, basting the side of my face with the heat of his breath.

"You deserve that," he admits, his voice rough. "Maybe it's best if I get it out now. So, we can move forward, and there's no more… Chaos."

He pursues his lips with renewed determination. As he cups my jaw against his palm this time, there is no hesitation. I shiver at the warmth emanating from it. Slowly, he guides my head back, forcing me to meet his gaze directly.

"The first day I saw you. Saw you again… My mind went blank. You were beautiful, yes, but that isn't what stood out to me. It was your eyes. Those fiery, hellcat eyes. Even if you weren't who you are..."

Both a Stepanov and Safiya.

"I would have been drawn to you regardless." His voice deepens, betraying a hint of that elusive truth he's avoided voicing out loud. The validation of the persistent part of me driven to find him. See him. Smell him. Taste him.

We're drawn together by something more than hate. He felt it too.

"Though, even in an alternate universe where we never met previously, your father would have every right to kick my ass for being attracted to you."

Not because of a shared horrific past, just that he's simply far older. That age is apparent more than ever in the wrinkles etched around his eyes. And yet, despite the weathered features, they're still objectively handsome.

I hate my body for reacting to him the way it does. My heartbeat quickens, my pulse hammering like mad.

Whatever this attraction is, it isn't reciprocated. He looks at me like he's physically in pain. Agony. As if the mere sight of me torments him in a way I could never understand. Finally, he withdraws his hand, spinning around to face the door of the balcony. He approaches it slowly, lacing his fingers together behind his back, head inclined.

"There is a future you could have, should you choose it. Either way, you deserve more than this. I should take you back home myself—"

I lunge forward, but it's like I'm not in control of my body. Something else has taken hold, and I can only watch on helplessly as my hand flies out, connecting with his cheek.

The slap startles him into silence, but I can't seem to lower my stinging hand. It hangs in the air between us as he roves his gaze from my twitching fingers back to my face.

"I deserved that," he admits. "I deserve a punch, too. Hell, far more than that."

He grabs my hand, startling me. Rather than bat it away, he guides the fingers into a fist, stroking each bared knuckle.

Alarm shoots through my chest, warning me to pull back. Retreat. Run.

Nothing good comes out of letting my guard down around this man. After everything we've been through, I can't risk losing any more of myself than I already have.

But he won't let me escape so easily.

I feel his breath on my shoulder before I even sense his face beside mine, his lips near my ear.

"The right thing to do would be to let you marry Vincenzo," he says, and only shock keeps me from recoiling as violently as I want to. I'm frozen in place, unsure of how serious he even is. Deadly serious, judging from the heavy exhale he releases next.

"A good man would insist that you do that. He would stand aside and know… Your future isn't one he should have any damn part in."

I'll never get over just how damn unpredictable he is. Open one minute, closed the next. Before I can react, he pushes past me, moving stiffly toward a hallway that branches off this part of the suite. "I requested two bedrooms," he adds. "You can have the larger one."

I hear a door slam, and knowing him, I'm sure he locked it. Not out of any gentlemanly concern, either. Merely out of his own selfish fear that I might defy him. That I might creep into that room after him and deny him the last word. That I won't let him hide from this or escape his guilt.

Why should he be able to?

When I can't.

I don't know if I'm surprised or relieved that hours pass without Mischa breaking down this door, or without Evgeni coming for me. It could be that Ellen took my note seriously enough to intervene on my behalf as I requested.

Or that Mischa's finally done what he should have years ago and written me off as someone else's problem. It was never his responsibility to take me in, and everything that's come after is my fault and mine alone.

The guilt I feel is like a noose, constantly pressing on my throat, but never quite hard enough to suffocate me completely. I can only imagine how both he and Ellen might feel. Leaving again is just constant cruelty to them.

And yet, the selfish impulse driving me all along insists that I have every right to handle this on my own. It's my life, after all. My future in question.

And Donatello Vanici has always been my cross to bear.

I can't seem to leave this main room of the suite, even as darkness falls, and the only illumination comes in the form of moonlight, paired with the neon glow of the city at its brightest peak.

I can't even read the letters I fish from my pocket and scan in the dark. Over and over, I stare at them anyway.

Over and over, my gaze flickers toward the exit.

I keep toying with the thought of running, and with every passing second, it seems more tempting. I even start to stand, wincing as my sore muscles protest after sitting for so long. Warily, I take a step. Then another. Another.

And almost as if on cue, I see his shadow, engulfing the mouth of the hallway nearby. Then I hear him, that perpetual low, heavy sigh.

"If you left now, I wouldn't blame you," he says, inching within a beam of moonlight that cuts across his face. I can make out his eyes, intense and yet unreadable. He takes another step, and I wonder if he truly intends to stop me. "But you must be hungry. We can talk over some food."

Talk. This illusive conversation we have yet to have. This time, however, he doesn't seem too willing to give me the chance to refuse. He crosses over to a phone perched on a table near the door. He must dial for room service, because a minute later, he's reciting a handful of meal items.

Once he hangs up, he switches on the main light and retreats to a small dining area positioned near the windows.

Perhaps it's the tension distorting time, but it feels like I've barely blinked before room service arrives. A smiling man enters, carrying our meal on a tray—various steaming items that I doubt he put any thought into ordering. Pasta. Fish. Fruit. Sandwiches.

As the server retreats, we both take places around the table.

And another battle in our unending war commences.

"Eat." Donatello snatches up something seemingly at random—a sandwich that he hastily takes a bite of.

I reach for a set of silverware and fix a serving of pasta on a plate. But I don't eat it. I observe him instead.

That strange sense of familiarity sinks in again. Like we're the only two in the world, nothing else matters beyond these walls, for better or worse.

"If you could live anywhere else, in or outside of the city, where would it be?" It's a question far different than any I would expect, catching me off guard.

Lost in thought, I turn my gaze to the window, inspecting the city beyond. The truth is I haven't pondered where I might wind up after my schooling in Vienna. Few places in the world seemed to hold the same allure of Stepanov Manor, or even Hell's Gambit. It's a rare gem—a mess of a city that glorifies its flaws as much as its beauty.

"This place is a cesspool," Donatello remarks as if reading my mind. "But it has an appeal you can't deny. Even if you go beyond its borders, you never truly leave." He follows my gaze, propping his fist beneath his chin. "I never thought I'd consider returning for longer than a few days at least, to help Vin settle in…"

He trails off, no doubt recalling one of the events he supposedly returned to attend. My debutante ball.

It feels like another lifetime ago. In another world, with far different worries than the ones plaguing me now. Back then, my only concern had been getting through that party and the few months I'd have home before returning to the conservatory.

"I could sell Havienna," he proposes, still facing the balcony. "Find another place somewhere else. A house in the country… A place fit to live in. Hell." He laughs darkly. "Before now, I'd thought my future living arrangements would consist of hopping from hotel to hotel. This place is hell on earth, but it's in our blood—" He nods to the jumbled array of concrete buildings and neon lights.

I stand, drawn toward the balcony to get a better view. The door opens easily, and the warm night air is a jarring slap in contrast to the cooler air inside the suite. Out here, the noise of the city assaults in a barrage of honking horns and distant voices.

It isn't loud enough to disguise the advancing figure who follows me out, coming to grip the railing beside me. He leans against it, tilting his head back to eye the impassive sky above.

"A change of subjects seems to be in order," he declares. "I never told you what sparked my change of heart, did it? Why I reached out to you in the first place…"

He didn't. I shake my head, sensing an ominous tremor wrack my spine.

"You remember Gregori Saleri? That pompous prick? Well, he's dead."

I picture the older counterpart of the duo we've confronted more than once.

"I never got the details, but the point is his granddaughter —remember her? Kisa? Well, despite being born into that godforsaken family, she might not inherit a damn dime. Poor kid. The point is, what use is money or power or any of that shit if it dies along with you?"

While most people would consider the emotional side of a young girl losing most of her family overnight, this is what truly bothers him. Her lack of resources to show for the tragedy. Not the monetary aspect, I suspect. Just the failure of a family's name for protection. The lack of control wealth or power gives anyone in the end. That reality disturbs him enough that his eyes are downcast, his knuckles protruding as he tightens his grip over the railing.

"You still have those letters," he says haltingly, and I feel my throat thicken at the audible pain he doesn't even try to hide. He has another reason for broaching this topic, it seems. "Did she write about how I was never there? That I told her I loved her at night, but spent more time at my desk than in our bed?"

He captures my wrist without warning, shifting to face me. From this angle, his features are bathed in shadow, robbing me of any hope of reading his intentions. Intuition is my only guide. His posture is relaxed rather than hostile, at least. The low, unsettling tone of his voice doesn't even near the enraged growl I'm used to. Even his touch is oddly gentle, providing more than enough give to pull away if I wanted.

"I was a terrible husband," he admits. "A selfish bastard who didn't deserve love."

My breath catches as sweat slicks the back of my neck. Is this his way of confessing what Mischa's alluded to more than once? That he played a larger role in Olivia's death…

"I don't think I'm capable of loving anyone," he continues, his nearness sending my pulse surging. "But I will make you a promise, here and now. No matter what happens, we can do this together—"

A noise sounds from inside the suite. Banging? I whirl around, recognizing the persistent thud—someone is at the door.

Donatello, however, sighs. "Goddamn it, not now."

His shoulders slump, and I suspect he recognizes who our insistent visitor is before he even reaches the door.

I follow him, but it doesn't take long for a familiar voice to emanate from the hall.

"You open this door, you son of a bitch!" If it weren't for the faint hint of polish to that voice, I wouldn't even guess it could be Fabio. He sounds furious, following up his demand with more fierce pounding. "Donatello? Donatello! I know you're in there. How the hell could you do this—"

Donatello wrenches open the door, revealing the man alone on the other end, his fist raised mid-pound. His voice aside, I barely recognize Fabio from his appearance. His usually crisp suit is rumpled, his hair tousled. His eyes look bloodshot, and the faint hint of alcohol wafts from him, another alarming change.

When he sees Donatello, he raises his still brandished fist, slamming it against the larger man's chest. "Have you lost your mind?" he demands as the other man grunts, rocking back on his heels. "You must have. You've gone fucking insane. That's the only possible explanation that might see you out of this with your life, at least. How the hell could you even think of doing something so reckless? Do you know the amount of ass-kissing I've had to do just to keep the Stepanovs at bay? And if you even dreamed of so much as touching the girl, I swear to God, I'll—" He breaks off abruptly as if realizing that I'm here. Blinking, he steps back from Donatello, smoothing his hand down the front of his jacket. "Willow. My dear, I'm here to take you home, and I apologize for whatever ordeal you've been through. I will—"

"No," Donatello says. The calmness of his tone alarms me more than Fabio's frazzled nerves. He stands tall, the picture of poise, and it's as if the two men have swapped personalities for the moment.

"You don't have a say in this, you son of a bitch!" Fabio curls another fist, but Donatello shakes his head before he can launch an attack.

"I don't," he admits. "But *she* does." He gestures to me, and Fabio blinks as if struck dumb.

"She?"

"You once warned me to let her have her peace," Donatello adds. "Why don't you listen before you gripe at me?"

Whether he intended to or not, his right hand is in view, exposing the missives I wrote across it, the ink now smudged and faded.

"You really think you have the higher moral ground right now?" Fabio scoffs at the idea. Still, he turns to me, and I can see him working to compose himself. "Willow…" He breaks off, glaring at Donatello. "I think it would be best if you let me speak to her in private."

Donatello ushers him inside. Then he strolls to the balcony, stepping out into the night air. His stance gives the appearance of relaxed confidence—but he didn't shut the door, ensuring he can still hear every word said.

Seemingly oblivious to that fact, Fabio sighs, raking a hand through his hair. "I'm sorry. God damn him…" He glowers in Donatello's direction, only to seem to remember where he is. "If he brought you here against your will, I'll kill him. But first, I will return you home. I have my men downstairs and a car ready. Your parents are aware, but I've managed to convince them to let me speak to Donatello first." He reaches for my arm, and I nearly trip in my rush to back away.

My thoughts are a blur, and I can't even make sense of them. Helpless, I grit my teeth, eyeing the wall in front of me.

"You don't want to leave?" Fabio sounds somewhere between shocked and fearful. "I… If you are afraid of Donatello, I can assure you that—"

I shake my head again and turn to find him gaping at me. I don't even know how to convey the rush of emotions racing through my head. Maybe shame is the best way to describe it. A fear that I can't go back to hiding in a room alone. Donatello Vanici is one monster I am no longer afraid of.

But shame? *That* is what haunts me. I can't bear the thought of what I've done to Mischa and his family. No longer can I burden them, either.

"I don't... I guess it's not my place to understand," Fabio admits, tugging at his collar. "You have the right to make your choice, and I can't stop you. Even if I don't agree. Not in the slightest." He clears his throat and raises his voice, presumably for the benefit of the figure on the balcony. "You can come back in, you son of a bitch—"

"Keep cursing, and you might shock yourself into a heart attack, Fab," Donatello remarks as he reenters the suite. I don't miss how he brings himself within the dangerous orbit of the bar cart, only to turn at the last minute and perch himself on a leather couch instead. His eyes flit over me before settling on the figure pacing a few yards away, but he hides whatever he might be thinking behind an impassive stare. "Maybe you should have a seat."

"Maybe you should stop fucking up the lives of everyone stupid enough to love you," Fabio snaps back. His cheeks flush the second the words leave his mouth. "I didn't mean it like that—"

"Yes, you did," Donatello says softly. "And you're right. I won't deny how much you've done for me. So, believe me when I say that this isn't your fault. I don't expect you to bail me out of this mess. Maybe that's been the problem all along. I've been too busy letting you fix my fuck ups. It's time that I take the helm on this one at least, don't you think?"

If anything, Fabio's cheeks become even redder. "Oh, don't be a fool," he snaps, throwing himself onto a nearby leather armchair. Groaning, he tips his head and exhales sharply. "Funny of you to want to be noble now, of all times. As much as it pains me to admit, this is a mess that even you, with your vast talent for fucking up, won't be able to get out of alone. You'll need a smooth talker just to buy enough time to develop a plan, let alone anything beyond that. Unless…" He swallows hard, darting his gaze in my direction before returning to Donatello. "You've settled on—"

"No," Donatello growls before he can even voice the option out loud. Then he frowns. "I don't know. It's not my choice to make."

"Yes, well, knowing, either way, will certainly limit our options," Fabio says grimly. "Not that I would be crass enough to voice an opinion either way—"

"Only one person can make that choice," Donatello interjects. I can feel his gaze on my neck as I turn away. It's far more unnerving to hear them dance around this mysterious final option rather than just say it.

Especially when this entire conversation might be moot after all.

"Yes, well, we don't have to focus on that now," Fabio says sardonically. "There are more pressing issues. Things that you and I definitely have control over. If you plan to go unnoticed, you can't stay here, that's for damn sure. Trust me, I'm not the first person to guess that you would return to this hotel. You aren't as brooding and mysterious as you think, Don. You'll need somewhere more secluded, but just as easy to secure. And not that god forsaken Havienna—"

"I'm open to other suggestions," Donatello says gruffly. "But don't use Mischa as your excuse. I plan on facing him directly and making my intentions clear soon enough."

"Like hell, you will," Fabio says with a harsh sound in between a laugh and a scoff. "No. That is one stupid decision I will override. The last thing you need to do is offend the man. I will handle all direct communication with the Stepanovs. And Willow, of course."

"So much for being done with cleaning up my messes," Donatello says with a grim smile.

Fabio doesn't return the expression. "This is so much more than a mere 'mess,' Don," he warns. "This is beyond anything I could have ever thought you capable of getting yourself into. Jesus Christ, a child—"

He breaks off abruptly, his eyes wide. "I'm sorry. God, I'm a fool."

No, he's honest. This is the first time anyone has put it so bluntly, rather than dance around the topic with wordplay.

A child.

Mine.

And Donatello's.

"Willow!" I hear Fabio cry out, but his hand isn't the one I feel cinch my forearm a second later.

"I've got you," Donatello warns, his voice a murmur. He easily rights my balance, but I pull away from him the instant I can.

His nearness is a taunting reminder of everything I've lost, and for a second, I wonder if Fabio is right. I should go home now.

"Whatever you decide to do, it's your choice," Donatello says as if reading my mind. "But know that you have my support no matter what. Whatever you decide, I will respect it."

I swivel my head to inspect him, skeptical of that. Could someone like him truly stand aside and let someone else take the reins of a decision that might go against his own desires? I can't help but think of Olivia and what was revealed in her letters. Did he respect *her* wishes?

Hell, he just confessed that he knew she was unhappy…

"I'm a fool," Fabio insists. I look back to find him returning to his seat, grimacing apologetically. "We don't have to discuss the particulars for now. What we really need to do is cement a plan of action. Make the necessary arrangements to keep you both safe and go from there. Perhaps it might be best to leave the city for a while—"

"We can't," Donatello says softly.

Fabio inclines his head. "Oh? And why not?"

Sighing, Donatello returns to his position on the balcony, letting his voice drift back. "Because I've already scheduled an appointment with a priest in two days."

The room goes dead silent, and I almost fear that Fabio did have a heart attack after all. He stares blankly, his head cocked in disbelief. Then he stands, smoothing his hands down the front of his suit. "And why on earth would you need to see a priest?" he wonders, his tone still composed.

"To arrange a marriage, of course," Donatello replies.

Of all the responses Fabio might experience, the last one I expect is for him to laugh. Loudly in long, booming cackles. He has to clutch his stomach, his head thrown back. Seconds into the display, he seems to realize that no one else is smiling. Slowly, his playful grin falls flat.

"You aren't serious," he says as Donatello reenters the room. "Tell me that was some sick attempt at a joke. Donatello?"

The man in question doesn't respond, instead returning to the bar cart for the umpteenth time. With determination, he snatches a bottle by its neck. Then he spins and throws it so hard it smashes against the wall in a spray of amber liquid and flying glass.

"Jesus Christ!" Fabio exclaims, covering his head. "Have you lost your fucking mind?"

Donatello eyes his trembling hands before wrestling them into twin fists. For a long moment, he doesn't move. Doesn't seem to react at all.

"I'm sorry," he says finally. "I'll clean it up."

"I know this is a lot," Fabio says gently. He crosses the room and cautiously places a hand on the other man's shoulder. "And while it is primarily your fault, I won't let you go through this alone. Either of you. But honestly, do you think that a hasty elopement will help to solve this mess any quicker? I can assure you that it won't. If anything, it will make life way more complicated."

"So, what do you suggest?" Donatello counters. "Keep hiding in shame and pretend this isn't happening? Wait until it's too late? Ignore this mess for another seven years and then deal with the consequences? I'm not willing to do that, Fabio. Not this time."

"Donatello…" Fabio throws himself onto the nearest couch. When he finally lifts his head, he's dropped his polished persona completely. He looks haggard and exhausted, a man pushed to his breaking point. "If you would stop barging into these situations head-on, you might actually realize that more people are on your side than against. You don't have to push me away. I will support you no matter what. But I also can't quietly stand by every time you act so impulsively. Have you considered what Willow might want? What her family would think? How this might play out a week down the road, or a month, a year?"

"I'm thinking of the here, and now; you're right," Donatello admits. "I'm wondering what would happen if I were to have a bullet slam into my skull this instant. How might Vincenzo and anyone else I care about be protected? Sometimes reckless decisions are the only way to circumvent the possibility that life won't always follow some neat plan devised by an accountant, or on a mob boss' timetable. I think you and I know better than most that life rarely follows a particular order. Don't believe me? Ask Gregori Saleri."

"So that is what this is about?" Fabio sighs for the umpteenth time. "You think a wedding solves anything? Though I can admit, this doesn't feel quite the same when it was a way to screw Mischa over and keep him from killing you."

"Which means it should be easier to plan," Donatello counters.

"And what about you?" Fabio turns his focus on me. "Though I assume that if you weren't at least partially in agreement, you wouldn't be here in the first place."

There's nothing I can do to counter that, not that he truly seems to want the reassurance.

"Running away, however, isn't the way to do this," Fabio insists, stroking his chin. "This should be handled correctly, through all of the proper channels—"

"You really think a sanctioned wedding makes much of a fucking difference now?" Donatello interjects coldly. "I don't think Mischa will be lining up to be my best man, either way, Fab."

"Mischa isn't the only one who matters here," Fabio says softly. "I think it's time you start to realize that. Take Vincenzo, for example. What the hell is he supposed to think if you go gallivanting off without a word? No, this must be handled in the right way. No more games."

"So, then what's your suggestion?" Donatello demands. "Keep groveling for forgiveness? I think it's a little late for that as well."

"No groveling," Fabio replies with more of his usual stoic calm restored. "No running away, either. Instead, I suggest you *inform*."

Donatello inclines his head, those dark eyes narrowed. "Inform?"

"I'll arrange another meeting with Mischa—but not to get his permission or agreement," Fabio hastily clarifies. "But merely to inform him of these latest developments and issue an invitation should he so choose."

"Which means?"

Fabio raises an eyebrow. "It means, you position yourself as an arrogant son of a bitch confident in his actions. Mischa could object, of course, but this way, you eliminate some of the appearance of guilt."

"How so?"

Fabio winces, visibly uncomfortable with whatever he's about to propose. "You set a date, but whether or not Mischa attends is irrelevant—" almost apologetically, he cuts his gaze toward me. "What matters is the appearance of propriety. Frankly, though, I'm disgusted with your behavior Donatello. Morally, I'd recommend that you cease this charade completely and make amends—"

"Or?" Donatello demands. The firm set to his shoulders reveals he has no intention of either outcome.

"Or you own the damage you've caused, and you live it. No more hiding. No more running. You own this choice, no matter how disastrous it may prove to be."

"Does that mean you'll help?"

Fabio's pained expression doesn't clearly broadcast either confirmation or a denial. "It seems I don't have much of a choice, do I? I can make arrangements with Mischa, but other than that, I can't control what happens from there. Only the two of you have that choice—and I do hope that it is a consensual choice between the both of you."

Again, he turns his gaze on me as if hunting for any hint of disagreement. When I don't give him one, he shrugs.

"I'll head to my office now and see what I can do. And Donatello? Be careful."

He leaves the suite, but everything looms larger in his absence. The distance between Donatello and me seems almost insurmountable, despite consisting of only a few short feet.

In the absence of Fabio, whatever confidence he displayed diminishes. Silently, he eyes the floor, his jaw clenched in thought. When he finally meets my gaze, I can't decipher his expression.

"Well, Fabio may be prone to theatrics, but he does have a point. What is it that you want?" He sits on the leather couch across from me, palming his chin. The look on his face is pensive but confused too. He's uneasy. God, it hurts how easily I can decipher him in some moments—and yet others, he's a stranger.

"Even if it's… The choice is yours."

I think he believes he's offering me some great favor. A glorified means through which he can wash his hands of any responsibility. His tortured expression suits that image perfectly.

Until he frowns before I even realize why—I've shaken my head.

"No?" He sits back, his head cocked in the way he used to inspect any of his men who dared to question him. "I'm assuming you don't mean that in the obvious sense. You're angry."

It's unfair. Even now, he can read me like an open book when his own motives are so hard to discern.

But he's right. Anger is exactly what I feel surging through my veins, heating my cheeks.

"It's not my place to demand an answer from you at all. Is that what you mean?"

I swallow hard. Then I copy him, leaning my head back against the leather cushions, observing him from this newer angle.

The action draws a choked laugh from him. "You're right." The hoarse note in his voice makes my chest clench. "I don't get to swoop in like some fucking hero and put you in the place of a child. You are not a child. I think you've made that clear more than once." He rubs his jaw as if recalling my most recent slap.

I don't remember if he's said those exact words so bluntly before. If so, they didn't resonate like they do now. It's as if that fact finally dawned on him. No longer can he regulate me to a position easily overlooked.

"Fine," he grates, still running a hand over the stubble on his chin. "We're on the same playing field. This is a fucking mess."

His voice loses the patient, gentle tone that strained it before. He's cold, but honestly raw. I never thought I'd crave to see this side of him so damn much. The unpolished, unrestrained Donatello Vanici.

The cruel bastard capable of leaving me behind. In this instance, he claims we're on an equal playing field, but I'd be a fool to take him at his word.

I sit forward, and his brows draw together with open curiosity. "You don't believe me."

I shake my head again, and he laughs.

"I shouldn't expect you to."

Damn him. This newfound freeness with me is a double-edged sword. His stoic mask slips further, his eyes openly wounded.

"You don't have a damn reason to trust me, do you? Especially not now. Fuck!" He stands, turning on his heels to pace. With this polished, luxury suite as a backdrop, he looks more imposing than ever—a man unraveling. Gone is the false confidence. That reassuring calm.

Perhaps all along, it was merely an act. The truth is, he's just as terrified as I am.

Because I am terrified. It seeps in when I least expect it, sending my pulse racing, coiling my stomach in knots. Watching him storm across the room unravels what little resolve I had. It's humanizing to see him like this. And disarming. This man is far more dangerous when he seems vulnerable.

For the next few seconds, we coexist in strained silence—with me watching him while he sneaks glimpses of me in return. His thought process is a chilling beast to behold. His eyes narrow, his brows wrinkling as his pace overall slows until he comes to a stop just feet from me.

"You don't want me to treat you like a child," he reiterates ominously. "Then I'll be as honest with you as I can. You're pregnant." He breathes out the word. "And it's mine. You can't even begin to understand how fucked up that is—" He seems to stop himself, grimacing as if he has to choke back the words and start again. "You should know how bad this really is."

The look in his eye catches me off guard. It's so stern, and yet that openness remains. For the first time, I can see beneath the cool exterior to just how unsteady he is underneath. He's shaking, his jaw clenched.

"Not only because of how young you are." He inspects me, once again grappling to accept what he admitted—I am not a child.

"It's who you are. Who I am. Frankly, if Mischa wanted to put a bullet in my skull, I wouldn't blame him—"

I'm not sure what I do to make him stop mid-word. Frown? Flare my nostrils? Whatever it is, draws his focus, and he sighs, his mouth tilting downward.

"You're right. Fuck Mischa. This isn't about him. This is about you and me…" He turns with a grace a man with his bulk shouldn't be capable of, coming to stand before me directly. "You don't want to be coddled? Then I'll spare you the false sympathy and the restraint. I'll tell you what I want —I want my child."

His voice rips through me, stealing my breath away. If I weren't convinced by the dark conviction in his tone, then the look in his eye would be proof enough. He's serious.

"I could lie to you and paint you a false picture of what your future will be when the inevitable comes to pass. That I'd step back. Give you time. That you could scurry off to Vienna and leave my child sequestered in Stepanov Manor, pretending I never existed. I'll tell you now—you're wrong if you believe that. No one will keep my child from me. I won't patiently lurk in the background. I will be there. Do you understand me?"

I do. And at the same time…

I don't.

Where the hell was this same man seven years ago? Though, it's not like I need any further proof of what I now know to be the truth. He never gave a damn about me.

And he still doesn't.

He stiffens as if sensing exactly what I'm thinking. Rather than counter me outright, he shifts his gaze to the window displaying the city's waterfront.

"There's more," he says gruffly. "You don't want to be treated like a child? Then enough with the naïve mind games. You tell me what you're after. The responsibility is mine; I'll accept that. But *enough*." He growls the word, his anger apparent in every grated syllable—and pain, too. It lurks beneath the gruff notes, reinforced by his heavy breathing. "I refuse to be the monster anymore in your little game—" He looks at me and grimaces at whatever he spies in my expression. "You don't know what I mean? Fine. I'll spell it out for you."

He advances, reaching me in seconds. Before I can react, he snatches my hand, drawing me to my feet. I sway, off-balance, as he grips both of my shoulders, leveling me with a stern, searching glance.

"Do you have that pen?"

I do. It's still in the pocket of the coat I have yet to take off. When I withdraw it, he snatches it, tossing the lid aside.

Then he lashes out with the nib drawn. I suck in a breath as I watch the metal tip connect with my palm. Within seconds, his intent becomes clear—not to attack but to use my own weapon against me in another way.

He writes, taking his time to form each word so that I feel the lash of ink with the same intensity as if he shouted. *You fucked me.*

"I'm not sick enough of a bastard to blame you for what happened," he adds, releasing me. We're close enough that his breath rakes over my cheek, searing hot. "I know better than that. But what I refuse to allow anymore?"

He strokes my chin with the pad of his thumb, tilting my face for his inspection.

"There it is. That. *That* innocent little glance as if you don't know damn well that you've been playing with fire all along. You know how babies are made. So don't pretend like you don't understand the pull you have. I'm not blaming you. I'm asking…" He looks down, exhaling harshly. "I'm asking you to show me an ounce of mercy in that respect. You stay here; there are boundaries to follow. Rules we will both abide by. Do you understand that? I've told you what I want."

He pulls away, his hands outstretched in a gesture of surrender. With a metallic clink, my pen hits the floor, rolling out of view.

"Just show me that one, small shred of fucking mercy and make it clear what you want. Do that for me, and I'll do whatever the hell it is. I swear to you."

He turns away, retreating swiftly toward the mouth of the suite.

"There are two rooms," he reminds me. "I'll take this one. You take the other. We keep them separate unless invited in."

No such invitation comes as he barrels down the hallway and out of sight. A second later, a slamming door alludes to which of the two rooms he's taken.

I should be relieved, I think. Flattered by his honesty. And his rules. And his assertions. And his lies.

Any other day before now, I'd retreat into the empty room and wait for the morning like a dutiful captive. But therein lies the flaw of his summation of our "situation."

I'm not a child. I'm not his captive. I'm not allowed to question his rules and ultimatums.

He merely expects me to behave however he wants me to—however is convenient to fit the narrative. He doesn't want a real equal playing field.

But if he accused this of being my game, then I alone can make the rules.

And break them.

I don't think; I just follow him down the hall and grip the knob of the only closed door. It isn't locked, opening easily the second I turn the handle.

His back is to me, his jacket already off. I spy it slung over a leather chair behind him as he wrenches at his collar next. Then, he must hear me because he freezes.

There are no words to adequately describe what I feel watching him. It isn't hate—not anymore. Something more wistful than that. Maybe it's simply frustration?

The man is a walking contradiction when it comes to me. *Do this. Don't do that. You're not a child. You're too young.*

There seems to be no in between among the extremes he's willing to slot me into. Not that I can blame him. I've let him take my voice in more ways than one.

But, as he said, *enough*.

The right thing to do would be to end this now. Show him the medical paperwork and let him revel in the fact that our futures might not be linked after all. Squaring my chin, I cross over to the chair sporting his coat and sit down, facing him with my hand in my pocket. The tumult of emotions crashing through his expression one by one are almost comical to witness. He's angry. Angry enough to grit his teeth, his nostrils flaring as he rebuttons his collar and lets his hands fall to his sides. Then frustration becomes evident as he clenches his fists. Finally…

His eyes take on that faraway hue of brown.

"What do you… I don't know what the fuck you want from me." His inflection shifted so drastically over those few words it's dizzying to decipher each nuanced phrase. It's as if he went from cautious coddling to callous and demanding, grappling with his promise yet again. We're on an even playing field, supposedly, but I'm not willing to let him retreat just yet.

It's not fair.

There are so many damn things I need to say, but the method eludes me. It's sadly ironic in a sense. He was the first person who ever made me feel as though I didn't need a voice to be heard. But now, interacting with him is much like trying to communicate through a wall of solid concrete.

I let myself wallow in the self-pity for a heartbeat before I recall the few times I ever managed to get through to him without the benefit of being his precious, charming Safy. I made him listen, either through violence or…

My cheeks flame as he clears his throat. I'd been so wrapped up in my own thoughts, I didn't notice him cocking his head as his expression finally settles on one overarching emotion. Hostility.

"I'm guessing this is your way of making it known you don't want boundaries. Fine." He stalks to another corner of the room, where a chair sits before a small desk. He grabs it, dragging it to me. Then he perches himself on it, leaning forward with his weight precariously balanced on his toes as if he's aching to leave. Run from me.

Instead, he snatches my hand, running his calloused thumb over my palm. I suck in a breath, though I already know what his real intention is. To unnerve. To rouse the shiver that snakes down my spine and make me second guess my own motives.

It's been his method from the start.

This time, I don't give in, leaving my hand in his grasp. Instead, I look up, holding the inquisitive stare that greets me.

"Alright. You have me," he warns gruffly. "So, what now? We rehash the past again? You threaten to leave. Or…" His eyes widen for a split second betraying that this next guess disturbs him more than he will ever admit out loud. "You've changed your mind."

The scary part is that I haven't. Sitting here now, I don't feel that oppressive need to run. Or the guilt or the pain that suffocated me for days. Alone in this room with Donatello Vanici, I'm just…

Tired.

He is exhausting, with his web of secrets and lies. My own experiences with him aside, there's the looming mystery of what happened to Olivia. And my birth father.

And to me.

So no, running isn't an option anymore. To prove it, I manipulate my fingers to squeeze his in return. He doesn't seem startled by the gesture. He stiffens, a sigh hissing through his lips. Rightfully, he sees it as the challenge it is.

"I promised not to coddle you," he reiterates. "Should I explain what that really means? I won't sugar-coat things, either. You go through with this, you marry me, and you won't receive some happily ever after. I could never love you in the way a woman should be loved."

He reverses course, withdrawing his hand from mine. I stare down at the pale, slim digits that seem so frail in comparison to his larger, darker ones, scarred with the remnants of the life of a crime lord.

"I can't," he adds, turning away. The windows in this room are smaller than in the main space, displaying a clearer view of the waterfront and the moonlight painting its delicate surface. He eyes the water with a desperation that chills a part of me to the bone. "I can't love you. I can't protect you. And… I can't give you the closure you want. I can't." He shrugs, but I've never seen a man look more helpless. "So, if that's why you're here, I suggest you leave."

He wants me to, more than anything. Sometimes, he's so good at hiding his real feelings. But every now and again, he slips, and the volatile reality peeks through. Beneath this stoic mask, he is in turmoil, scrambling to cling to that composed bravado he's sported for so long.

He wasn't lying—there is no more coddling, just cruel honesty. But it doesn't sting the way I thought it would.

He's right. Love isn't the name for whatever festers between us; it's something uglier and stubborn that refuses to diminish even in the face of logic. It's greedy and selfish, and hateful.

It's honest and real.

It's… It's better than nothing at all when it comes to him.

Abruptly, he bolts to his feet as if sensing the direction my thoughts have taken. A restless energy radiates from him as he crosses to the window, bracing his hands against the glass, leaning his full weight forward as if he wants nothing more than to crash through the structure entirely and fall.

My throat constricts as I stand and follow him, copying his motions, watching my palms flatten over the cool, unyielding surface. The words he wrote reflect off the polished glass.

You fucked me.

Even with our combined weight, we don't go crashing through.

We just stand in silence, waiting for destruction that never comes.

11

EVGENI

This is my fucking fault—there is no escaping that truth. As expected, Vanici's gift had a more nefarious aim, and now Willow is missing. Nothing should be enough to draw me from the search for even a second. Nothing.

Save for an order not from Mischa, but from Ellen Stepanova herself.

The second she returned to the manor, I was there waiting, ready to send out every resource at our disposal.

"No," she said tiredly. "Here."

She then handed me a slip of paper I still can't take my eyes off. It isn't a detailed list of Vanici's crimes, but a note, presumably written by Willow herself.

I need to speak to him alone, please. Give me a day. I'm not running away, but I need to do this for myself. I hope you understand.

But I don't. More importantly, I don't understand how Ellen managed to convince Mischa, either, because while I wait for his signal, it never comes. When I finally approach his office, ready to demand an answer, I just find him seated at his desk, his head bowed, hands braced over the wooden surface.

"A day," he grates without looking up. "In the meantime, you follow whatever leads you have on the Saleris. Gregori's death was unexpected—and I don't like it. Something feels off. That being said…" He lifts his head, and I swallow hard at the visible exhaustion etched into his features. "We stay in the shadows for now. That means no attacks on the Saleris or anyone else without my permission. In the meantime, I will cultivate other resources."

"You really think I'm more useful to you playing wild goose chase with a conniving witch?"

He purses his lips as if mulling it over. "I wouldn't trust anyone else to find the truth."

A more tactful way of stating the obvious—find out what Briar Winthorp is hiding. Now.

But after last night, I'm not in a hurry to interact with the woman again.

To buy more time, I enter the service wing, where most of the guards spend their off-duty hours. I've barely stepped inside the modest suite assigned to me, when a knock rattles the door.

"Please," a woman demands, her voice tense.

Damn. When I finally face my unwelcome visitor, I'm unsurprised by who I find. This time she's fully dressed at least, sporting a black shirt and modest skirt.

"Shouldn't you be somewhere gloating?" I demand.

If Vanici weren't a big enough threat on his own, I'd assume she was somehow behind his stunt with the flowers.

Surprisingly, she lets the jab go by without even a smirk in response. "Not gloating. Begging. Trust me, soldier, it hurts my pride far more to ask for your help than you know. But there is no other choice. So, hear me out."

I raise an eyebrow at her gall. "You mock me. Lie. Spin your mind games and somehow believe that you can still manipulate me to your will."

Some of that elusive coyness returns to her gaze. "If I wanted to manipulate you, I'd be willing to try far more desperate methods than asking you outright," she hisses. "But I know that you are far too prideful to be seduced. Even if I presented myself to you naked on my hands and knees, the great Evgeni Volkov would take greater pleasure in denying me. This way robs you of that ability to gloat, at least. Nonetheless, the effect is still the same. Help me. I think that Saleri bastard holds the answer, and I need your help to capture him."

"Why not ask Mischa?" It's a question gnawing at the back of my psyche, lending credence to the suspicion that her true aim in requesting my "help" is far more nefarious.

Then again, she could be telling the truth. Something big is lurking on the horizon—I can feel it. Like the unending calm before a storm when lightning crackles in the air. The only question is, will I be ready when the rains begin, or caught off guard, unable to withstand the onslaught?

Irritatingly, the key factor to everything seems to be Briar fucking Winthorp.

"Frankly, I'm not in the mood for a suicide mission," I tell her, preparing to slam the door in her face.

"No!" With surprising strength, she forces her way in, slamming the door after her.

"No one else will get me close enough. You will." Panting, she faces me, her chest heaving, cheeks speckled pink with exertion. Those blue eyes blaze, and my suspicion grows. She wants far more than a lapdog to accompany her on a wild goose chase.

"I'm to believe Mateo Saleri matters that much to you?" I snarl.

"No." She doesn't even flinch. "And you are smarter than I want to give you credit for. You know how men like this operate, and I don't trust anyone else. Not with this."

I recognize ego stroking when I hear it, despite how much of a shock it is coming from her.

"Get out." I reach past her, aiming for the brass knob still clenched in her grasp.

"Wait! Fine. I'll tell you the real reason I'm willing to undergo this suicide mission. Ali is Jonathan's last and most important leverage. Without him, the bastard has no claim to the Winthorp fortune—"

"So, we switch gears to your son instead of the Saleris," I point out, increasingly skeptical. "Now you've suddenly decided to shoot for mother of the year?"

"Of course not," she says coldly, meeting my gaze without a hint of guilt or shame. "I haven't been a mother to him since the day he was born. But without him, Jonathan has no tool to secure more money. Without that influx, he can't secure the allegiance of fools like the Saleris. They've joined him for their own gain. If that house of cards looks like it might topple, they'll be the first to scatter from the ruins. You can unravel whatever scheme he has in place simply by intercepting my son when he arrives. After that, it will be too late. He'll have him surrounded by security—"

"And you don't care about the risk you might be putting him in if we succeed in getting him out by your so-called brother's men opening fire?"

"He won't," she declares, but I can see the doubt in her eyes.

"Tell me the real reason. Now. Stop dancing around the issue. I want to hear you say it. Do you plan to ransom your own son back to him for a cut of the profit? Or do you want to lead me into a trap while your little cohort mounts an assault on Stepanov Manor? Don't lie and claim that your motives are anything but selfish."

"Oh, they are very selfish," she hisses. "Pride."

The intensity in her voice alone is what stops me from shoving her into the hall. Her cheeks flame as if she regrets that admission, eager to play it off as a coy bit of manipulation.

But somewhere in the forming of another playful grin, her lips fall into a frown instead.

"Congratulations, Mr. Volkov," she says softly. "You've wounded my pride with all of your petty little jabs. I am a terrible mother with no real love for my son. I'm a horrible, selfish bitch, and I only care about myself. And I care if some smug murderer calls my character into question because he has no idea what it is like to birth a child. To be willing to do anything for that child, even if you don't know how. You think you know me, and maybe I'm bitter enough to lure you into a trap out of spite. Or maybe…"

Her voice softens, and I brace myself for the shift in her demeanor. I'm expecting her eyes to take on a more limpid sheen and the low purr she slips into when she's priming to manipulate. I have this woman nailed down from head to toe.

Until she raises her hand abruptly, sending it colliding with my cheek. *Thwack!* The stinging pain draws a hiss from my throat. She didn't hold back.

"You are a fool, and I'm forced to relent to the fact that of all the brawn Mischa employs, you happen to be the smartest, but not by much. You want me to beg and plead?

I'll do you one better." She saunters past me, her eyes on the window. I can't name the emotion I sense from her—something more elusive than anger, perplexing enough that I don't chase after her and wring that slender neck.

"I believed that Ali and I had no allies. That we were alone in a cruel, cold world. Being here, while I do believe that Mischa is a brute, I don't think my dear sister would let him turn away Alexander even if he tried. That makes this place a better home for him than being used as a pawn by Jonathan. Think of this as a mother's prudent judgment, but the game has changed. I don't care what you think of me, or what assumptions you've come up with. But you should realize that I could still go crawling back to Jonathan if I believed he were a better option."

"Even after he's tried to kill you?"

She scoffs. "I've done worse. You have no idea of the ways I've debased myself. All for…" She bites off the words, her eyes blazing.

I could blame curiosity for what draws me to her side. "For what?"

"Oh, dear." She hums low in her throat, that smile quicker than ever. "Isn't this the part where you comfort me, and I seduce you and convince you to help me in my little crusade? All without telling Mischa, of course. Because a man like you can't resist the chance to play the hero."

"Who is the one being pretentious now?" I counter. "I keep warning you. You don't know a damn thing about me."

"Oh?" She places her hands on her hips. "I know that your father was a rebellion leader in a small European country most people have never heard of. Especially not in a city like this one. That you fought for him, and in the process, you participated in the murder of an unarmed family of farmers, including a young girl, barely seventeen years old. Some would consider you a war criminal, Evgeni Volkov. They might wonder how such a man could ever judge anyone, let alone someone like me. I may be ruthless, and spoiled, and cunning, and so on. But I can tell you for a fact that I have never directly killed anyone."

She steps up to me, boldly prodding the center of my chest with her finger. That mocking smile is brighter than ever, her head cocked in contemplation.

"And I wouldn't presume to think I'm better than you because of a few rumors whispered by men every bit as unscrupulous as you. I wouldn't take their word for something I could see for myself. You are a vicious, dangerous man, Evgeni. But for some silly damn reason, I keep believing that you might not be like the rest of them. Hellbent on killing out of the pursuit of money or fame or prestige. Dare I say it? I think you might be a tiny bit less repulsive in your motives. So, sue me for believing that."

"You aren't that trusting," I counter, aware of how damn close she is. The stench of her floods my nostrils. Faint perfume that she must have hidden somewhere in her room. Fresh air. Lies.

She's such a good damn liar that it's almost too easy to forget her original aim. She's more cunning than I gave her credit for, nowhere near as shallow—which isn't a good thing. A shallow woman wouldn't be quite this shameless.

"I see that you've resorted to your so-called plan B," I point out, matching her grin with one of my own. "Seduce me. Manipulate. Spin a sob story about how you've had a revelation. You've changed. And you need me to put my life on the line as your hired muscle. I'm not that gullible—"

"Will you stop?" Her nostrils flare, her hiss too unbecoming to be faked. "I don't want gullible. I want reliable. You followed through for me at the docks when you could have looked the other way. I need someone like that to even have a hope of breaching their security. Too many men will tip them off, and Mischa's hoard has been breached once. Who's to say that more men haven't been bought to the other side? It's not very heroic to have me beg, but I will if I have to. Come with me. You know I'll go on my own otherwise."

"No." I step back, but I see her coming for me, her hand grasping for a fistful of my shirt. I don't know why my first impulse is to suppress the urge to fight. Why I let her scramble to stand in front of me.

"Fine," she snarls. "I shall have to resort to my plan C."

Her lips are on mine before I can process the motion. My hand goes around her throat reflexively, and her teeth graze my lip in a warning. But she never bites. She tilts her head instead, taunting me to chase her. Step into her. Tighten my grasp on her throat so that she has nowhere to go.

I've denied women like her before. Sexy as hell. Tempting. Lying bitches.

None ever got this close, and maybe I should have entertained those previous trysts. At least then I'd have something to compare her to. This lying mouth…

It's a goddamn sin. She beckons with her tongue, inviting me in. The second I relent, her teeth clamp down without an ounce of restraint. *Shit!* As I recoil, her laugh slips into this mocking excuse for a kiss, and her fingers latch onto my collar.

She tugs so fucking hard she could choke me, sucking in a breath as I flex my fingers in return. Her body conforms to mine, and I'm painfully reminded of how long it's been since I've slept with…

Anyone. I can't even remember the last woman, her face a blur. Some one-night stand met at a bar.

Women are a vice I've learned it's best to ignore. No cunt is worth the heartache. The headache. The hell.

Certainly not her.

She grinds her hips against mine, shameless. Damn good. Her nails scrape my chest as she readjusts her grip on my collar.

"Stop." I shove her back, blinking to get my bearings. "Just… Get out."

Turning to the window, I wait for the sound of her retreating footsteps and another sly jab at my expense. The soft hiss of fabric is unexpected. I crane my neck as alarm tightens my spine. Either she just wrestled a gun from the folds of her skirt, or…

Or she shed the fabric entirely, the next pair of soft footsteps marking the moment she stepped from the pile left on the floor. Even as I drag my gaze over her narrow frame, it doesn't sink in that she's fully naked. Not until she advances, her head tilted, her eyes shrouded in shadow.

I've seen her stripped before, but in those times, it was a more obvious ploy. A blatant game on her part. In this moment, the expression on her face differs. She's not smirking. Her throat quivers around a hard swallow as she draws even with me, but her eyes glow with more determination than I saw in her the day I fished her from the water at the docks.

As though she's pledged herself to tackle a new enemy, no matter the cost.

"Don't deny that you want it," she warns, taking another step while reaching out to cinch my collar in her fist. "There's no honor in playing coy now. You get your fix, and then I'll leave to do what you are too much of a coward to do. But don't pretend as though you don't want me. After tonight, we will never see each other again, unless I deign to come and laugh over the smoldering remains of your precious Stepanov Manor."

"So why sleep with me?" There's only one obvious answer to that question, but she laughs.

"I'm selfish and childish. I want some way of proving that I got one over on you. I got you to break down your precious boundaries—" She tightens her grip, wrenching on my collar so hard a ripping sound issues from the fabric. "You aren't so high and mighty, though you certainly do a good job pretending to be. You still want me. Like any man, you are just as weak."

"You are beautiful; I will give you that."

I risk taking another glance at her, hissing through my teeth as my abdomen tightens in appreciation. That was a lie. She's heads above any other women I can remember. Too beautiful.

That's her problem.

"But I wouldn't dare stick my cock in you, even for a quickie."

She should laugh, unbothered that I refuse to play in her little scheme. Her expression ripples instead, her lips pressing into a firm line, her eyes an even colder blue.

She doesn't recoil and saunter away. She holds my gaze unflinchingly, probing for whatever she expects to find.

"I was wrong," she says softly, disentangling her fingers from my shirt. "You aren't as brave as I thought you were. You are a coward. So afraid of breaking your little rules and straying from the straight and narrow. You think that I'm the selfish, foolish one, but I at least know my limits. I know who I am, and I don't go around pretending to be someone that I'm not. I can admit that I'd want to fuck you if only to see what it felt like. But I can only assume that your flaccid personality extends to other parts of your being. So fine. You get out—" She strolls to my bed and makes a show of stretching with her back to me. From over her shoulder, she nods to the door. "I'm tired. That bed in my room is atrocious, and I'd rather get some sleep before I leave. Oh, and tattle to Mischa if you'd like. Don't think he or any one of his goons can stop me. So long Evgeni Volkov."

I'm tempted to deny her. Drag her out of this room by her hair. Or push her onto that bed and show her how heroic I can be. But that's exactly what she wants—to play her game to whatever ultimate end she has in mind.

Well, I'm done being her patsy.

"Goodnight, Briar Winthorp." I head for the door, wrenching it open without looking back. Until I do.

She's still standing by the bed, her body glistening in the moonlight, her eyes fixed in my direction. Her prideful, confident laughter should be what chases me from the room as I finally leave.

Not a sigh.

DON

I've committed hundreds of crimes in my lifetime —and I deserve to suffer for every one. This latest transgression merely adds a few more sins to the massive pile, but in contrast to the rest, they stand out. Corrupting the daughter of Mischa Stepanov. Roping an innocent woman into a mess, she doesn't fully comprehend…

I should burn in hell.

The guilt is all-consuming, threatening to swallow me whole. Until I make the mistake of looking over into a pair of watchful brown eyes. Condemnation isn't what I find there. Just a similar guilt she shouldn't reflect so easily.

I may be a fucking animal, but there isn't a damn thing "innocent" about her. She wouldn't be able to inhabit the same room as me if she were. Not for hours, with only our breathing to pierce the quiet.

I keep waiting for the second she'll demand the answers I've promised her. Answers about Olivia. About her. About her choice.

Instead, she watches the sunrise, her cheek pressed to the window, her legs outstretched in front of her, our bodies side by side with only a sliver of space between us. So much for boundaries. We've broken them already, despite no real physical contact. Yet, I might as well have touched her. I feel just as dirty, just as selfish.

Hearing her soft breaths scrape at the air is a corrupted intimacy I know I shouldn't extend. Every time I inhale her scent in return just reinforces how twisted it is that I get to experience this moment at all. Nearness with another person. A night spent in the presence of someone else who doesn't aim to scold or stab me.

It's a fragile peace I'm too much of a coward to break—so I never tell her to leave as I should. I don't exit the room, either.

I relish one more sin, and my damaged soul buckles under the weight of it.

Finally, a ray of sunlight pierces the cloud cover, intruding upon the shadows like a warning. This reprieve is over.

It's time to face the consequences, whatever they may be.

"We should go." I stand, smoothing my hands over my rumpled shirt.

It's no use. I still look like shit, but luckily fashion isn't my aim today. Aware of her watching, I cross over to the chair and grab my jacket, pulling it on. I turn to find her unmoving by the window, those eyes as unreadable as ever. "We'll leave Fabio to attend to his meetings and politics. If you don't mind, I'd rather not deal with your father just yet, either."

Frankly, I'm surprised no Stepanov agents have come barging in during the night. Beyond the window, the morning looks pale, with dark clouds heralding rain looming over the horizon. It's as good a day as any to make yet another bad decision.

"We should discuss our course of action together before involving anyone else," I suggest. "In the meantime, we get out into the city. Keep our ears to the ground for anything out of place. Gregori Saleri's death could be the start of something bigger. You'll be safer with me."

It's a pathetic fucking lie. If there were any intel worth scouting, she would be the last person I'd bring with me. Still, I can't escape this impatient itch biting at my spine. I need to move. Think. More importantly…

"We need to continue our conversation from last night."

That gets a rise out of her. She stands, smoothing a hand down her rumpled dress. A good man would procure her fresh clothing to wear—and something to eat. She needs to eat.

God, my head hurts. I haven't entertained these concerns in a long damn time, perhaps outside of nagging Vin. Caring for someone apart from myself. Remembering the simple things that a human being needs, like nourishment and liquids other than alcohol. It's strange, like flexing a muscle I haven't used in years. So long, in fact, that it's atrophied from neglect.

"I should take you to lunch," I say. "We can get a few things for you to wear too before getting down to business."

Thanks to Fabio, I still have my money and access to my accounts, at least. Shopping will be a good excuse to leave before the accountant returns to continue his scolding.

"You can wash up," I suggest, entering the foyer. "I'll wait."

I've barely left the room when she appears by my side regardless. The stern tilt to her mouth makes her thoughts painfully clear. She doesn't trust me.

Not yet.

Rather than argue, I exit the suite, sensing her fall into step behind me.

I'm half-suspecting to find an awaiting Stepanov cavalcade as we descend to the lobby. Silence greets us instead. The muted tones of classical music playing throughout the lobby feed on this unstable paranoia. I can't shake the need to scan the empty hall, hunting for anything out of place.

Or it could be that I'm just that damn desperate for a distraction in any form. I crave a fight. A confrontation.

She presents the next best thing, though. I can sense her, watching me with those unspoken questions dancing in her eyes. Two months ago, if anyone asked me who I feared most—though a bit too strong a word—I'd probably say Mischa Stepanov.

Now? It's her. This woman from my past, haunting me with that soulless gaze. Looking at her is like reliving Liv's death over and over again. Not just because she shares that twisted history with me. At the core of it, I feel guilt. Guilty as fuck for betraying the only woman I ever loved.

For replacing her with someone who shouldn't be with me in the first place.

This isn't the time for self-pity. Not anymore. It's time to prove to Fabio, and anyone else who might be skeptical that I can function like a normal man for one fucking day at least. The blond head I catch a glimpse of in my peripheral vision serves as the only person who should command my focus right now.

I owe it to her.

As we enter the hotel's garage and find the car where I'd left it, climbing behind the wheel feels ghoulishly symbolic. It's time to take the reins of my own life again, starting with something deceptively simple.

"Today, we'll set the bullshit aside for a moment," I tell her as she claims the passenger's seat. "We'll just…"

I let the statement hang there, unsure of how to finish it. A sloppy beginning to a shopping trip, but hell.

It's better than kidnapping her.

13

EVGENI

I spent the night in the van, watching the house from the shadows, ready for the moment she'd sneak out in the darkness. By morning, there's been no sign of Briar Winthorp.

Either she's developed the gift of teleportation, or she never left.

By the time I reach my room in the service wing, an answer comes in the form of a slender woman lounging on my bed, eating from a bowl of grapes she presumably stole from the kitchen.

She's dressed herself again, her blond hair tied back into a poised bun. To anyone on the outside looking in, I'm the intruder, determined to disrupt her peace.

"You're still here," I say gruffly. My throat is dry after inhaling the crisp night air. If I slept at all, it was for an hour at most. Cautiously, I keep every inch of her in view, envious of the lack of shadows beneath her eyes and her seemingly well-rested state.

"Change of plans," she says, shifting into a sitting position. "If you won't help me take on Mateo Saleri, perhaps you need a demonstration of just what he's capable of."

"And what would that be?" I cross my arms, leaning against the doorframe.

"If the man killed his father, it means he's becoming impatient." Her tone takes on a scolding note reminiscent of a teacher informing a problem student of a difficult subject. "If I know the man—and I do—it's only a matter of time before he strikes out on his own. And if he does, I think I know where he'll attack."

"And where would that be?"

She leans back, smoothing her hands over the rumpled sheets beneath her. "I couldn't help but overhear that poor little Willow's run away again."

I bristle at her mocking tone. "I'm surprised you haven't run to your master to let him know."

"Ah, but I'm sure he does know." She wags a finger at me. "While you were gone in the night, I took the liberty of pilfering this—" She reaches beneath a nearby pillow, withdrawing a slender, black device.

I curse in recognition. "Son of a bitch." It's a cell phone—not mine, but a similar model, most likely taken from another guard.

"I'll return it," she says with a playful giggle. "But Louie wasn't my only special friend capable of providing information."

"A fact that you purposefully hid," I point out. Not only that, but I'm sure she saw through my plan to track her last night.

"The point is, my contact let me in on a little secret you might want to be privy to."

"Which is?"

"Take me shopping, and you'll find out." She tosses the phone at me and lurches to her feet. "And by that, I mean, let me shop in peace while you watch from the shadows like a good boy. Bring your weapon, and I'll even let you keep the rest of your hoard on standby."

My interest is instantly piqued—as is my alarm. "This sounds less like a shopping trip and more like an assault."

She winks. "You're the fool who left me alone all night. Blame yourself."

Damn her, she has a point. I thought to gain the upper hand by calling her bluff and following her straight to her master.

But—grudgingly, I'll admit—she managed to turn the tables.

But to what end?

*B*riar Winthorp is many things. She's reckless and impulsive like a child denied a sweet. And she's apparently suicidal.

But what does that make me? The idiotic bastard tracking her movements from afar despite every ounce of common sense warning me away. The only upside will be if I catch her red-handed in a scheme against the Stepanovs.

So far, I'm forced to admit that outcome doesn't seem very likely in this location. Rather than a yacht or a crime lord's mansion, she's dragged me to a boutique just near the city's center. More puzzling, it's not located in Saleri territory or within the boundaries of another power player.

I'd almost assume she decided to partake on a carefree shopping spree in between supposedly running for her life.

But she's too smart, and for her to risk being out in the open…

She must have a good damn reason.

Or, she's led the Stepanovs and me into yet another trap.

To distract myself from the folly of trusting her, I take in my surroundings, hunting for even the smallest detail out of place. The boutique itself has a front formed entirely out of a row of large windows that provide a clear view of the interior. There are several similar establishments up and down this block—and by noon, she's visited most of them.

This could all be a game on her part. Watching her observe a red dress near the back of the store, I'm starting to believe that.

The suspicion makes me turn away and scan the rest of the street in the hopes that Mateo Saleri himself will come strolling into view, if only to prove that this isn't a waste of my time.

And, hell… I must be so desperate that my eyes are playing tricks because, while not Mateo Saleri, the figure exiting a black car just a few blocks down looks strikingly familiar. So familiar, in fact, that I push through a passing couple to get a better look.

A man and a woman step onto the curb—with him bracing a hand protectively over her waist. Together, they enter a nearby boutique. Only then, do I get a good look at the man's face. Wait…

Son of a bitch.

There is no mistaking the bastard. Donatello Vanici—nor is there any denying who the small, blond figure accompanying him must be. Willow.

Does her family even know where she is?

I reach for my pistol while grasping for my cell phone with my other hand. I've barely pressed it to my ear when a flicker of movement draws my notice.

Briar Winthorp has positioned herself at the front of the store, seeming to admire a dress hanging in the window display. But then she looks up. I swear those blue eyes find mine despite the decent foot traffic and the distance I am from the store. I even see her lips move, mouthing a silent command.

"Wait."

Maybe it's shock that stops me in my tracks. Either way, the hesitation gives her enough time to hurry from the boutique empty-handed.

I cross the street, braving moving traffic, and head for her, stealth aside. The second I'm close enough, she strains on tiptoe to murmur against my ear, "Easy now, soldier. Put your anger aside and use that brain of yours."

"You knew they would be here."

Her coy smile confirms the accusation.

"How the hell did you—"

"They aren't important," she says dismissively. "But those men? They are." She inclines her head a few blocks down.

I hesitate only a second before following the line of her gaze, down the street to where a gray van lumbers around the corner. Something about it raises the hairs on the back of my neck, and I feel the woman tug on my arm, pulling me into the mouth of an alley so that she's out of the driver's line of sight.

Whoever they may be. The windows are tinted, obscuring a view of anyone who might be lurking inside, but no one exits the vehicle. Instead, it lingers near the store Willow entered.

Waiting.

"You see how gracious I can be, soldier?" Briar taunts. Her voice is that characteristic mocking purr, but I can sense the tension ripping through it. She's worried. Hell, maybe more than that. She's terrified. "You want proof of the danger you and your precious employer are in? Here it is. Now I suggest we stay out of sight and see what they might be planning."

"You think it's an ambush?" When she doesn't answer, I take my eyes off the van long enough to snatch her wrist. "What the hell are you playing at?"

She smiles, though her eyes widen. "You want to spurn my gift? Or do you want to save lives? There isn't much time."

Common sense tells me to break her wrist and grab Willow now. My gut instinct, however? I can sense the unspoken danger tainting the atmosphere, warning me to stay on guard.

The question is, how did she know?

"I asked you what you're playing at." She doesn't resist as I grab her throat next, applying pressure to her windpipe.

Her eyes meet mine boldly without a hint of fear. Either she has a death wish, or she's convinced I won't hurt her. A foolish mindset either way on her part.

I grip her tight enough to make those beautiful eyes bulge. Hard enough to cut off her air completely and risk drawing notice from anyone passing by. Only when her cheeks turn an alarming shade of pink do I let go.

"You have five seconds to tell me what we're doing here—"

"You want to know?" Wincing, she rubs at her throat before shrugging off the discomfort entirely. Then she advances, rising on tiptoe to bring her mouth to my ear. "Then I suggest you employ some *patience*. So, let's get in that van of yours and stay out of sight."

It's stupid to trust her.

But I don't have much of a choice.

14

DON

Considering my credit cards go through without incident, Fabio hasn't cut me off out of spite just yet. All for the better. It's been so damn long since I've done anything this…

Normal.

Every piece of clothing I've owned the past few years was procured by Fabio in some fashion. In this arena, I'm woefully out of practice, and it's funny in a sense. Willow believes that I think of her as a child, when I've barely had control of my own life as of late.

And in the same amount of time, she's matured into a different person entirely.

Setting off on a mundane errand feels almost as momentous as the day I bought my first suit with money earned from my work with the *famiglia*. This store isn't a shady tailor, but a ritzy boutique in the upscale part of the city specializing in women's clothing.

As it turns out, I'm not that invested in shopping after all. I barely notice whatever the saleswoman sends our way.

I only see her face.

She looks just as out of place as I feel. Hours later, she still does, seated across from me in a restaurant somewhere on the city's outskirts, hopefully far enough from Mischa's domain that he won't risk barging in unannounced. Though if Fabio worked his magic, the *mafiya* leader should be swayed from any murderous plots.

For now. Not that being out in the open feels any less risky. Because of the danger of outside enemies, and the danger of interacting with her. Alone. Sitting in this chair across from her is a struggle. It's too quiet. Too damn close in this private dining room near the back of the restaurant— secluded enough that Fabio can't make a scene should he come strolling in unannounced. I've covered every base but the obvious.

I'm still dancing around the topic at the heart of this matter.

What will her ultimate decision be?

I promised not to influence her choice, and I meant that. That doesn't stop my brain from dwelling on it. I lost one child, and it damn near killed me. Is it selfish not to want to experience that pain again?

Maybe not. Ignoring my feelings on the matter won't help anyone. Oddly enough, I don't even know how to put it into words. I just speak. "I bought him a toy once."

She's staring at me—probably has no fucking clue what I'm talking about. I feel this impulsive need to keep speaking anyway.

"Nico. A ball, I think it was. A baseball with a tiny mitt he wouldn't be able to fit for years at least."

I laugh, startled by the sound. It sounds genuine.

"I think that was the happiest fucking day, buying that stupid ball. I could already see him as a grown man, playing in the major leagues. Though hell, he could have wound up like Fab. Still, I would have loved him. I still do. I'm not telling you this to guilt you," I add, looking up.

Her eyes are like mirrors, reflecting how I must appear to her. Unwashed. Unshaven. A man barely capable of taking care of himself, let alone a baby.

I can't argue that it might be an accurate portrait of who I've portrayed myself to be until recently.

"I've spent nearly the past decade letting my life go to shit. If I wasn't surviving on beer and liquor, then it was something far stronger. It's no secret that Fabio's been the one chasing after me, wiping my ass and cleaning up my messes. He got my life back on track, and I know what he wants me to do now."

I don't feel the need to clarify. Her grimace is confirmation enough that she knows damn well what I mean.

"Let you go. Let you take care of this problem and fly back to that polished little school of yours and forget I ever existed. He'd lock me away himself if he thought that would work. He's afraid. I can see it in his eyes. Afraid that this might tip me over the edge and history will repeat itself."

And he has a point.

"I'm not going to pretend like I know any better than he does, and, either way, you don't owe me a damn thing. Whatever your choice is. I can't stop you. I can't even promise you a better future. The reality is you might have to put your entire life on hold and deal with me for God knows how long. But what I can tell you is this. We're in this together."

I reach for her hand—and instantly regret it. She's on fire, radiating heat that burns as if in punishment for daring to touch her in the first place. I want to rip my hand away.

But I don't. I grit my teeth and let the contact linger, sensing every nuance and curve in the delicate fingers trapped between mine.

"I don't want to be bound to the past. I want a fresh start."

Even if I'm not entitled to one in the slightest.

"Do you want the same? Yes or no?"

She hesitates. Then her chin jerks downward, and I have my answer. *Yes.*

"Fabio will be pissed," I admit, feeling a corner of my mouth twitch upward. "Perhaps your parents as well, but what they want doesn't matter. All that does is—What the hell?"

A scream comes from the front of the restaurant. I start to stand as the sound of breaking glass echoes. More screams. Shouts…

Before I know it, a shadow falls over the doorway, moving swiftly in our direction.

There isn't time to think.

"Get down!" Instinct kicks in as I lunge across the table, grabbing a slender wrist before we both plummet to the floor.

I've barely pulled her beneath me when a deafening roar confirms my suspicion in the worst fucking way—this is an ambush.

The potential attackers are too numerous. The Saleris? The Rossis? Someone else? It doesn't matter who.

They're good. I've barely gotten my bearings when another shot whizzes past my head, taking chunks of wood out of the wall. Instinct saves me as I withdraw my gun, aiming blindly.

"Stay down," I hiss to the woman beneath me. Then I stand, racing to put as much distance between us as possible.

Boom!

Pain rips through my shoulder as I stagger to my knees—but the bastard still in the hallway is already falling to the floor, his body lifeless. His face is bared, but I don't recognize it. Groaning, I haul myself upright, raising my weapon as someone else comes to take his place.

Only, this man I recognize instantly—and only one fact keeps me from pulling the trigger.

He works for Mischa Stepanov.

EVGENI

$\mathcal{A}$ detour to the hospital is too risky, given the attack. That's the excuse given to Vanici for why he has to settle for a private doctor to inspect his wounds, anyway. The good news is that he was only grazed by a bullet, not hit. He'll live.

The bad news is that his exam takes place in an abandoned wing of Stepanov Manor under the watchful eye of at least a dozen guards—all of whom await Mischa's arrival. I'm not a fool. The fact that the bastard came here of his own accord means he has his own motives for meeting with Mischa on his territory.

Either way, Willow is home where she belongs, and Vanici won't be here for long if I know Mischa.

"Is your job to play nursemaid to me?" Vanici himself snaps as he pulls on his bloodied shirt. A row of bandages encircles his left shoulder, but apart from that, he's unharmed—though apparently not very grateful to the man who saved his ass. He glowers in my direction, his posture tense. "Or to find who the fuck did this?"

"We're searching the bodies now," I snap, but he has a point. It wasn't a coincidence that I happened to be there in time to intervene.

And for such a sloppy hit to take place in broad daylight...

Well, if Mateo Saleri was behind it, that only gives more credence to Louie's claim that the man has lost his fucking mind.

Though one person was able to predict him—and I don't think it was due to her innate gift of feminine intuition.

"Watch him," I tell one of the men posted near the door.

Before I step into the hall, I look back at the only occupant of the room other than Vanici. She leans against the wall unobtrusively. Our eyes meet, and she flashes a weak smile, but she doesn't move to follow me out.

I don't push her to. There will be plenty of time to speak to her later.

My nostrils flare as I turn my attention to another woman, trying to picture where she might be. I move swiftly, intending to hunt her throughout the manor. Instead, I find her staring from one of the windows just a few rooms down.

"You knew," I say coldly. "How?"

She inclines her head as if she didn't notice me until now. "I assume you appreciated my gift," she says coyly. "Believe me or not, but that was just the first attempt. There will be more. There is only one way to stop them. You defeat one cell, and another will spring from the ashes. The game is only beginning."

"Stop speaking in riddles." I grab her wrist, spinning her around to face me. "I want answers."

"And you'll get them," she says, stone-faced. Her eyes don't even blink, and it's a rare show of resolve on her part. "Once you uphold your end of my little request. Help me find Alexander. No extra force. No sloppy tactics involving the *mafiya*. You help me alone."

"It's sounding more and more like you really want to isolate me in particular, Ms. Winthorp." I don't intend for it to sound as suggestive as it does. "I have to wonder why that may be."

"Don't flatter yourself," she says with a simpering smile. "Your skillset is of use to me, nothing more. Considering your current standing with your employer, I doubt you'd be of use for any relevant information. Even under torture. I need you because, frankly, you're the only man capable of performing this task that I have leverage over."

At least she's honest.

"And, Mr. Volkov, time is running out," she adds. "If you refuse, just tell me now, and I will most definitely do it on my own. But you might not catch the next time a strike team is called on one of the many, many Stepanov family members."

"You want my help?" My common sense bristles at even entertaining the prospect. I'd only be springing the trap she no doubt has in mind. "Then tell me one damn thing. How did you know?"

She smiles, but her eyes take on a hard gleam. She's on edge. "I already told you. You have your 'friends in low places.' So do I. I had a hunch, and it happened to pay off to your benefit. You should be thanking me for being so thorough."

"So much for your story of being a poor, hunted woman all alone in the world."

"I never claimed to be lonely. Your imagination is running away with you, Mr. Volkov. All I claimed was to be desperate. Desperate enough to keep tabs on whoever may be of interest to the men 'hunting' me."

"If I do this, you tell me more than a few hypothetical hunches and riddles. You give me everything. All of the intel you know."

"I thought you'd never ask," she counters. "But I'll honor that request, only regarding what is necessary to complete your task. Be a good boy and do your job admirably, and you might earn another reward."

"And if I were to go to Mischa and tell him of your little scheme—"

"Pardon my use of such trite phrasing, but that would be the equivalent of sending a raging bull into a china shop. You do anything to risk Alexander's life, and a sniper team will be the very least of your concerns."

"Does that mean you aren't planning to bring your son back to the bosom of this manor? You plan on going on the run."

"And if we do, trust me, it will be better for everyone in the long run. You deny your enemy of his leverage, and I miraculously get out of your hair. Everyone wins, as they say."

And yet, I get the sense she's deliberately holding one or two details back. The suspicion gnaws at me, clashing with curiosity. But I can't take the risk of another attack.

"When?"

Her smile falls, and a hint of her genuine fear crosses her features for a split second. "Tonight. Thanks to you, we've lost ground and time. I'll need to meet with my contacts and devise a new plan of attack—"

"That undercuts your desperate narrative."

"Desperate, but not stupid," she snaps. "A trait I'm sure you can appreciate."

"So, I'm supposed to just turn my back, let you meet with your 'contacts' in secret, and blindly do your grunt work like a good boy."

"Now you've got it." She places her hand on my shoulder. "Be ready by midnight."

"You think I could just sneak away after what's happened?" The guards will be on red alert tonight.

"That's your problem," she counters, swaying her hips with every step. "Don't be late."

WILLOW

This homecoming unfolds nothing like the first. Ironically the circumstances are no different. Violence. Bloodshed.

With my life precariously in the balance by a cruel twist of fate.

It's as if I'm being punished for my crimes, too numerous to name individually. This chaos is all I deserve.

But I wish I could undergo it alone.

It doesn't feel fair that the Stepanovs keep getting caught in the crossfire. If anything, only one man deserves to be punished alongside me.

Donatello Vanici.

He promised me answers, but they feel more elusive than ever. In the end, I'm not even sure which outcome would provide closure. If he played a hand in Olivia's death, it would cement every vile, horrible thought I had of him and then some. I would be justified in hating him.

But if he were capable of such a heinous crime, then everything I thought I knew would shatter right along with his lies. The memories of my past will collapse. Everything will have been an elaborate lie colored by my own naivety.

Another fear is more selfish. He loved Olivia enough to forgive even a transgression of that magnitude.

And yet, he condemned me for something that wasn't even my fault.

In both scenarios, I wind up hating him.

And yet, here I am, watching him wince through the pain of his injuries, still striving to live up to his unshakable persona. I'm getting better at seeing through the act, though.

He's in real pain. Though the bullet grazed his shoulder, the wound stings whenever he moves. He must crave a painkiller to take the edge off, and yet I saw him deny what the physician offered. His stoicism could be the cause, but I doubt that in this case.

Much like me, he's punishing himself, though he doesn't feel the need to resort to dwelling on the past and his own shortcomings. He prefers to suffer.

"Let me guess," he says gruffly. "I won't be able to stroll off this property, huh?"

A man lurks near the doorway, gazing stoically ahead. I know that look. He's received his orders. Now he's merely enforcing them.

"Thought so." Donatello scoffs, and I can't tell if he's apprehensive at all for the inevitable.

I am. My palms sweat, my throat so tight it hurts to breathe. While Donatello seems content to wait patiently for his punishment, I'm not so calm. I'm dreading seeing Mischa again, knowing I put his family in danger.

And I'm afraid he'll ask me to stay.

I can't ignore a growing part of me determined to resist that request no matter what. Shame is merely part of the reason. The other is greed.

I'm so close. To what? I have no idea, but it's a taunting, elusive prize. Deep down, I sense that I'll never be able to move on without facing it.

The truth?

Mischa could beat an answer out of Donatello for me. He is more than capable of that.

But I don't want him to. It needs to be me, and I can't avoid the confrontation anymore. Donatello owes an explanation to me and me alone.

He stiffens as I stand and approach the old bench that's become his makeshift hospital bed. This room is in the lower level of the manor, easily accessed by the servant's entrance—and out of earshot of the main part of the house where the children might be.

Coming here was strategic, but I can tell by looking at his rigid stance that Donatello doesn't intend to stay here for long. Hissing through his teeth, he shifts to face me.

"You can go if you want," he grates, wincing. "I'm not keeping you here against your will. I can face Mischa alone without using you as a shield."

I blink, thrown off by the statement. Belatedly, I dissect it, homing in on his coarse, grated tone. Go. He thinks that is what I want. To scurry away and let him leave.

No. I shake my head, weighing the option of brandishing those letters again. I still have them. With him bloodied and trapped, I could force him to read each one. Make him react. Make him answer.

"I don't think you'll have a choice," he says, and I flinch at that. Even now, he keeps forgetting the promise he himself made me. To let me stand on my own.

His eyes narrow in alarm before I realize why—I've jerked my chin defiantly. But that's only part of what has him on edge.

Footsteps approach our direction swiftly, echoed by a voice.

"Get back," Donatello warns just as the door flies open.

I don't even recognize the man standing on the other end. Mischa? Or a monster. Only a flash of blond hair registers before he surges, crossing the room in a heartbeat to reach Donatello.

A monstrous crash shakes the very foundation of the house. At the center of the commotion stands Mischa, grappling with a man every bit his equal in terms of bulk and size. The only difference?

Only one of the men is actively attacking the other.

"Mischa!" The shout comes from another figure racing through the doorway. "Stop!"

Ellen—but I doubt he even hears her. Fully enraged, he's singularly focused on driving his fists into every part of Donatello he can reach. Over and over again.

Impulse drives me forward, within his line of view.

And he goes still, his fist raised. "Willow… Leave," he commands in a harsh tone I've never heard him direct at me. "Get her out of here!"

"I suggest you listen to her," someone interjects.

I don't recognize the voice at first, nor the figure speaking. His nose is bleeding, painting his face in swaths of scarlet that obscure any defining features. Except for his eyes. That hue of brown is unmistakable. "I'm not here to fight with you—"

"I know why you're here." In the blink of an eye, Mischa is composed again. Only his disheveled blond hair reveals the violence he enacted just seconds ago. That, and the blood on his hands.

"Willow." He meets my gaze, his jaw stern. "Go—"

"I said you should listen to her," Donatello warns, swiping at his jaw, painting the sleeve of his shirt a brighter crimson. "She isn't a child."

"And you claim to speak for her?" Mischa pivots toward him, his fists clenched. "I think you've done enough—"

"I second that." This voice isn't Ellen's, but the newer figure who appears in the doorway, briefcase in hand. That's right. Fabio was meeting with Mischa originally. Both must have been aware of the ambush soon after it happened.

"In case you gentlemen have forgotten, an attack was just launched on both families in broad daylight. That was an elite team. No identification. No easy way to trace their origins. Hell, they don't even seem to have fingerprints. Paired with our recent troubles, and the death of Gregori Saleri, to say I'm concerned is an understatement. Now isn't the time to fight." He enters the room, broadcasting his trademark confidence, but I note a tremor in his usual swagger. He's on edge, more than just a little shaken.

"I received a message," he says thickly, proving my suspicion true. With a sigh, he looks up, his expression grave. Anxiously, he wrings his hands together before finally clearing his throat. "A warning, more like. Mischa has already heard this little missive, Donatello, so brace yourself. Our enemies didn't beat around the bush. They've demanded a trade."

"A trade of what?" In an instant, Donatello transforms into the man capable of running a crime syndicate.

"They want the Winthorp woman. Supposedly you've already met her acquaintance."

"Winthorp woman?" Donatello raises an eyebrow, but I can easily picture just who he means.

Briar Winthorp. Ellen's estranged sister.

The same woman we got a bloody introduction to while on a stolen yacht.

"And what if we don't 'trade'?" Donatello snaps.

Fabio sighs again. "They specify they'll take a life if their terms aren't met within twenty-four hours."

"Interesting that they would specify some woman rather than Gregori's own goddamn granddaughter. Mateo's made his priorities clear. So, whose life is on the line this time?"

"They didn't specify," Mischa interjects, and I jump, turning to him. "But it doesn't take much to guess."

I feel a shiver wrack my spine as his gaze flits in my direction.

"It would be bold for them to target her outright," Donatello says, but his tone is less hostile. He's thinking, employing that trademark cunning that always allowed him to zero in on a target. "Not to mention mount an attack in broad daylight. It's stupid, too, knowing the reach of the *mafiya*. It's reckless—"

"I wouldn't call any of this opponent's actions anything other than reckless," Fabio points out.

Donatello shakes his head, still actively bleeding, not that he seems concerned by the constant stream dripping down his chin to the floor. "No, what I mean is, this doesn't exactly square with the patience used to plan an attack on the harbor. Or the hospital."

"There was no tact," Mischa agrees, grudgingly thoughtful. "They're getting desperate."

"Or this isn't the same person," Donatello suggests. "What once was a cohesive operation is splintering. Someone's getting impatient and trying to tie up loose ends, most likely without the input of their other partner who's been helming the plan from the start."

"Infighting?" Fabio says. "We could use that to our advantage while homing in on the leader of this scheme."

"Or," Mischa adds. "This could spur them to be bolder and take more risks. We can't take any more chances."

Donatello nods. "Agreed."

It's astounding how quickly these men can morph from enemy to ally when presented with a larger threat. All three stare pensively into the distance, working through a million different plans and tactics in their heads.

At some point, they must remember the still simmering hostility because they stiffen, training their gazes on each other.

"So, what is our next move?" Donatello asks.

"Our?" Mischa echoes, his tone an octave deeper.

"You can't possibly intend to honor their demands," Donatello surmises. "So, what is your real plan?"

Mischa frowns, mulling over the possibility. Suddenly, his eyes cut in my direction. "We shouldn't discuss this here."

"She's not a child," Donatello says offhandedly. "She deserves to know what's going on as much as anyone else."

"So, you think you can dictate how I raise my own daughter?"

"No." Donatello stands fully upright, rolling his shoulders back. "I'm saying, she can make her own decision without being ordered like a child. Do you forget who saved your wife and son? I haven't."

It's ironic to hear him say this considering he only made that determination for himself within the past twenty-four hours. Still, it serves to shift the mood of the room entirely.

Though, he's only half right. If I'm truly entitled to my own choices, then he shouldn't speak for me either.

Inhaling deeply. I step forward, sensing all eyes turn to me.

"Do you want to stay?" Mischa asks.

My mind is racing with so many opposing thoughts. *Lurk in the shadows. Don't.*

In the end, all I can do is nod.

"That settles it then," Fabio says, stepping forward to coincidentally place himself in between the two men. "Whatever we do, it needs to be quick. I suggest we don't give our enemies any chance to regroup. We strike fast."

"What do you suggest?" Mischa demands.

Fabio begins to pace. "We mount a silent assault. Something deceptively simple, but that will give us the upper hand. We know the docks have been a consistent point of interest for this enemy."

"You want to strike there again?" Donatello asks. "But where? I doubt Mateo Saleri will let us board his boat so graciously this time."

"No. But we know that they have their sights on one area in particular. Your harbor office, Don."

"Yeah, which is now mostly in ashes," he grouses. "So, what should we do? Blow it up our damn selves as a warning?"

"No. I'm thinking something a bit more literal," Fabio says with a devious smile. "If they want it badly enough, we can use that to our advantage. We can't waste time going after every rogue mercenary operation or dead-end lead. We need to cut off the head of this snake."

"So, you offer the territory as a trade instead?" Mischa asks. "I don't see how that presents a better option."

"Not as a trade," Fabio counters. "Donatello offers it for sale at a price too tempting to resist."

"You want me to sell that property for a steal?"

"But that will lure them out," Mischa says, his head thoughtfully inclined. "They won't expect it."

"And they won't be able to resist," Fabio adds, nodding. "If I can trace their accounts, with my various contacts, there is no end to what I could accomplish. Transaction logs. Links to any private airfields or any other purchase. We could use those records to pinpoint their movements and perhaps discover where they might be staying while within the city."

"Then we pay them a visit," Donatello says darkly. "And confront them head-on."

"Won't that take time to arrange?" Mischa sounds skeptical.

"In usual circumstances, weeks," Fabio admits. "But with my contacts, I can arrange to have the property listed within hours. If advertised via the right channels, our mystery buyer will be alerted soon after. I suspect they won't wait long to make a move out of fear that someone else could purchase the property and add a wrinkle to their plans."

"It's sneaky, Fab; I will give you that," Donatello admits. "But, while I'm not a vaunted money man, even I could see that it screams 'trap'."

"Yes," Fabio concedes. "But if they truly need this property—"

"They won't be able to resist. They might try to purchase via a proxy, though."

"Yes," Fabio concedes. "A possibility I'm prepared for. In that respect, the true buyer wouldn't be untraceable, but it would take more time."

"Which we don't have."

"It's better than nothing."

"We need a backup option." Mischa takes the floor now, his brows drawn together in contemplation. "Something to lure them out on two fronts."

"So, you think we should hand over the woman as well? Ruthless, Mischa. I didn't think you would be that cutthroat."

"We don't give them a damn thing. Just *appear* to," Mischa says. "I doubt the ringleader would show his face so easily, but it could leave them unprotected."

"Which could be a decent strategy if we can trace their main location. It would be an attack on two fronts, and they wouldn't see it coming."

"So, we take matters into our own hands," Donatello says. "We set the time and place for the trade within three days. At the same time, the sale goes live, and we wait it out."

"There is one problem with that strategy. It could look like coordination," Mischa says. "Especially if it seems we are in communication."

"Yes." Fabio strokes his chin thoughtfully. "Which could definitely complicate things. However, if the feud between your families appears to be alive and well…"

"They might not second guess either the sale or supposed trade. In fact, they might even feel cocky if both the *mafiya* and Donatello are willing to offer up two vital parts of their strategy."

"So, we need to stage a fight," Donatello says, warily eyeing Mischa. "One that will convincingly show we're not close in the slightest."

"Might I suggest…" Fabio seems to hesitate, his expression dark.

"I think I can guess where you're heading," Donatello says grimly. "It's a dramatic tactic but not entirely implausible."

"Care to enlighten me?" Mischa cuts in.

Fabio and Donatello share a glance before the former says, "A wedding would suffice. One that seems as though it comes at the cost of good relations between both families."

"So, you want to use my daughter as bait?" Mischa's voice is so cold I can't tell what exactly he's thinking.

"Frankly, I was planning on marrying her anyway."

The silence that falls is chilling.

"Mischa…" Ellen steps forward, reasserting her presence. She places a hand on his shoulder, but he gently shrugs her off.

"And you think admitting that now changes a damn thing?"

"It was for security," Donatello says. "Inheritance. So, she could have complete access to my assets should anything happen—"

"Your assets…" Mischa turns to me, his brows drawn.

Of course, Ellen must have told him what the doctor revealed. I wait for him to voice as much.

"An archaic solution, but strategic," Fabio says before he can. "And, to be blunt, it wouldn't be the most egregious part of this situation by far."

"In your opinion," Mischa growls. "But you aren't the grown man with a failed career and no prospects who preyed on the woman who was supposedly like a daughter to him. After, of course, you sold her into slavery and left her to die."

Donatello flinches as if struck, but my cheeks flame. I've never heard him talk like this. Judging from the gleam in his eye, this is only a fraction of what sparked his hostility when it comes to Donatello.

"Not to mention, the rumors," he adds in a dangerous hiss.

"Oh, don't play coy now, Mischa," Donatello counters. "Lay it all out, gossip and all."

"Well, the *gossips* claim that you killed your wife in a blind rage, your son along with her. That you sold your young ward not out of petty revenge, but out of prudence. Those same gossips claim that the girl witnessed your crime, or had knowledge capable of incriminating you. Rather than kill her yourself, you took the coward's way out."

So much for the fragile comradery. The shift in the atmosphere is so palpable the temperature seems to drop. It's degrees colder, but no one moves or reacts. We're all frozen.

Fabio recovers first, clearing his throat. "Given the subject matter—" anxiously, he tugs on his collar, his cheeks reddening. "I don't think this conversation is appropriate to have right now after all—"

"No," Donatello says hoarsely. His expression is stoic, but those eyes betray him, wild and narrowed to slits. "Let's hear his so-called gossip, which sounds far too outlandish and specific to have been thought up on the fly. I wouldn't have pegged you as one to fall prey to rumors, Mischa."

"Not a rumor. Let's call it secondhand information that came directly from a source with firsthand knowledge of at least one of your crimes. They don't have the best reputation, but in this case, they have no reason to lie, either. And paired with your current actions? I'm more inclined to believe them."

"And what does that mean?"

"That I wouldn't put it past you to manipulate a woman who might hold the key to ruining your name for good. Manipulate and seduce her into ignoring the past and keeping her silence. Before, you sold her to gain leverage, but now you use more underhanded tactics. Does that sound too 'outlandish' for you?"

I watch as Donatello processes the accusations one by one. Whether intentionally or not, his expression shifts to visually convey alarm, then disgust. And finally…

Guilt? The tension in his jaw makes my breath catch. Just as quickly, he quashes all traces of the emotion behind an iron mask.

"I shouldn't dignify that bullshit with a response." Real anger breaks through his fracturing composure. "But I will anyway. I would never hurt my wife. Ever. Funnily enough. You have. The scars are visible for anyone to fucking see, and yet you want to insinuate that I'm the monster?"

"Enough," Fabio exclaims, once again scrambling to insert himself between the two men. "All this fighting will do is waste more time, and nothing will be accomplished. Set your differences aside. There will be plenty of time for name-calling later. At present, all that matters is neutralizing this threat and finding out their true aims before more bloodshed is unleashed. Understood? First things first, I believe the wedding plot will be the perfect way to throw off suspicion and potentially lure them out. In fact, we should go a step further. Set the wedding on the same day as this supposed trade. I don't think they'll be able to resist such a tempting arrangement. They could launch an attack, secure the harbor and their target in one go."

"Which means they'll pool most if not all of their resources on that location," Mischa says, switching into the mindset of a tactician with a chilling ease. "Which could also increase the risk. But we could head them off. They won't be expecting the full resources of the *mafiya*."

"But that will all require careful planning," Fabio says. "No room for deviation and no room for mistrust. Whatever the details are, we need them nailed down securely. We won't be able to communicate until the day of to avoid rousing suspicion. We need full transparency and trust."

"I'd be risking my neck while you get to stay safely within your manor walls," Donatello points out, his face still partially bloodied. "It wouldn't be hard for you to turn the tables and join forces with our enemy to take me out for good. I doubt working with an arsonist and crazed murderer would be any different than taking intel from a human trafficker."

Mischa scoffs. "You forget, those bastards tried to kill my son."

"I could say the same when it comes to you."

The tension ratchets up again, until Fabio claps his hands loudly. "Enough! If the threat of carnage and death isn't enough to cease this infighting, then nothing will. So go ahead. Kill each other here and now and save anyone else the trouble. One would think that nothing would trump seeking out an enemy who has managed to catch you both unawares not once, but several times. I understand there are…complications. But for fuck's sake!"

"You're right." Donatello clears his throat. "We will have plenty of time to kill each other later." He laughs, but it doesn't reach his eyes. "In the meantime, we need to settle on logistics and fast—"

He winces, rubbing at the bandages around his shoulder.

"We'll need to leave the property unseen," he grates. "Then we need a base of operations. Somewhere in the city that won't raise alarm."

"No doubt they'll be watching our every move," Fabio says. "But if you *were* to elope in three days, the hotel suite wouldn't be out of the realm of possibility. I've already had your suite surveilled for sniper access, and it's relatively safe from that kind of assault. I could arrange to buy out the nearby suites for your men."

"It's more secure than the house," Donatello admits.

"So that's settled," Fabio says. "Then I'll find a way to make it known that tensions are higher than ever between the two of you and that the impending wedding is a powder keg."

"But won't they question it?" Mischa says. "My daughter is attacked, and I let her go with you without hunting down the attackers?"

"We'll need a way to throw off suspicion," Fabio admits. "A plausible way to explain why you wouldn't join forces."

Donatello clears his throat. "Well... If I thought you had sent them after me, without realizing Willow was nearby, that would explain it."

Mischa nods, his expression thoughtful. "It would give me an opening to contact them seemingly on friendly ground."

"And plenty of opportunity to forge an alliance," Donatello adds. "Not that you would."

"This is a game of wits, gentlemen," Fabio insists. "We must keep ours and remain one step ahead. Now, with that settled, we need to put our plan into action. Soon. I'm sure our enemies are watching this manor and have already noted Donatello's presence. If we delay any longer, their suspicion will be piqued before we can even get a real plan into motion."

"Fine," Donatello grudgingly says. "How to beat a madman at his own game? Where to begin?"

DON

I've learned the hard way that there is no benefit to being sentimental. The past is a weight around a man's neck and to dwell on it is to tighten the noose.

Or maybe that's just what I told myself to cushion the blow that I barely remember those bitter days around Liv's death.

I could write off Mischa's accusations as petty jabs. But not her reaction. Not the look in her face as he voiced each one in cruel detail. There wasn't alarm or even horror to be found in her eyes. Just fear.

Terror.

As if she already knew.

To her credit, she's tried confronting me herself with Olivia's letters, and, like a coward, I used that desire as leverage.

I should be grateful to whatever sick motherfucker has me in their sights. They've bought me time to stall, but I can't avoid the truth forever. It gnaws at me, playing on the gaps in my memories and planting festering fears in those spaces. As bullshit as Mischa's little explanation sounded…

It also makes sense. Fuck, it makes *too* much sense—that I'm a worthless monster who killed his own wife and tried to silence the sole witness.

That would explain her pain. Her hate. She sought me out intending to kill me, and I more than deserve that retribution. If I hurt Liv…

I'd deserve death.

Yet, I still can't bring myself to face those accusations directly. Instead, I hide. Not even in our shared suite but the one below it. Under the guise of clearing the premises, I've been in this room overlooking the bay for nearly a fucking hour. It's cowardly, but I can't bring myself to leave. Not until I've gathered the nerve to face the truth, no matter where it may lead.

"Sir?" One of my men calls from the doorway. "Any trouble?"

"No." I turn toward him, heading into the hall. "All clear. You can bring the others in."

"Right away, sir."

Out in the hall, another holdout from Antonio Salvatore's forces stands guard, falling into step behind me as I approach the elevator.

Thank God for Fabio. The man must list God among his many connections because barely two hours after our conversation at Stepanov Manor, he's managed to clear out the necessary rooms in the hotel and arranged to have part of my men meet me here.

All that's left now is to enact stage two of the plan.

"Give me a minute," I tell the guard once we reach the upper floor. He stands at the ready as I withdraw my cell phone. Typical Fabio, he answers on the first try, but I can hear the tension in his voice.

"I take it you're back at the hotel. The rest of your men should be arriving shortly, along with your 'guest'."

Judging from his strained tone, he's referring to Kisa Salvatore.

"I think you'll be pleased to know that a buyer has already expressed interest in your harbor offices. Several, in fact."

It sounds too damn good to be true.

"Any clue on which one might be our mystery man?"

"Not yet," Fabio admits. "Frankly, I think I underestimated the popularity of that particular location. You've gotten far more inquiries than I expected. It shouldn't be hard to weed them out. It's simply a matter of who is willing to pay more."

"So now what?"

"Now we wait," Fabio says simply. "In the meantime, might I suggest you go over the plans for your sham wedding? It needs to be convincing, after all. An event suitable of rubbing Mischa's nose in your dastardly scheme."

"That's one way of describing it," I croak. While I haven't been able to get the bastard's taunts out of my mind, it seems Fabio hasn't either.

"In any regard," he says, "feel free to drain your emergency accounts all in the name of making this event convincing. Financial ruin wouldn't be the worst situation you've put yourself in by far."

"Thanks for the encouragement, Fab," I snap. "What about the church? Think it will work as a suitable trap?"

"I have a team on it now," he says, serious once again. "We won't be able to completely eliminate the risks. I suggest that we take every precaution."

"What? You mean a bulletproof vest?"

"Can't be too safe," Fab says. "But… There is one more thing."

"What?" The change in subject has me gritting my teeth in grim anticipation. "You've sounded off from the second you picked up. What's wrong?"

He sighs. "I take it you haven't heard, then."

"Heard what?"

My guard is up instantly. Has Mischa decided not to play nice after all?

"I honestly don't know if you'll see this as good news or bad, but… This wedding might turn out to be more of a sham than intended, which is a good thing in my estimation."

"What the hell are you getting at?"

"Willow might not be pregnant after all, according to the tests run at her last exam. It's a longshot, but this all might have been a fluke of blood work explainable by other factors."

"A fluke."

Jesus Christ, he wasn't lying. Good or bad doesn't seem like the right characterization of this news either way. To be honest, he could have stabbed me, and I'd process it better.

On the face of it, Willow Stepanova gets her perfect life back and a future without me in it.

On the other hand…

"Don?" Fabio's voice is a fraction louder, as if he's been repeating my name with increasing alarm.

"Yeah… I'm here."

"This is the worst possible time to go, I know—but I think it might be best if we don't communicate regularly for now. Before I hang up, there is one more thing."

"That you think I killed Liv?" I'm only half joking. All things considered, he has every right to suspect me of the worst. His hate would be easier to handle than whatever I feel swelling in my chest.

"No! Vincenzo."

"How is he doing?"

"He's fine," Fabio says. "Itching to leave the hospital, in fact. I've doubled his security detail, and there is no sign that he's been targeted."

"Is this your way of telling me that I can't see him until further notice?" It's hard to keep the irritation from my voice.

"Not at all," Fabio says, surprising me. "In fact, I think you should see him. Perhaps tomorrow. Anyone with the slightest bit of reliable intel would know that if you truly believed Mischa was partly responsible for the attack on your life, nothing short of the Devil himself could keep you from checking on Vin."

"Point taken. It isn't like you to be so accommodating."

"You're right," Fab concedes. "I'm merely hoping you take that juicy carrot and won't complain as much when I bring out the stick. Given how tenuous relations are, and your past history, I believe it would be best if you and Willow settle on a few boundaries."

"You mean that if she isn't pregnant, don't use this timeframe to make it so," I taunt—only my tone isn't even close to joking this time.

"I'll let that gross insinuation slide because even you aren't that sick," he says tiredly. His polished persona slips, revealing the true man beneath. One so damn exhausted he can't even bother to put energy into his voice.

Damn. I've been so selfish I didn't stop to think how hard this might be for him, constantly hearing Liv's name dredged up.

"I'm sorry," I say, not that it matters any. Still, I feel compelled to offer him something, no matter how small. "You know I would never hurt Liv—"

"Of course, I know that," he starts. "Don't even think I would—"

"But to be totally fucking honest with you, Fabio… I don't remember. Everything is in bits and pieces. I don't think I would…"

I eye my free hand, scowling at the divots and marks scarring the palm. A blue patch represents the sole remnants of a sprawled message written in ink. Only one word is still legible—*truth.*

And the truth is…

I have no fucking idea what I could have been capable of. The memories of that time are a jumbled mess with no real clarity to be found. But I do know one thing.

Mischa Stepanov won't be the one to throw whatever truth there is in my face. I'll seek out the answers my damn self, starting with the most obvious.

"You were my rock in those days, Fab," I say hoarsely. "Tell me what you remember, no matter how fucked up it might be."

Hell, I'm even holding my breath.

"No," he snarls. "You need to be focused only on the present. Looking backward won't solve anything. All it will do is just bring up more pain for everyone involved."

"I know where I can get some answers, though," I say, turning in the direction of said answers, and the person wielding them.

"What are you talking about?" Fabio demands.

"Don't worry about it. I'm sorry you ever got dragged into my shit. You're the best, Fabio."

"The best," he echoes faintly. "Don't forget it. I always have your best interest in mind, and that when you forge into these situations alone is when things tend to go wrong. Don't shut me out. What answers are you talking about?"

This affects him too, doesn't it? He deserves to know something.

Swallowing hard, I croak, "You know about Liv's letters?"

His silence is disarming. It isn't like Fabio to be speechless. After a few more seconds, he clears his throat. "I do. And I thought we both agreed that it would be better for everyone if they weren't disturbed. The past should remain in the past."

"Easy for you to say. You aren't the one who could have killed his own damn wife."

"Do you really think I would have stuck by you all of these years if I believed that?"

"Fab…"

To be brutally honest, I don't know why he has stuck around all this damn time. He doesn't owe me anything, and after all of the hell I've put him through.

"Some people might say you should have cut me loose years ago."

"Some people are dumbasses," he counters. "All that matters is getting through this current peril unscathed. To do that, we need total honesty. Where are the letters?"

His reference to them irritates me for some unknown reason. It could be his cautious tone, the same one he might deploy when dealing with an unruly child.

"I'll deal with them, don't worry about it. Take care, Fab. You're right; we shouldn't talk much."

I hang up, sensing in my gut that something is off. Unbalanced. Despite Fabio's insistence to the contrary, the past is alive and well, and I will never outrun it.

The only way to leave it behind for good is to overcome it.

No matter the cost.

Stowing the cell in my pocket, I finally enter the suite, ready for anything.

The entrance hall is empty. The only other occupant lurks in a study overlooking the harbor, her back to me. There are no pretty words to ease into this conversation. No way of avoiding the hard reality, either.

"The letters," I blurt out gruffly. "I'm ready to read them."

She spins to face me, an eyebrow raised. In the space of time since leaving the manor, she's changed into one of her new outfits—a plain black dress with long sleeves. It might only be her proximity to the window that allows the faint daylight to paint the panes of her delicate cheekbones, but she looks older in a heartbeat. Someone who has seen too damn much in her time, aged by pain and trauma.

"I'm ready," I repeat, crossing over to a nearby desk.

I wait for her to leave and retrieve them. Instead, she turns to face me fully, revealing that she already has them pressed to her chest.

I swallow hard as the old handwriting catches the light. My nostrils flare, sensing the faintest hint of sweet perfume. Each breath guts me. For a second, I'm there again. The woman before me morphs into one with a similar build but dark hair, her gaze accusatory.

Did I hurt her? Every fiber of my being tells me no. I never would. Damn Mischa for ever insinuating as much.

But deep down…

Doubt infects that confidence, festering with every passing second.

"Please." I extend my hand, and the specter of Olivia morphs back into Willow Stepanova. She approaches me warily, placing the letters before me one by one. What I at first mistake for a haphazard arrangement soon reveals itself as something more deliberate.

"This is the order you want me to read them in?" I ask, meeting her gaze.

She nods, but her expression isn't gloating or triumphant. If anything, she looks resigned. Like someone lighting a match, intending to set off a bomb—but with no excitement toward the impending boom. Just dread.

Unlike Fabio, she isn't afraid to set things into motion though. Finished with her placement of the crumbled letters, she steps back, turning her gaze to the window.

I stare at her for a dangerous few seconds. Far longer than I should. I'm only stalling from the inevitable, but I stubbornly let my gaze linger, hunting for any signs of hatred or disgust that I might have missed. She should be brimming over with both, to be honest. She should hate me.

And if I truly hurt Olivia and sold her to hide my own guilt...

She should want me dead, and she'd have every fucking right to.

EVGENI

For one woman to so thoroughly throw my plans into disarray, chaos must be a talent of hers. Along with destruction and deception.

Unfortunately for her, her luck might have just run out.

They're keeping her on the lowest level of the house—a layer of security that might be unwarranted for someone of her stature. Unless, of course, they want to keep her protected rather than merely keep her prisoner.

It's a thought that won't stop weighing on my mind as I make my way through the labyrinthine halls to reach the old wing where two men stand guard. They nod wordlessly as I approach and let me past.

"I've seen worse forms of captivity," I announce, taking in the spacious room and the sole woman occupying it.

They didn't give her any windows, instead shutting her within an old storeroom lit only by an overhead lamp.

Someone cleaned the cobwebs from the rafters, at least. Fresh sheets drape the lone bed, and she was provided with a table and chairs to sit on.

Regardless, I suspect that Briar Winthorp finds these lodgings far beneath her standards. I've never seen her stare quite this cold. She doesn't even flash a charming grin as I advance. Instead, I can almost see the hair on the back of her neck rankle.

"You seem stressed, Ms. Winthorp," I say, though nowhere near as nastily as I could.

Regardless, her eyes flash, and she's practically on tiptoe. "Damn you. Unless you've come to uphold your goddamn bargain, then get the fuck out."

I feel myself raising an eyebrow. "That's not the usual greeting I've come to expect from you."

"Do you think this is a game?" She gestures wildly to the plain white walls surrounding us. "You think this will hold them off? God damn you fools. I warned you, and now we're all nicely packaged for the slaughter."

"Explain."

My tone startles her into silence. She blinks, raising an eyebrow of her own.

"As if you didn't orchestrate this idiotic excuse for a plan," she snarls. "I'm sure your hand was all over this, but I will warn you now, it won't work. God, I should have left when I had the chance—"

"I don't know what the hell you're talking about," I say over her. "So, I suggest you start talking before you pepper me with insults."

Her lips flatten into a hard line as she inspects me, her head cocked. I can see her suspicion warring with confusion. Finally, she inclines her head further. "Your beloved master aims to use me as bait in a trade. The idiotic fool doesn't seem to realize that he's fallen for a very clever trap. They won't settle for biding their time for a neat handover. They want me dead, and they don't care who gets in their way."

"A trade?"

Her eyes narrow, and once again, I sense her questioning my motives. I wish she had a reason to be so skeptical, but the twisted part is that…

I don't fucking know what the hell she's talking about. After his meeting with Vanici, he and Mischa left the compound, and none of the men left behind seem to know a damn thing. Until he returns, I'm in the dark.

But I know better than to let her know that.

"You don't know, do you?" she surmises. Rather than taunt me over that fact, the line of her mouth grows even tighter. "It seems you still haven't wormed your way back into your master's good graces."

"Then I suggest you drop the act and enlighten me if you hope to have an ally in this mess."

Her eyes widen for a split second before more suspicion displaces the shock. "Is this part of the trap? Feign innocence to get me to reveal what I know?"

"You say that as if you haven't been honest up until now, Ms. Winthorp."

"And perhaps I haven't." She steps up to me, her lips still pressed in a stern line. "I wanted you to help me find my son so I could leave this godforsaken place and never look back."

"You could have left without him," I point out. "And you yourself admitted that you aren't the maternal type. I'm supposed to believe that overnight you had a change of heart?"

"No," she says softly, and something in her gaze shifts, darkening the hue of those blue eyes. "You're supposed to believe that I am prudent and ruthless but not heartless. Have you stopped to think what drove me from them in the first place?"

"You learned something," I say, hazarding a guess.

She nods. "And I'm sure that even a man as literal as you can guess what that was. Think. If you were a man who stood to gain everything, what might you do to anyone or anything you felt might impede your progress?"

"Your son," I say. "He threatened him?"

"Not in so many words." She looks away, and I'm sure it's to hide her expression. She's lying.

I grab her shoulder, wrenching her around to face me. Her expression conveys an emotion alright. Fear.

"Maybe I was stupid enough to be tempted by his lies," she admits, her chin jutting stubbornly. "That I could have my family's wealth and prestige returned with the flick of a pen."

"It sounds too good to be true," I point out.

"Of course, it does," she snaps. "But I don't think you've ever known what it is like to go from having the world at your fingertips to ruin overnight. To having to rely on the very people who ripped your life apart to pick up the pieces."

"I think you should be careful when it comes to insinuating things about me, Ms. Winthorp," I counter.

"The point is, I didn't realize the full extent of their plan."

"But you knew it involved a child, Eli Stepanov, losing his life in the process. You just didn't think you'd have to get your hands dirty to carry out that part of the process when it came to regaining the world at your fingertips."

"I knew he had to be removed from the line of succession," she clarifies coldly, her expression stone. "I didn't think he would have to be killed to achieve that. Use your imagination, Mr. Volkov. Everything isn't so damn literal."

"And the real world doesn't cater to the blind naivety of a penniless socialite desperate to regain her family's fortune, either. So, you joined in with this grand scheme and got cold feet. Then what?"

"Then, I realized that there was never any real choice presented to me, either. If the plan did succeed and Alexander stood in line to rightfully inherit what is his birthright, that bastard had no intention of sharing the wealth any more than Mischa and his brood."

"You would find that both you and your son were the new obstacles needing to be 'removed'."

"Exactly," she hisses.

"But it's more than that, isn't it? A child can be manipulated, but not if his ambitious mother is there to whisper in his ear. No… You found yourself becoming the obstacle. It wasn't the case that you miraculously gained a conscience overnight. It's that you realized sooner or later, you would be next on the chopping block."

"So, what if I did?" She shrugs in defeat, but her gaze is suddenly averted from mine. There's more to this she isn't saying. "It doesn't matter now, does it? I've been here too long, and they've probably suspected the course of action I'd attempt to take next."

"Retrieving your son, you mean?"

She nods, meeting my gaze again. Her eyes blaze with a fierce, vicious energy, but for the first time, I suspect it isn't directed my way. "They won't take any chances now."

"You mean they'll move him?"

She nods. "He's probably out of the country by now."

"He might be," I say. "But I think you're overlooking one key detail."

"What?" Her brows draw together, her irritation palpable. "Don't play games with me, soldier. Just spit it out."

"Unlike you, I'm not partial to shrouding everything I say behind word games and a riddle," I snap. "He bought him here for a reason. What was it?"

From the way her eyes narrow in contemplation, I have my answer. "You don't know. Do you?"

"I assumed he wanted him close out of smugness at his impending victory," she says dryly.

"But it might be for something else. What?"

When she doesn't answer, I grab her wrist. Fear flits across her features, and it takes her longer than normal to recover. I feel her stiffen, every bit of muscle going rigid beneath my grip.

"You think manhandling me will get you the answer?" she asks tersely, still jutting that chin.

"No." I release her and turn toward the door. "I think you don't have any fucking options left but to give me an answer. Or watch me leave knowing that all of your efforts spent manipulating me weren't worth a damn—"

"I know where he might attack next," she says.

Damn her. I stop short, still poised to take another step. "Where?"

Slow, confident footsteps march in my direction. I don't look, but I can easily picture her reassembling that stoic mask piece by piece. When she finally comes to stand before me, I realize I'm right.

"Wouldn't you like to know?" she says with a coy tilt of her head. "But that would require cooperation, Mr. Volkov. Frankly, my patience is running out trying to get that through your thick head."

"It also requires honesty," I say. "Something you seem to be reluctant to give. No more. Either you tell me the truth, or I leave. Better yet, I'll convince Mischa to go along with the trade, no backup in mind. Then I'll see firsthand just what your old master has in store for you."

Her eyes widen, her lips pursed. I've struck a nerve, it seems.

"The harbor was just the beginning," she says. "A distraction. He's laid the groundwork to take over the city quickly, but now he needs to put it to good use. If you were a man intent on running the world, what might you deem necessary to enact your devious plan?"

It's another fucking riddle, but at least this one has a more obvious answer.

"I'd disable my enemies," I say cautiously. "Then position myself to replace them at a rapid pace. Make it impossible for anyone else to compete."

"And if you were using the Saleris as your cover, what business might you be interested in?"

I mull it over, feeling my eyes narrow as I home in on the most likely target. "Trafficking. I'd trick the Saleris into thinking I wanted to help them broaden their reach and clientele. Then I'd bring in my own resources on top of their head. By the time they realized what was happening, I would have already parasitized their network for my own."

"Exactly." Is that grim approval I catch in her tone? "But even more ruthless than that. To take over an existing network, you need allies, but you also need resources. Such as…"

"Manpower," I say, not liking where this is headed. "I would feel confident if I knew I had other allies hidden in the background, waiting to advance and push the previous partners out. He's aiming to bring them in."

"And soon," she says. "My suspicions tell me they must exist outside of the country, but with access routes via water that should be easier than ever to utilize given the precious destruction."

"And you don't know any names? Any organizations?"

Though a few come to mind already—none of them reassuring.

"Now you see the reason for my urgency?" she says. "Once he gets those reinforcements in place, it will be a numbers game, and I can assure you that the math isn't on our side."

"Shit." She could have mentioned this all sooner, not that it makes a damn bit of difference without knowing any of the specifics.

"What if there was a way to alert the Saleris? Get them to turn if only in their own self-preservation?"

"I don't see how," she says. "They seemed pretty convinced. I don't know what he's told them, but it must be enticing enough to ignore the many red flags. They won't see the betrayal coming."

"But they might if it comes from the right person," I say, warily. "I think I know someone who could fit the bill. We don't need them on our side. We just merely need them to withdraw their support or at least try to circumvent their destruction. It could buy us more time."

"All this use of 'ours' and 'we'," the woman says, her smirk returning in full. "It's very heartwarming, soldier."

"I don't mean you," I snarl, ignoring how her face falls. "Mischa. You can still serve your purpose as bait."

Her upper lip pulls back from her teeth, her hands in fists. I half-expect her to lunge at me, given her fierce expression. Instead, she scoffs.

"Still playing the role of a thick brute, I see."

"Bait, for appearances purposes," I say. "While I do your dirty work and gather intel. Isn't that what you wanted all along?"

She frowns, startled by the shift in subject. Her eyes tell all as she wrestles with the idea of trusting me or not. In the end, she seems to settle on the only solution available to her. She doesn't have a choice.

"Give me locations to check and anything else you remember. I'll need to do reconnaissance on the Saleris while also trying to discover who the other ally might be."

"While I get to sit here and look pretty?"

"Don't tell me you'd prefer to be out there getting your hands dirty?" I toss back.

"Fine. I will tell you what I know," she says, but I can sense the caveat coming a mile away. "In return, you add one more task to that little list of yours."

"And what is that?"

"You find where my son is, and you get him back."

"He's the key to this whole masterplan, isn't he?" I ask. "Without him and the promise of a Winthorp fortune to pay off his debts, your old master can't fund his devious little plans. That might leave him in a bind with a lot of dangerous enemies."

"Rationalize it how you'd like," she says without revealing a shred of emotion either way. "Just promise me you'll do that."

"I don't make promises." I turn to the door and knock once. Meeting her gaze from over my shoulder, I add, "Especially not to someone like you."

"To a 'threat' you mean?" she counters.

"No. A dangerous liability."

WILLOW

It's wrong. But I thought I would get a sick sense of satisfaction from watching him relive the past, finally. As he does, I witness the same realizations dawn over him in the exact order they must have affected me the first time I read them.

Shock. Confusion. Then utter despair as he fully surrenders to the throes of agony, having to face the consequences of his own actions.

And yet, this isn't the same as holding him to account for his betrayal. What happened between him and Olivia was more personal. Intimate. Something that I know in the pit of my soul I have no right to see unfurl.

I'm not entitled to the kind of pain that contorts his body the more he reads. It started in his face, with his brows drawn tightly in concentration and his lips pursed. Then disbelief. His jaw went slack, his eyes widening. I thought he'd drop the letter entirely, but he didn't, finishing the page before woodenly grabbing another.

Then another.

The most terrifying thing to witness in him is the grudging acceptance. It steels into his expression, hardening every line. Before my eyes, he's stone, impossible to discern anything from.

I don't know how long he stares at that final page, crinkling the paper beneath trembling fingertips. It feels like an eternity before he finally lowers it, cradling his face in his hands.

Once, I prayed to witness the destruction of Donatello Vanici with my own eyes. I craved to see his despair. Weep. I wanted to gloat over the bastard at his lowest point and be the one to have driven the knife in deep.

Faced with that very sight, I don't feel the triumph I thought I would.

It's cruel. It's harrowing.

It's pain.

"Is this what you wanted?" His voice is so deep I can barely make out the individual words among the mass of grated syllables. "For me to know that my wife was unfaithful. That my son… That he wasn't mine. Is this what you wanted me to see?"

He looks up, but the anger I expect to find is absent from those worn features. He just seems old. Exhausted. A man at his limit, unwilling to carry on a step further.

And my heart aches, bruised and swollen with guilt I shouldn't feel.

"I deserve this," he admits with a weary sigh. He smooths his hands over the letters as if grasping for any trace of the figure who wrote them. In the end, his trembling fingers come up empty. "Every fucking bit… But—"

He breaks off, gritting his teeth, his gaze on the window. Watching him is like viewing the ravages of time on a man in mere seconds. He ages, hunching over as if life is draining from him.

"I didn't know. Or I didn't fucking remember. Fuck." He rakes a hand over his jaw, drawing notice to the dark stubble growing there. It's been days since he's shaved. His eyes seem darker in contrast, haunted by the horrors he's survived until now. "How could I not remember?"

It's something I've been dwelling on since he first made that assertion. How? It seems improbable that something that's shaped my entire life could conveniently leave his memory.

But now I see the truth. He hasn't let himself remember. He's blocked off that space of time, building mental walls around the pain and drowning his present thoughts in whatever vice he could to dull the pain.

"I loved her." He stands, gripping the desk. There's a harshness in his movements that wasn't there before, as if every step—

every breath—takes all his effort. He sways unsteadily as he crosses to the window, and he braces both hands over the glass as if it's the only thing in the world capable of holding him up.

That uncomfortable feeling in my chest throbs the more I watch him. Sympathy? Or remorse?

This seems…wrong. All wrong. Like I'm seeing only a small piece of a larger, more complex puzzle—and it's jagged, liable to cut anyone foolish enough to handle it without knowing the fuller context.

"God, I loved her," Donatello says, scowling down at the city he once claimed for himself. "Can I even blame her if she felt alone? Neglected? I loved her, but I can't deny that she came second. There was always something else in the way."

Another bastion of control to take. Another bit of power to snatch. Another piece of the world to conquer.

"I knew what it was doing to her," he adds. "What it did to all of you."

He turns, meeting my gaze, and I stiffen at what I find lurking behind those dark irises. Agony. His eyes glisten, threatening an inevitable outcome.

And yet, I don't believe it when the first few tears fall, painting a sparkling trail down his cheek.

I have to inch forward and touch one for myself, catching a fat bead of moisture. It's so warm and wet, bursting open over the pad of my thumb.

He doesn't cringe from me or attempt to hide the aftermath. At the same time, the sight doesn't reduce him any. A crying Donatello is every bit as fearsome as the smirking man, wielding a knife, painted with blood.

"You think I did it?" he asks me gruffly. "That I killed her? I couldn't blame you if you did. Hell…" He shrugs me off, turning back to the window. His fingers flex against the glass as he repositions them, and he looks less in need of stability and more…

Assertive. As if any minute, he intends to barge right through the barrier and plunge himself into the world waiting below.

Fear bites through me, shocking in its intensity. I think he's capable of it. In fact, he's liable to do far worse. No man should look like this. As though the entire world is a weapon at his disposal, and he wants nothing more than to use it.

But not against any perceived enemies. Just himself.

I reach for his shoulder before my brain even processes the motion. In shock, I register the hard plane of muscle rippling beneath my fingertips. At times, he seems so strong. Untouchable.

Laws of nature don't apply to him. He can embody two sides of the same twisted coin. Like being both repulsive and irresistible. It's wrong to step closer to him the way I am now. To let my guard down even a fraction wherever he is concerned.

I can't help it.

I know pain. Even so, I can admit that whatever he's feeling is beyond my comprehension. It goes deeper than a physical wound, or betrayal. It guts him.

Despair hollows out those usually fiery brown eyes, and he's an empty shell gazing blankly at the outside world. Sympathy should be the last thing I feel toward him, but it infects me regardless.

In this moment, I identify the source of the pain in my chest. It's compassion. Before I know it, I'm even closer, bracing my body against his.

He lets me linger by his side for longer than I should. This form of nearness is dangerous. Addictive, comparable to a child sticking their finger in an electrical socket out of curiosity about what it might feel like.

Electric is the answer. A potentially lethal mixture of shock and alarm that darts down my spine as if someone traced it with the tip of a knife. He must feel it too, because he abruptly shifts beyond my reach, putting a hairsbreadth of distance between us.

And yet, it feels as wide as the gulf between the sea and sky.

"You don't have any more?" he grates, referring to the letters.

I shake my head, feeling the same desperation that has him groaning out loud.

"So, what the hell do I do now?" he demands from the darkening sky. "Turn myself in? God, if I hurt my wife…"

He breaks off, but it's only when I feel a shudder run along my palm that I realize why. I've touched him again without meaning to. It's like some part of me is driven to comfort him, and I feel my cheeks flame when I contemplate why that might be.

He's right. We're linked together whether we like it or not, and the past no longer feels as looming as it once did. The future is far more terrifying to face.

"You should go." He shrugs me off a second time, only to sink to his knees, pressing his forehead against the window. He looks like a man due to be executed, eagerly awaiting the feel of the blade slicing into the back of his neck. So intent on suffering, he doesn't even react when I crouch beside him.

"I know," he says with a grimace.

My pulse stutters at the soft accusatory note in his voice, but he doesn't seem angry. If anything, the sound he chokes out next could be a broken imitation of a laugh.

"I know that you might not be pregnant. So go home. I won't hold it against you, and we can find some other way of luring out the attacker."

Perhaps it's morbid curiosity keeping me here now. What my brain chooses to interpret as sympathy is really a twisted sense of satisfaction. I must enjoy this.

"You're right," Donatello says with a dry laugh. I stiffen. Has he read my mind for real this time? "If anyone deserves to stay, it's you. You deserve to see me burn in hell for what I did to you. This is merely the start. So, take it in. Maybe your father has more evidence than he led on. That I killed Liv. Why I did what I did…"

He trails off, lifting his head enough to eye his hands. They're both bruised and battered from recent events. I keep replaying those scenes in my head. How he threw himself in front of me without a second thought. Rather than grateful, I'm annoyed. It seems more desperate than selfless. Even Fabio insinuated that the man has a death wish. That could be all there is to it.

But I don't believe it.

He's too calculating for that. He did what he did because, in that instant, his sole intention was to save my life, no matter the cost.

I'm too lost in thought to notice him moving at first.

He lurches as if intending to stand, but he staggers. Alarmed, I reach out to stabilize him, and before I realize it, he's on his knees. Then on his side and his head lands…

On my lap.

We both go rigid. I'm holding my breath, my hands held awkwardly at my sides. From this angle, I have a close-up view of him that drives home just how close to perfection he is—even beaten down and worn to the bone. His timeless features are reminiscent of a statue's, apparent even after the decades have taken their toll.

Misery suits him unfairly well. The grief enhances the stern line of his jaw and the moisture glistening on his cheeks just seems like delicate touches of natural highlight.

I hate the curiosity he rouses in me. It distracts from the hate, displacing it before I'm ready. If I don't loathe him as much, it's far easier to trail a fingertip along a wayward strand of dark brown hair. He hasn't brushed it in days, but it still feels so damn soft. Silk that easily parts as I smooth all five fingers through it.

He stiffens, and I freeze. Once again, we're nearing those dangerous boundaries we both know so well. I can tell he doesn't want to cross them, not now. He tenses as if he means to stand and shrug me off. Then he sighs.

"I wanted to erase you."

Barely a whisper, his voice still resonates beneath my skin down to the bone.

"I thought if I could relegate you to nothing, you'd cease to have a hold over me. You *shouldn't* have a hold over me," he adds. "It's my own damn fault, but still… I thought if I could break you down, I wouldn't have to look back and face what I've done."

He's said this line before in so many words, but this time feels more real. Final. This is part of the disjointed thought process swirling around his mind. But this isn't for my benefit. No.

There is no polish, no softening of the harsh reality. He's speaking to himself.

"It didn't work," he admits.

I feel his jaw flex against my upper thigh. The heat of his breath easily scorches through the fabric of my dress, warming the skin beneath. I draw in a ragged breath. Even with our past interactions considered, this nearness feels the most dangerous. The most unnerving.

"You found a way to worm inside my head regardless. Do you want to know what the worst part of this all is?"

He gestures aimlessly with his hand as the weight of him settles more firmly in my lap, as if he let his body relax without meaning to.

"I'm not a monster. I know what this looks like. I know you don't even have a clue as to the hell I've set you up for. No idea. You might think you do, but you don't. I know that. It's wrong. I deserve hell for what I've done. But pushing you away… Shouldering the blame or acting like the noble asshole for taking responsibility, that just makes it easier on me. The hard part would be to let you take the lead. To give you control. I'm too damn old. You're too damn young. But I can't act like I have all the fucking answers, because I don't. Not now. Not ever."

It's hard for him to admit that out loud, and shock forces the air from my lungs in a single exhale.

"It wouldn't be fair of me to act like I do." His eyes are magnetic in this moment, piercing and electric. "I don't have the right to push you away. I can't ask for anything from you. I can't tell you a damn thing as to how to think or feel."

He reaches up hesitantly, giving me plenty of time to anticipate what he intends. I'm riveted as his fingers waver near my cheek, inching closer before pulling away. Finally, he bridges the gap, stroking along my jawline.

I feel that touch in every inch of my body down to my toes. It's gentle enough—but the texture of his calloused flesh awakens a million dangerous sensations and bothersome thoughts. My heart feels heavier, and when I remember how to breathe, the air scrapes down my throat as if laced with glass.

"I'm not a moral authority," he admits. "All I can do is be honest with you. So, believe me when I tell you that I will never love you the way you deserve to be loved."

He frowns, disappointed by the admission leaving his own mouth.

"I won't. I will never be able to care for you. I will never be able to return any affection you might have for me. I will only bring you pain. I can't expect you to understand what that means, not now anyway—" He breaks off with a grimace. "Fuck. I'm doing it again. Playing the higher authority. The point is. I'll let you make your own choices, but I can never make you happy."

He says that like it's some great revelation I should be thankful for. He's finally admitted his role as the villain in this story, good for him. Donatello Vanici is every bit the heartless, selfish criminal I always believed him to be.

But this is yet another cop-out. Another way to skirt any real responsibility. Another way to undermine his own claim to surrender control to me.

I don't want him to martyr himself.

I want him to try. I deserve that. I want him to fight against the doom and gloom he's prophesized because I know that would be harder for him. I want him to want me even though he shouldn't. He deserves nothing less than hating himself every damn second of every day because he's happier chasing a fantasy than living a lie.

It's the same fate he's damned me to for almost a decade. A living hell of playing pretend, all while knowing that the one person you crave is the very monster responsible for ruining your fragile peace in the first place.

I want him to chase chaos for the rest of his life and never again resign himself to the role of victim.

Just stop.

Reacting on impulse, I flatten my palm against his chin, sensing the unruly stubble beneath. His face is so expressive that even a frown takes a concerto of muscle and tissue to achieve. I feel each one straining in harmony as he inclines his head, letting what little light there is illuminate his features.

God, I hate this man. It's unfair how beautiful he is. How ugly he makes me feel.

More than anything, I hate what he's made of me. After everything we've been through, I shouldn't be this spiteful. But I am. I relish the way he flinches as I capture the other side of his face with my opposite hand.

Alarm dances across those dark irises before a grudging resignation settles over both. I can see myself reflected in his gaze. Angry and vengeful, like an angel from hell with golden hair.

Tears still fall from his eyes, painting a silent trail that doesn't diminish him any. If anything, the vulnerable display of emotion just makes him seem stronger. Invincible.

Some petty part of me wants to test that theory. When I lean down and drag my mouth over his, he shouldn't budge an inch.

But he does.

A groan rips from his throat that I can taste on the tip of my tongue. His flavor is a rich, dangerous spice that clearly conveys just what he's feeling—pain. He wants to pull away, but only sheer force of will keeps him here. Keeps him with me.

Good.

I don't take mercy on him. Instead, I continue my exploration, dragging my fingers along the rugged panes of flesh and bone that make up the stern expressions of Donatello Vanici. With every inch of him I trace, his brows draw further together. Like black holes, his eyes seem darker, and his mouth is so rigid that it doesn't give, as the tip of my pinky smooths over it.

When I draw back, he sighs.

"You always were so damn stubborn." His voice resonates with the grim finality of a man on his death bed. He knows he's doomed; there's no use in fighting it.

So, he doesn't even try.

A flutter of alarm runs through my belly, but some part of me is driven to ignore it.

So, I prove him right and *stubbornly* probe his mouth again.

The second time our lips meet, he hisses, coming alive in a burst of movement. His fingers latch onto my skull, fisting through my hair. My heart hammers as I wait for him to tug me away, but he doesn't. The contact seems intended to reinforce his presence more than anything. He's still desperate to maintain control at any cost.

But he restrains himself, though it must kill him to.

Frozen at this awkward angle, we coexist in a strange sort of limbo. Our breaths mingle, our bodies contorted. My hair falls forward, creating a cocoon that shields us both. In this shadowy sliver of the universe, previous rules and boundaries mean nothing.

But he's the one leaning forward this time, bridging the gap. I don't know what drives me to do it—seize a corner of his lip between my teeth and bear down.

He grunts, bringing his other hand to my chin. His fingers twitch as if it's taking all of his strength not to push me away. Instead, his thumb slips out, stroking along my jaw, and shock makes me release him.

But I don't pull back, and neither does he.

I wouldn't call this a kiss. It's too sloppy for that. Too hesitant. In a sense, it's just another form of exploration. I get to poke and prod at Donatello Vanici in this aspect, and he can't bring himself to stop me. Lust isn't what I sense from him, either. Just resignation.

He promised me power, and this is how I choose to claim it.

By tasting him. By deepening the kiss. By making him endure every probing jab from my tongue. I can feel the tension ripping through him, coiling in every muscle.

And somewhere amid it all, he turns the tables.

We collide in a mass of twisted limbs, and I'm in the air. In his arms, pressed to his chest, my legs around his waist…

A heartbeat later, I'm blinking up at the ceiling, feeling the mattress conform to my spine. All I can do is stare as he comes into view, moving to settle over me. My heart flutters, and for a second, something bubbles up within my chest that might be fear.

Until I see the look in his eye, tortured and broken. He brings his face near mine, but his breaths are labored. He doesn't touch me, bracing his hands on either side of my body instead.

For what feels like an eternity, we just coexist, sharing the same thinning air.

I don't know what it is in my expression that makes him finally raise one hand, stroking it along my chin. Maybe it's that I don't push him off. Or how my lips part, remembering his taste.

When his fingers ghost the side of my throat, I can't stop my spine from twisting toward his touch. It's as if he is magnetic, calling to some twisted force within me.

The nearer he is, the more it burns. Ignites. Explodes.

I'm shaking, my teeth chattering, though I'm far from cold. If anything, I'm overwhelmed by his heat, dizzy and breathless.

Slowly, he rears back, bracing his weight on his thighs instead. I can feel him settle over my hips, and the unfamiliar weight draws my attention to the space between my legs. I'd almost forgotten what this feels like.

Dangerous intimacy. Foreign fire and an uncomfortable pressure that aches. My thighs twitch, desperate to rub together. Soothe it somehow…

But my memories taunt me with the only force capable of providing relief—the last time, at least. His fingers. His touch. The pressure only he can apply…

The images flood my skull one after the other as my eyes drift shut, robbing me of my view of him—but I can still hear. It's as if in the absence of one sense, the others grow stronger. I can perceive every raspy inhale he takes. Every ragged exhale.

And I can feel the way his fingers shake as he brings them to my thigh, snatching fistfuls of my skirt, lifting it. An inch at first. Then higher. Higher…

It should make me feel weak as he bares me to him, removing my dress altogether. Weak and pathetic.

But the way his breath catches makes me shiver in return. When his calloused fingertips trace my inner thigh next, I don't clamp my knees together against the intrusion.

I spread them, letting him coax my quivering knees further apart.

I marvel at the power he has over me as he fingers the hem of my panties.

With a single touch, he has me holding my breath, shuddering in time with the shifting mattress. I hear the rasp of fabric over skin before the texture of his shirt vanishes, replaced by bare skin. The purr of a zipper next warns that another piece of his clothing has met the same fate.

But it's a testament to the enigmatic pull he has that I'm not afraid.

I'm ready as he pushes inside me with a single thrust. We both go still as my body stretches around him, forced to accept every inch—desperate to.

I open my eyes again and feel my breath catch at the sight of him pressed against me, every inch of him on display. Almost as if taunting me, the scarlet letters etched into his chest gleam.

I run my fingers over them one by one, feeling a tremor run through him.

S. A. F...

And with every letter I trace, his groans deepen, becoming guttural. Broken. Growls.

Until he loses control completely. Desperate, his hips rock against mine in a fierce rhythm that takes my breath away.

Our gazes lock, his swollen with an emotion I can't decipher right away.

But it's dangerous.

A promise.

And a warning.

We're bound together more deeply than even this act.

Whether we like it or not.

20

———

DON

I'm going to hell. Admittedly, my descent began years ago, so why resist the fall now? The only thing left to do is brace for the inevitable fiery ending.

If only it didn't feel so damn good. Hellfire burns sweeter than expected. There are no hordes of demons to torment me with searing flames—just one angel.

She lords her goodness over me, daring me to corrupt it. Take it. Claim it.

But I already have. Is it really a sin if I touch her again, raking my fingers through her hair to draw her closer? Is it wrong to slip my tongue between her lips, stealing the startled breath she intakes?

In short? Yes.

I'm going to hell.

Every second I extend this moment just increases the amount of damnation attached to my soul. The sick part? I'm not the least bit repentant. Hell feels far better than that torturous road toward forgiveness.

But I don't make excuses. Even as I further the kiss, I don't explain away the wrongness of it all. I don't make it easier by drowning this under the guise of being out of my mind. I make myself feel it.

All of it.

There is plenty of time to burn later.

And plenty more sins to commit before then.

By the time I leave the suite, it's noon, and I'm alone, forced to face this next test of my sanity with no one to hide behind.

Will I tell him the truth?

I don't know. The hospital doors feel like a portal, transporting me back into what my life *should* be. A clinical maze of neutral colors and blank sterility with Vincenzo at the center. No distractions.

No secrets.

No lies.

He's sitting up in bed when I enter his room, and the sight stops me in my tracks. "Vinny…"

A few weeks, and he's damn near back to his usual self. The only glaring reminder of what he's been through is a bandage still wrapped around his skull.

"They say I might be able to leave in a few days," he says by way of greeting. His tone is accusatory rather than triumphant. "You haven't been here pushing for that to happen soon," he adds, the apparent source of his suspicion. "So why not? It isn't like you. Unless you don't want me out."

"What?" I force a smile he doesn't return. "Don't tell me you're sick of the free food, constant supervision, and having a pretty nurse at your beck and call already."

Shit. His mouth flattens into an even sterner line. Of course, he sees right through my bullshit.

"I'm not an idiot, Donatello," he scolds in a tone reminiscent of Fabio's. "I know you. If you think I'm safer in here with a thermometer shoved up my ass every six hours, then it's because you're more afraid of whatever is out there—" He jerks his chin toward a window displaying the concrete jungle that is Hell's Gambit. "You told me that everything between you and Mischa was settled. So, what did you leave out?"

I can't even look at him. *Fuck.* I cross over to the window he indicated and glower at the stormy horizon. If everything Fabio put into motion is to be believed, then in just a few days, this war will come to a head. Afterward, Vincenzo will be home free and on his way back to his studies.

In a perfect world.

That's the fantasy I'm clinging to, regardless. It doesn't include the possibility of him finding out about a maybe-future Vanici who will rival his place as my sole heir. Vincenzo isn't that petty, though. The only thing about the addition of a new family member he'd take offense to is who the father is.

And the mother.

I could tell myself the same bullshit I have been all along. That she is an adult, and so am I. Our relationship, however twisted it may be, is our business. No one else's.

Until last night, that is. Besides, no excuse erases one glaring fact. I know how Vin will react. I know my boy. I know…

He'll hate me for this. He'd have every right to.

"Do you think I'm an idiot, Don?"

I look over at him, taking in the subtle details I missed before. They've let him wear his own clothing, and he has a book open on his lap, displaying a dedication to his studies that no Vanici before him ever possessed.

"I've had full access to the internet as well as the news channel while I've been here," he adds, crossing his arms, the book forgotten. "Everything going on in the city right now could be written off as typical chaos, but I don't believe in coincidence. What aren't you telling me?"

His tone alone sets me on edge. I know to tread carefully.

"What do you mean?"

He frowns and adjusts his glasses over the ridge of his nose. The beeping of medical machinery creates a chillingly mellow backdrop—though this conversation is shaping up to be anything but.

"It wasn't as hard as you might think to bribe one of the men on my security detail to tell me the latest gossip. One of my night nurses let me use the internet on her computer to verify. It's not on the mainstream news broadcasts, of course, but the local forums catch everything."

Oh fuck. Does he know? I fight to keep the panic from my expression, praying to God my voice sounds steady. "Like what?"

"Like a wedding," he says without any inflection.

His frown is skeptical, but the boy is as sharp as ever, and like a dog with a bone, he won't stop until he satisfies any curiosity. After all, that's exactly how I taught him to think.

"*Your* wedding, Don. Which would be strange, since last time I checked, you didn't even have a girlfriend, let alone a fiancée—"

"The amount of money Fab and I pay these bastards to guard you, and they spend their time gossiping?" I make a show of faked indignation, forcing a laugh. "Sounds like I need to visit you more often if you're that damn bored."

"Don't coddle me." He's never spoken to me like this. For a heartbeat, I swear I see something flit across his gaze before vanishing. Hurt.

"You're right," I concede. "I shouldn't coddle you—but I should protect you. Whatever's going on out there—" I jerk my chin toward the window. "That's out there. All you need to focus on is what is in here—getting better so that you can return to that fancy school and earn enough money to take care of me for the rest of my fucking life. Got it?"

I know my tone is convincing enough. I've told him lesser lies with twice the ease before. But this time…

He smiles as he typically would, but it doesn't reach his eyes. "Whatever you say, Uncle Don. Maybe you do have a point—because you would never lie to me, would you? About anything, no matter how trivial or how big. You would never lie to me."

But I have. We both know it. Whether I could justify it at the time as in his better interest, it doesn't fucking matter. Still, I force a chuckle and lie to him again.

"You're damn right; I wouldn't. Now, are we done with the third degree? Why don't you tell me more about that night nurse of yours? It's about damn time you notice something other than those stuffy medical texts."

He doesn't even blush. Instead, he shifts to sit on the edge of the bed. When he looks up, none of the piercing intensity has left his gaze. Not one damn bit. If anything, he seems more determined to probe whatever issue has him so unsettled.

"Willow," he says softly. "She didn't come with you?"

I flinch, knowing damn well that he can read that slip-up for what it was. I turn away, choking out what I hope passes for another laugh.

"Invite a woman whose presence might hamper my ability to tease the shit out of you? Hell no. I can have her come later, if you want," I add.

"I do want her here," Vin says. "We're a family, aren't we? Or at least… We were."

Shit. Not now. I don't have the right to beg for more time—and stave off the inevitable—but I don't have a choice. Where he's leading is a road we both aren't equipped to travel.

As much as it dings my pride to admit, I wish Fabio were here.

"You never told me what happened," Vin adds. His voice wavers, and I look over my shoulder to find him attempting to stand.

"Don't." I scan the room for an alarm button. "Let me call a nurse—"

"I can stand on my own," he snaps, proceeding to do just that. "The doctor's ordered me to take laps around the wing every couple of hours. You'd know that if you were here more often. If you weren't so busy."

I wince. He could have punched me, and it would hurt less than the pain in his voice. "Vin…"

"I'm not a child, Don." He sounds less angry, just exasperated. Against my suggestion, he unhooks himself from whatever devices he's connected to and stands fully upright with a steadiness that leaves me dumbstruck.

He's right. I haven't been here often enough. I missed the subtle signs of him regaining his strength. He moves easily, and perhaps he isn't wrong to question why I haven't inquired about his discharge.

"Look at me."

He's by my side within seconds, and I do a double take. He looks so much like his mother. Though Donella would never give a damn whether or not I kept her in the loop. She'd have her own ways of finding whatever information she sought. A true Vanici, she trusted no one.

If only Vin could have inherited that trait from her.

"I am not a child," he repeats. "You don't have to protect me anymore. Gone are the days when I'll blindly accept that people die without a funeral, or wonder in silence why I couldn't outwardly mourn the person I loved like a sister. You have your secrets; I understand that. But where my life is concerned? No more. I am done standing in the dark because you think I can't handle the truth."

"It's not that," I admit hoarsely. "Come here."

Before he can resist, I throw my arm around him, drawing him close. Despite his bravado, he's not as strong as he wants me to believe. He sways, easily knocked off balance, too weak to pull away.

"I know you can handle it," I tell him. "But I can't. I can't lose you too. I won't. So, if that makes me a fucking coward, then I'm sorry, Vin. Just give me time."

"You want to know the only way you'll lose me, Don?" He pulls back, meeting my gaze directly. "If you lie to me. I have my own ways of finding out the truth. Please don't make me do that. I want to hear it from you."

Now he does sound like his mother. Could he possibly know the truth already? Even the prospect makes my blood run cold, and I shake my head to clear it. *No*, he couldn't. Even a gossipy soldier wouldn't be able to tell him, because supposedly no one outside of Mischa and his immediate family knows. And Fab.

I couldn't see him telling Vin, either. Though hell, my perception of everyone has been so shit lately; who knows what secrets he could be hiding?

"Don?" Vin sounds further away as if he returned to the bed. Sure enough, he's seated there when I finally face him.

"You can tell me anything," he says. "I know that sometimes you aren't the best decision maker in the world, but you always have the best intentions in mind."

Do I? I think one woman, in particular, might take offense to that characterization. Two, perhaps.

"Enough of this gloomy talk," I say with a smile. "You're right. It's about time that we find out when you can get the hell out of here. How about we call that doctor over and discuss it, huh?"

Like me, Vin is good at disguising his emotions. Even so, I still identify what sentiment causes his mouth to turn downward—disappointment.

"Yeah," he says softly, no longer looking my way. "Whatever you say, Don."

We both continue to sport our fake grins, but I know in my gut that I've horribly mis-stepped.

If only I knew how.

By the time I finally leave Vin, I've convinced myself that everything is fine. Whatever I sensed before was just paranoia. Considering how he was laughing as I departed, whatever plagued Vincenzo's mind has been put at ease.

So why the hell am I so edgy, glancing over my shoulder as I exit the hospital? It could be common sense warning me to be on guard as Fabio sets his plan into motion. There is a wedding to organize, after all.

But I can't shake the feeling that something's off. The dread haunts me every inch of the drive back to the hotel, and I nearly race up to the suite. The first person I find inside is Willow, apparently unharmed—but she isn't alone.

"You," I blurt, frozen in the doorway.

"Hello, Mr. Vanici," the visitor replies. There is no mistaking those blue eyes, and while I know they aren't related—with her daughter beside her—it strikes me just how similarly they carry themselves. That stony confidence must be a trademark of the Stepanovs.

"Mrs. Stepanova," I say, stiffly returning the introduction. My gaze darts to Willow, but she doesn't attempt to make eye contact. Doubt creeps into my thoughts. Did last night snap some sense into her? Or is there another explanation… I have to wonder if Fabio is behind this.

Whatever the reason, Ellen Stepanova doesn't seem to be in a hurry to reveal it.

"I've been meaning to talk with you," she says, her tone cold but still cordial. Even without her husband in view, she cuts a striking figure, commanding respect. Apart from the slight paleness to her skin lingering even now, no one would be able to guess the ordeal she went through just a few weeks ago. She's steady on her feet, her hands folded neatly over her waist. But those eyes blaze, removing any doubt that this is a friendly visit.

"You're welcome here," I say thickly. "Please, have a seat."

She nods and claims one half of a chaise. In silence, Willow joins her, and that sense of dread continues to build. Looking at her face alone, I can't tell what she might be feeling—a warning sign if there ever was one. As the seconds pass, her eyes remain averted from me, her gaze distant.

"My husband doesn't know I'm here," her mother says to preface her speech. "So, I come to you entirely of my own accord, if only to make one request."

I fight to keep my tone as polite as possible. "And what request is that?"

"I want you to leave."

I wait for the threat that must surely accompany that statement—but either she's shrewd enough to think she doesn't need one, or just simply that confident in her family's power.

"This isn't a threat," she adds, though her tone isn't any softer. "It's merely me speaking as one mother to a father."

Though I doubt this newest child is whom she refers to. Either her husband's kept her out of the loop when it comes to his gossip mongering, or she has far more tact than he does.

"I'm listening," I say, but my focus is on the woman beside her. Her lips purse, flattening into a thin line. I assume whatever her mother intends to say has already been discussed between the two.

"I'm not telling you this out of a maternal sense of protection, or even because of the morality. I'm telling you this from the viewpoint of a woman who knows what it is like to have a child with a man of power. A beautiful blessing—but also a sentence to a life of pain for everyone involved, especially the child in question."

"I take it you're not referring to your current husband," I say dryly.

"No," she admits. "There was another man before him, and there isn't a day that I don't regret letting him control me the way he did. My only solace is my oldest son. I wouldn't trade him for the world. But I hate that his life will always be burdened by the sins of his father. There is no erasing those ties."

"And you think my child is doomed to the same fate?" Gone is the politeness. I can't keep the anger from my voice, hearing it leech into every word. The worst part? The rage isn't directed at her.

She's regurgitating what I already know.

I can't stop myself from glancing at the woman in question. Maybe I expect to find agreement on her face? Not… annoyance. Her teeth capture her bottom lip, though she stares straight ahead.

Her reaction tempers some of my anger—but not all of it. "I would caution you to remember that, despite your past relationship, your current husband is no saint," I point out, returning my focus to Mrs. Stepanova.

That draws a rise out of her—not Mischa's wife, but *her*. Willow. She's looking at me now, her gaze like a razor blade slicing through my brittle resolve. God, I want more than anything to banish this stranger from the room and draw out the thoughts on her mind. Still, I have enough sense to know that she wants me to hear this spiel, whatever it might reveal.

She wants to see how I'll react to it.

"Mischa is many things," his wife admits. "But he is selfless when it comes to his children. He knows when to protect them and when to let them go—" She looks at her daughter briefly, but I can tell from her tortured expression that she might not cleave to that same principle. "He knows when to let them make their own mistakes, and he isn't afraid to show his love. But do you want to know what truly sets him apart from my previous husband? I chose him. Despite the circumstances and the chaotic backdrop against which we met, I still had a choice. I wasn't threatened or coerced. There was no fear. No imbalance of power."

"With all due respect, Mrs. Stepanova," I say, clinging to what little civility I have left. "I've heard the rumors, and your love story with your husband isn't half the fairy tale you want me to believe it is. I know that he kidnapped you. Tortured you. Scarred you. God knows what else he did. In your capacity to forgive him, I'm sure you can imagine that other women might be able to do the same for less."

"You are entitled to your opinion," she concedes with a graceful nod. "And I am entitled to mine. I think if you truly care about Willow, the best thing to do would be to leave. To allow her to cut you off completely and move on."

"And this is your *expert* opinion?"

Both women flinch. My tone came out too harsh.

"This is my biased opinion," Ellen admits. "But one honed sharp after years of dealing with men like you. I know how your world works, Mr. Vanici."

Everything from her tone, to how she carries herself reveals a glimpse of the woman rumored to equally rule Mischa's empire. She's good at playing calm and meek; I'll give her that. But she's right. No woman could survive in a shithole like Hell's Gambit without sporting a few claws of her own.

How sharp are Ellen Stepanova's? I suspect I'm about to find out.

"I'll speak to you plainly, Mr. Vanici," she continues, her pink lips turning downward. "You know your actions have been wrong, predatory even. And yet you continue to play these games and manipulate those in your orbit."

Picturing last night, I might not be the only predator in this equation. My gaze flits to her again, and my stomach tightens. Faint color paints her cheeks, and I know I'm not the only one reliving that shift in our dynamic.

"I think you should speak to your daughter." I start to stand.

"Wait." It isn't the commanding note in her voice that stops me. It's the rage blazing in those light blue eyes. She's disguised it well until now, but it's there, every bit as violent as her husband's temper.

Maybe guilt is what makes me stop and listen.

"I love my daughter, and you've hurt her more than you will ever know. By staying in her life, you will only continue to hurt her, and I refuse to sit by and watch it happen—"

Glass shatters, and the woman falls silent out of shock. I'm already on my heels, my eyes on the window in case of a sniper. Belatedly I register the absence of a gunshot. Then, my gaze settles over the apparent source of the commotion —a broken glass lying on the floor inches away.

There's another glass and a pitcher of water on the coffee table—presumably, the women had both been drinking from it before I came in. Considering the whole cup is positioned closer to Ellen, the person nearest the broken glass might be responsible for it falling.

When I turn to her, she finally faces me, her cheeks red, those brown eyes ablaze with that chilling, quiet intensity. She's angrier than ever, but it isn't directed at the woman beside her.

Just me. Always me.

"Willow?" Ellen Stepanova clears her throat. "I'm sorry. I know you don't like being spoken over—"

"She doesn't like being treated like a child," I interject without thinking. "Which she isn't. Therein lies the flaw of your argument toward me. Whether I stay or leave, it isn't my choice to make. The door is there. Both of you are free to go if you want. And to stay."

Ellen frowns, but Willow…

She seems to sigh, exhaling a sharp breath. The rage leaves her gaze, revealing the confusion left behind. The same way she looked as I kissed her last night. As if she was unsure what in the hell possessed her to kiss me back.

"I'm sorry, Mrs. Stepanova. I do appreciate you coming here, but there are other pressing issues to deal with at the moment. There will be plenty of time for familial drama later."

"There is another reason why I'm here," the woman admits, clearing her throat. "One more tactical. Mischa couldn't take the risk of coming here himself. There is information you should know."

"Such as?"

"How close are you to the Saleris?"

I raise an eyebrow. Switching from the topic of my predatory nature to the Saleris is a subject change I didn't see coming. "'Close' being the operative word, not very," I admit.

"Could you still arrange a meeting with them? Or at least draw their attention?"

The gears in my mind shift from anger to calculation. "For what purpose?"

"We have reason to believe their distribution network is being used in a larger scheme. One they might not even be aware of. We need a way of testing that theory without alerting them to the bigger plan."

"Did you stop to consider that Mateo might have been the bastard who arranged that little hit the other day?"

I grit my teeth at the thought. My eyes return to Willow. She could have been killed, and it would have been my fucking fault for letting my guard down for even a second.

Guilt isn't what I find on her face, however. She's watching me in return, the gears in her mind turning. I think she's come to the same conclusion I have regarding her mother's suggestion.

"Playing detective by arranging to meet with the son of a bitch doesn't seem like the smartest plan," I say, voicing it out loud.

"I didn't say it had to be a friendly meeting," Ellen says tacitly. "In fact, it might be better to goad him into making a mistake and exposing his role in this scheme."

Even I can admit that she has a point. But what might goad Mateo into making yet another reckless move? One plan comes to mind.

"I think I have an idea," I say grimly. "It might be a little unorthodox, though it's a good thing for you that you seem to enjoy the company of children."

She raises an eyebrow in confusion.

"Gregori Saleri has a granddaughter who happened to fall under my care."

After I killed her father—a fact that I'm sure she's aware of because her eyes widen in horror before she manages to school her expression again.

"I could always make an overture to him under the guise of arranging a trade to return her to her family. But I would need backup as well as intel of where Mateo is holed up. *And,*" I add, feeling bold, "I want assurances from Mischa that he'll be ready to hold off another attack."

"Using young girls as leverage in your twisted power struggles. That must be a preferred tactic of yours."

I wince at that, glancing at Willow once again. Despite myself, I'm also impressed. While Mischa may be more physically direct in his attack strategy, his wife, it seems, prefers words as her weapon.

Ironically, much like her daughter.

"It isn't like that," I reply.

But it is. Isn't it?

One of said pieces of leverage is watching me again, her expression impossible to read. I don't even have to run the plan by her to know she doesn't approve.

I compose my reply carefully and direct it toward her more than anyone else. "Using Kisa is the best method we have of drawing out Mateo Saleri without alerting him as to our other motives. I don't intend to ever put her in any real danger. She'll be safe."

Does she believe that? I can't tell. Damn, I almost feel blind. Though, at second glance, her nostrils flare with a resigned exhale. She understands.

"Fine," Ellen says expressionlessly, of the same opinion. "I'll make the arrangements with my husband and have one of our guards contact you."

I can guess who that might be; the same bastard who always seems to turn up in the nick of time comes to mind. Evgeni. Without naming him, Mrs. Stepanova stands, smoothing her hands down the front of her skirt.

"I have one other request of you," she says. "Though, if you do want to prove that you don't assert your influence in a predatory way, then you'll allow my daughter to leave with me, right now. Do I have your word on that?"

"If she agrees," I hiss through clenched teeth. It takes everything I have in me to keep from glancing in the direction of the person in question.

Because that's exactly what this woman expects me to do. It's ironic. From an angle, the faint scars marring her cheek are visible—clear evidence that her husband is no better than I am. Yet, she thinks he is without a doubt. In a world of monsters, I'm no better than the devil to her.

"Fine." She turns to her daughter, extending her hand. "You can come home with me," she says.

I don't witness the exchange that transpires in silence. I only know that when Ellen Stepanova does finally leave the suite, head held high, she's alone.

I look back. The woman behind me doesn't acknowledge my presence, but her shoulders slump, robbed of that tense posture. I think she's relieved.

So am I.

"I meant it," I croak, regardless. "Whether you stay or go, it's your choice."

She inclines her head, turning that impassive stare my way. I might imagine the slight nod she gives me. Either way, she doesn't make a move for the door, and I have my answer.

Ellen Stepanova and me aside, she made her own decision.

But with her own aims in mind. For all I know, those reasons might have nothing to do with me.

21

EVGENI

Following a plan devised by Donatello Vanici is as laughable as it is foolish. But said plan, once relayed by his accountant Bocelli, seems…

Well, it might be just crazy enough to work. Or at least, draw Mateo and his puppet master out of hiding. Either way, it's better than nothing.

In the meantime, I have my own task to undertake, however reckless it may be. Ironically, it might help benefit Vanici's scheme in the long run—and prove if Briar Winthorp is worth trusting yet again.

To spare my last shred of patience, I didn't bring her along on this detour. Instead, I work alone, using the cover of nightfall to my benefit to infiltrate a home just beyond the city boundaries.

In theory, the mission is simple—get intel on the Saleri mansion myself and determine if Briar's son could be here after all. While I'm at it, any information on the distribution network would be a plus.

That's assuming I don't get shot to death in the process.

This mansion in the hills overlooking Hell's Gambit seems unremarkable at a glance—opulence aside. It's as gaudy as any other property connected to the Saleris, with a towering three-story home atop an expansive stretch of land. For once, the excess plays to my advantage as the ornate gardens, complete with towering shrubs and bushes, provide plenty of places to hide once I breach the outer gates.

The only thing standing between me and the main house is at least twenty guards patrolling the grounds, each one armed to the teeth.

It's odd. Given the current tragedy befalling the family, I'd expect to find the mansion draped in black crepe and flowers, signifying mourning.

Not assault rifles and armored vehicles.

A parade of dark vans streams through the property gates in an almost constant caravan. They circle around to the back of the house and enter a multi-car garage—only to drive off minutes later, heading toward the city.

A strange occurrence, even if Mateo wasn't under suspicion for sending an assassin after Vanici and killing his own father in cold blood.

For hours, this process has been underway. I've counted at least five such departures by the time I finally decide to leave my hiding place near a row of shrubs for a better look.

Slowly, I creep up to the house, avoiding the steady stream of patrols.

Mateo Saleri, for all his pomp, is still a smart bastard at heart. His father's death hasn't shocked him into skimping on security. In fact, it looks as though he's tripled their usual detail. Either the man prefers to be overly prepared, or…

He's afraid of something. Which only brings up the plausible possibility that Briar hasn't told me everything. Am I surprised? No.

Gritting my teeth, I shirk the tree cover for a row of hedges, my eyes on the garage. It's reckless to risk being seen, but I can't shake this impulse driving me to get closer.

Gravel crunches beneath the wheels of an oncoming truck, and I look up, spying yet another vehicle turning through the gates. I take the chance to follow it, keeping to the shadows cast by more overgrown hedges lining the central driveway.

Up ahead, a guard marches past, a weapon displayed openly across his back. Even Mischa's guards aren't this alert. As soon as the man's back is turned, I take my chance, lunging closer to the garage just as another guard storms into view.

I slip around the back and through an open door, right before the van continues its approach, pulling into one of the few empty parking spaces. The entire garage is filled to the brim with boxes stacked one on top of the other. Overall, the space is lit only by a strip of overhead lights that barely provides enough illumination to see by.

A benefit to the clutter is that I easily find a hiding place behind a row of crates near the back of the building.

On the other hand, it doesn't look like long-term storage—but a temporary makeshift depot meant to hold items in a pinch.

Or in preparation for something.

Briar's warning itches at the back of my skull, and while I haven't searched the main house, I feel in my gut that a child isn't on this property. At least not now.

These men are guarding something else, ready to shoot anyone who comes too close.

Eager to find out what, I turn my attention to the van and crane my neck for a better look. One of the guards opens the van's trunk, revealing a glimpse of what lurks within the back—at least two more crates, made of the same black material as the rest.

A pair of guards lowers one to the floor, ripping off the top.

And I now have a better idea of just what Mateo is hiding.

Weapons.

A shit ton of them.

"You lied to me." I don't aim for coy. My voice reverberates around the room, and the only other occupant shrinks, pressing herself against the wall. Just as quickly, her mask is reassembled, her head thrown back at a haughty angle.

"Did, I now? Are you truly surprised?"

"No," I say, trespassing further into the room she's claimed as her own. "I just feel pity for you that your worried mother act was a lie. Even a stray dog has a stronger maternal instinct than a dishonored heiress, as it turns out. There isn't a child on the Saleri estate. I can tell you that for a fact."

Her eyelids flutter—a rare glimpse of confusion. Another act? Of course, it is. "Care to enlighten me as to what exactly I've been lying about?" she asks.

I scoff, turning on my heel. I can't even look at her. "There wasn't any sign of a child on the Saleri compound," I reiterate coldly. "I doubt a mouse could get in there with the amount of security. Is that what you wanted me to see? Or were you far more tactless and wanted me dead."

"I think *you* are the one who is lying." Her voice loses that polished exterior quickly, deepening into a hiss. Head held high, she braces both hands on her hips, jutting her chin defiantly. "Either you aren't as good at reconnaissance as you think, or you took too damn long, and they've moved him by now—"

"I'm telling you, there was no hint of a child ever having been there. It's like a fortress. They're planning for war."

Rather than accept defeat, caught in her lie, she…

Looks panicked. Her eyes widen as she shakes her head. "No. Then he is somewhere else."

I frown at the hoarseness in her voice. It could be yet another disingenuous ruse—but… She seems driven more to tears and hysterics to get her point across. That was unwarranted. I've caught her by surprise, and she's genuinely thrown off.

The look on her face furthers that assessment. She's glaring, fighting to keep her confident mask intact.

"I should have known that a murderer ought to be the last person on earth sent to rescue a child. You could have taken me with you, at least. I would have known what to look for. Thanks to your bullheaded actions, I can't even find him myself, and we are running out of time!"

Her voice rises in pitch, a convincing display. I must fall for the ruse, because I find myself asking, "Where else might he be?"

She stammers. "I-I don't—"

"If he isn't with the Saleris, and you truly believe he is here, then where?"

Her eyes flit around the room. Then, suddenly, they widen. A laugh trickles from her throat next, and I steel myself for a quip or a joke at my expense.

Instead, she slaps her own forehead. "Damn him! I am such an idiot for not seeing it before."

"Seeing what?"

She whirls on me, an eyebrow raised. "Where would you go if you were desperate to assert your ties to a family that refused to acknowledge your existence?"

An answer comes to me, but it isn't relevant to this scenario—a modest, crumbling farm that is probably wrecked by now. But then, I approach that same question from the viewpoint of a spurned bastard, and it clicks.

"Winthorp Manor."

Briar nods. "I've heard it's in ruins, but that could be where his main base is."

"Or a trap," I add. "Someone as clever as you portray this man to be might assume we'd head there first."

And I'm sure that either Mischa, or Vanici has kept tabs on the property. They would know if it were overrun in the recent weeks. Right?

"I heard the place has been burned to the ground," Briar says dryly. "Perhaps, he's found a way to infest whatever is left behind without drawing notice?"

It could be worth the risk to take a closer look. Or just another line spun in her twisted little web, meant to ensnare me further.

"You should take me with you," she says. "If I'm wrong, you can throttle me in person—"

"Or you could throttle me." I'm sure the idea has crossed her mind more than once. To her credit, she disguises any murderous intent well behind a harsh laugh.

"If I wanted to kill you, there have been plenty of opportunities before now, you must admit. And if I wanted to lead you into a trap, why would I help you circumvent what could have been a very nasty assassination attempt on your precious ward? Believe me or not, but hear this—I'm going there, one way or another."

"Fine," I relent. "But we do this my way. That means on my terms and via my rules. Tonight, is too risky," I add, thinking up a plan on the fly. "We go in the morning and not without backup."

"You soldiers and your goddamn protocol." She rolls her eyes. "I wouldn't expect anything less. Don't forget to get permission for our little adventure from your master as well."

"I won't," I warn. "Because we aren't going alone."

Alarm flashes across her gaze. She doesn't like that idea, but to my shock, she doesn't argue. Instead, she merely points her chin in my direction, an eyebrow raised.

"Well, let's not waste any more time, then. Why can't we go now?"

"Tomorrow," I insist, thinking through the logistics. "Better to minimize the risks of an ambush."

"Of course," she says, nodding. "And to make sure that you adhere to the stereotypical rules of a dutiful soldier. No risk. No ingenuity."

"And little chance for you to escape," I add. "I'll indulge your little hunch one more time, but I'm warning you. If it doesn't pay off, you won't see the chance to attempt a third."

"I'm so scared," she says softly. "I best be on my most perfect behavior, then."

22

WILLOW

I am young. If I hear that phrase again, I might scream. I want to rail against the constraints that being nineteen seems to place on me. I hate having what feels like the entire world walking on eggshells to ignore the obvious.

I am young, but so were they once. Mischa, Ellen, Donatello, Olivia…

They made their mistakes, and they can't shame me for doing the same. We all have our weaknesses and our vices.

Why can't mine be him?

I want to know more, and that terrifies me. I want more of this world I've only gotten a glimpse of. If I'm going to be condemned for it, I deserve to experience it all.

Not out of rebellion or hate. Perhaps it's plain masochism. He warned me what a future with him on the periphery would be—but it's no different than how it's always been.

Having him at a distance, brooding over a past that neither of us has any control over.

The thought emboldens me as I reach the door he's hidden behind. Slowly, I push it open, unprepared for what I find on the other end.

I exhale, feeling my fingers tremble over the doorknob. He's sprawled over the bed, still wearing his dress pants, and rumpled white shirt, the tie partially undone and askew, with his collar open beneath.

A sliver of his chest is visible, coated with a thatch of dark hair, as well as a strip of white near his shoulder, alluding to his bandages. His eyes are on the ceiling, his mouth pulled into a twisted grimace of concentration. At a glance, I doubt he's slept. Whatever Ellen told him must weigh heavily on his mind—not to mention the revelations Olivia's letters revealed.

He's so lost in thought; he doesn't hear me come in at first. I make it all the way to the foot of the bed before he finally notices. His nostrils flare with my scent first before he cocks his head, lifting it from the pillows to aim that scowl firmly in my direction.

"Is something wrong?" He starts to sit up, but I shake my head before perching myself on the end of the mattress.

With my back to him, it's easier to ignore the glaring reality in which we exist. He's a man. I'm a woman.

And yet, there is so much between us that sets those simple facts at odds. We're enslaved to the past. The truth is that, outside of that box, I have no idea who I really am anymore. The role of Willow Stepanova feels as distant to me now as Safiya Mangenello. Both were shells of a scared little girl forced to find her place in a drastically different world from what she previously knew.

But now…

The world seems more or less the same, but I've changed in too many ways to name. I'm not braver, or more mature. If anything, I've regressed in those aspects, becoming more selfish. Curious. Rebellious. Questioning.

Spiteful.

It doesn't bother me one damn bit that when Donatello releases another heavy sigh, I can hear the dread in it. He doesn't want me here.

But I'm through letting him dictate our dynamic.

Because as much as it stings to admit, I feel closer to whoever I'm meant to be near him. Someone angry and vengeful, unwilling to be restrained. With his scent in my lungs, every breath feels sharper, and I sense my pulse quicken as if my heart is eager to send that tainted air to every inch of my body. We melt together into a twisted musk that lingers in my nostrils, potent enough to taste on the tip of my tongue. Like fire and smoke. Something spicy and dangerous but warming at the same time. A thin layer of sweat slicks my skin in the aftermath, relieving any chill I may have felt.

"You're not here for any particular reason," Donatello declares suddenly. It's as if he's driven to narrate my thoughts out loud, so confident in his abilities to read them. "You couldn't sleep either."

He isn't wrong. I tossed and turned in the other room, unable to quiet my racing thoughts. The present danger wasn't what taunted me, though. Just him. His face as Ellen spoke. The weight of his head on my lap. His pain. His anger. His taste.

I can still remember the heat of his mouth and the way his hands felt running over my skin. That quiet moment in the dark plagues me still. Maybe because I can't decipher it. Was it a trick on his part—a subtle manipulation meant to unnerve and confuse me? Or was it merely a lack of control.

The sick part is I almost prefer that scenario; that he compromised those lofty morals for me. In many ways, I'm no different than him, just as sadistic.

And just as cruel.

"There is a lot to set into motion," Donatello says, a subtle hint that dealing with me isn't on that list. "We need to deal with the Saleris, and plan the diversion—" I notice that he doesn't say "wedding." Already, he's craving the outcome that this was nothing more than a lab glitch. A mistake. "Not to mention dealing with Fabio and his many requirements to pull this off. We should probably get a move on soon."

He breaks off, and my heart stammers as I realize why—I've shifted toward him fully.

That elusive tension returns, robbing him of whatever he meant to say and stealing my senses. I inch closer despite every cell in my body warning me not to. I can't help it. He is magnetic, but the pull to him is a painful mixture of anger and…

Curiosity. I'm reaching out without permission from my brain, swiping my fingers across his jaw.

"What are we doing?" he croaks, but I sense it's a genuine question.

His eyes are puzzled, his lips twisting into that trademark frown. I ghost my fingers along his mouth until those lips part instead. I drag myself closer, trying to decipher for the umpteenth time why he inspires these emotions in me.

My throat feels tight, my tongue damp. Every breath I take feels heavy. He disrupts my body in the most intimate way, and I hate him for it. At the same time, some sick part of me must be addicted to his nearness.

I keep advancing, rising onto my knees.

He lets his head fall back against the pillows, almost as if in surrender. His hands fan out over the sheets until I come within his reach.

I shiver as his palm captures my waist, dragging me closer. One look at his eyes tells me this isn't aggressive on his part.

It's a dare. He wants to see if I'll pull away, perhaps to satisfy his own curiosity.

But I don't move. Instead, I lean into the movement, inching even closer. My thigh brushes his, my fingers contacting his arm. I inhale, and the rise of his chest warns he's doing the same. His gaze seeks out mine, his eyes narrowed in a way I can't interpret. Thoughtful and yet calculating. Dark circles betray just how tired he really is.

Last night aside, he hasn't slept well in days.

Wordlessly, he watches as I settle in even closer. My cheeks flame, bitten by the impropriety that's been driven into my skull by him and everyone else. It's wrong to be this close to him. To seek him out. To let my body contort into what feels like the most natural position to watch him in.

From above.

He grunts as if biting back a refusal. For whatever reason, he doesn't voice it. Instead, his hands shift to support my weight as I straddle him, bracing my hands over his chest.

His pulse hammers like a song. Despite hours of study of musical notes and composition, this is one tune I can't decipher easily.

His breaths scrape at the air, heavy and yet steady. "You can stand to be this close to me?"

I blink, caught off guard by the line of questioning. He could be referring to so many different topics. Then I remember the most recent revelation that might be weighing on his mind.

Olivia and her letters.

"What does that make you?" he wonders, his tone dangerously soft. "If I'm the monster. Are you the prey, or something worse?"

I don't think he expects me to answer. Communicating with him like this is a game of roulette. I never know which way the dice will fall.

Still, I feel compelled to answer him in the only way I can. I reach for his right hand, and he curls the fingers into a fist.

"Prey," he says, naming the option that hand signifies.

My throat tightens as I make my choice, entwining my fingers with his—but the ones on his other hand.

"Something worse," he declares in defeat. "Either way, I'm responsible for whatever you've become."

He can't resist asserting control, even under the guise of taking the blame.

"Why do you want to stay here with me?"

His tone deepens into a throaty rasp. Suddenly, the air feels thick between us.

"I know why." He untangles his fingers from mine, bringing that hand to my cheek. "To punish me," he says, laying out one option. "To hurt me."

There is no in between in his mind. Every motive must contain him at the center. The reality, however, is far simpler.

I shake my head, and with another tortured sigh, he lets his hand fall.

He inclines his head, eyeing me more skeptically. Something in the intensity of his gaze sends a shiver through me. Sometimes it's alarmingly easy to tell what he's thinking.

This time, his gaze contains a single dare that sends another tendril of unease down my spine.

It's a lot like the look I presume a wolf might give a prospective rabbit caught in its path. To bite, or to let it hop in blissful innocence a little while longer?

But what this wolf doesn't know is that the rabbit isn't prey. It's an equally dangerous hunter.

"I think you should leave," he murmurs, close enough that his lips brush my jaw with every movement.

When I don't, he pulls me beneath him, looming above.

I swallow hard, aware of his strength. His thighs dent the mattress on either side of me, forming a prison from his body heat.

I choke down the apprehension and run my hands down his chest, feeling his heartbeat. My fingers find the edge of his shirt to touch the skin beneath. He feels so hot—like a live wire.

His lids grow heavy as he looks down, tracking every movement of my trembling fingertips.

I go lower. Lower. Too low.

He sucks in a breath snatching at my wrist. Then something flits across his eyes, and he returns my hand to its position.

"You want to play with fire? Then play."

I take him up on the dare. I can barely manipulate the zipper, but when I finally get the latch freed, he inhales, every muscle rigid.

I tug the material down inch by inch and let myself view what lies beneath.

The first time is so vivid in my mind, but even those images barely do him justice. Beautiful is the only term to come to mind. Beautiful and dangerous.

Until he takes it upon himself to turn the tables, palming my hips.

My body burns in ways I'm not familiar with. His heat becomes a weapon, igniting parts of me I've barely explored. He teases me above the fabric, almost daring my hips to shift against his palms in a silent invitation.

He takes his time winding the thin material between his fingers, dragging it up...up... Then he removes the thin barrier beneath, until his eyes are on the part of me that makes my cheeks flame.

"You are so beautiful," he breathes out as if the confession is too dangerous to voice too loudly. "So damn beautiful."

But he doesn't touch me, only utilizing his eyes to rake over every exposed inch.

I take it upon myself to touch him first, and he groans, his head shooting back. His fingers latch onto my wrist again, restraining where I can wander. Only the faint light gives me a glimpse of him, and I trace the shape.

"Slow," he grates, his eyes wide.

I strain his grasp instead, shivering as his heat burns even hotter. In this arena, he's held the lion's share of control, I can admit. Partly due to my own ignorance, and maybe a little fear as well.

Sometimes, he can seem so damn untouchable. Like there isn't a hint of softness to be found beneath his skin. I run my fingers over the ridge of his collar bone, and that belief is instantly proven false.

The man is more dangerous than a solid, unmoving mass. He has the ability to melt like molten steel, molding to my body perfectly. When I brace my hands under his chest and shove, he falls back easily, those dark eyes glinting with confusion.

My heart quivers against my ribcage as I follow him, using my body to pin his this time.

With a low groan, he lets his head fall back, his hands by his sides. I'm forced to mount him unassisted, navigating the planes of muscle alone. His shirt is a hindrance, and I reach for the buttons.

His throat cords as I undo one. I can see a refusal playing on the tip of his tongue. It's unnatural for him to cede control like this without a fight.

Still, he lets me undo the rest and drag the material from his shoulders.

Now, there is nothing to stop me from exploring him in full, tracing the divots along his ribcage before finding the jagged, raised line of his tattoo.

I'm too lost in exploration that I don't realize he's continued his own investigation of me. Not until the pad of his thumb grazes my nipple over the fabric of my dress, freezing the air in my lungs.

"You are so beautiful." He doesn't put effort into his voice. The growled, gruff syllables betray who he is at his core. Someone who eyes my body hungrily with an intensity that doesn't match the gentleness with which he finds my belly, pressing his palm flat against it.

He looks up, hiding nothing. Regret should be what I find there. Not…

Desire. And hope. And a desperation that seems impossible for one man to harbor toward another being. A warning sensation pricks the back of my eyes. My eyelids flutter as it takes more effort to breathe. Think.

To counter the wave of emotion, I feel driven to a reckless action I don't have time to think through. I reach down, finding that dangerous part of him that throbs greedily against my fingertips.

His nostrils flare, his eyes narrowing as that hope gives way to another emotion. One a part of me hesitates to name—but I do so anyway.

Lust.

"Slow," he reminds me, his words barely audible.

Instinct takes over instead, driving me to curl my hand around him completely. Stroke, sensing him harden.

I can't imagine how he fit within me the first time. Or the second...

Until he eases a finger inside me now and my body has to make room.

Our eyes meet as he fills me, hissing at the feeling.

It's different than before. Less a rush of sensation and more concentrated.

We move together in a way that feels too natural for words. Like I was born for this. For him.

And he was made for me.

23

DON

It's wrong to savor this. Her heat. This moment. The snatches of sleep we've managed to steal despite everything looming beyond this room. Lulled by the soft sound of her breathing in my ear, it's too easy to ignore it all.

I haven't felt this way since… Not since Olivia and the days when sleeping in was a rare treat considering our growing household. This isn't quite the same. The woman beside me is smaller, her presence quieter than Liv's playful chuckles. Her scent is lighter, the air poisoned with it. One inhale, and I'm under her influence, drunker than a million bottles of alcohol could ever achieve.

This form of intoxication isn't a crippling blanket, meant to blind me to the state of my life. Instead, everything feels enhanced to a painful degree. Magnified. What once looked dark and grim, now holds a hint of color I never noticed before. There might even be some beauty lurking within all that grime.

Like that of the woman beside me. She rests on her side, inspecting me with those watchful eyes. Only a thin sheet covers us both, but she has her end tucked beneath her arms, wrapped tightly around her torso with a modesty that reinforces just how new this is for her.

Intimacy.

A good man would ease her into this. Instead, I cross the sliver of space between us, brushing the flat of my palm across her belly. She shivers, her eyes meeting mine, but I ignore the eye contact, for now, watching the thin material shift with every breath she takes.

Another life could be growing right beneath my hand, and it strikes me that I haven't stopped to consider what that might mean—beyond the negative connotations anyway.

It means a potential person with eyes like hers or a nose like mine.

I feel my lips quirk at the mental image of him or her. I'm tempted to lie here for as long as possible and embrace this new outlook, putting off whatever waits beyond this bedroom door.

As always, fate seems to have other plans.

Muffled noise comes from the front of the suite, like that of a door opening. Then a voice, "Donatello?"

That familiar baritone penetrates this warm cocoon, shattering the peace instantly.

"Shit!" I bolt upright, sensing my companion startle beside me. There isn't time to do anything more than bark, "Stay here," and lurch to my feet. Cursing, I snatch my pants from the dresser, pulling them on while stumbling into the hall.

And I nearly run into Fabio, who pivots in time to avoid me.

"You're late," he says as his eyes skim over me with disapproval.

I barely manage to slam the door in his face, praying to God he didn't see inside.

His exasperated sigh doesn't relieve that fear one bit. "Not even dressed yet at this hour?"

"This hour…" I spy a glass clock hanging on the wall of the room behind him and hiss through my teeth. It's almost noon.

Hours spent in bed listening to someone breathe—something I haven't done since…

Too damn long. I'd forgotten what it feels like to sleep—truly sleep. My head feels clearer, my movements easier. It could be that sobriety is finally kicking in. I'll blame that, nothing else.

"In case you've forgotten, we have maybe a few trivial things to take care of today," Fabio says, gearing up to scold. "Such as, oh I don't know, finding the person who made an attempt on your life, more than twice now. I'm sorry if you don't find that issue pressing enough to get out of bed for!"

"I'm sorry," I say. There's no arguing with him when he's like this. He's more composed than yesterday, but the bags under his eyes are darker than mine.

"Don't be," he says softly. Then he cocks his head, his eyes narrowing. "You look different. Better, I think. Maybe it's not such a bad thing you've set us behind schedule if you aren't scowling at me. Now come on, let's get you dressed properly."

He reaches past me for the door.

"W-Wait!" I surge down the hall toward the main room, sensing him on my heels. Thank God. I fight to keep my voice steady, fishing for any change in subject. "Remind me again. What's the game plan?"

"I don't understand you, Donatello," Fabio snaps, shaking his head. "Did you just happen to forget the bullet wound on your arm?"

The funny thing is I have. The pain sears like an afterthought, easily drowned out by the remnants of another's body heat.

"Don?"

"You're right, Fab. Which is why you should jump at the chance to talk logistics."

"I've made the arrangements for the sham wedding," he states, his disgust evident. "But it's up to you to put your plan for the Saleris into play. Mischa's man found something strange at one of their estates."

I hazard a guess. "The answer to our mystery man and what he's after?"

"Not quite. Only a weapon's cache with enough firepower to supply a small army," Fabio says deadpanned.

I nearly choke. "Shit—"

"Exactly," Fabio says, grimacing. "Which is why I think it's best if we accelerate our timeline and lure out our enemies into a trap as soon as possible. Mischa told me that you have a way to rile Mateo? It's a risk to provoke him, but if we can get a lead on their accounts, we can track them down more accurately."

Which brings up another point. "Any news on the real estate front?"

Fabio sighs. "Not yet. Still too many interested parties to home in on one for sure, but I'm winnowing the list as we speak. If you can goad Mateo into making a more blatant offer, perhaps? That could give me the clue I need."

"Done," I say. "Firepower or not, I can handle Mateo Saleri."

"Let's hope so," Fabio says softly. "Now… Where is Willow? Still sleeping? Usually, she's up well before this hour. Anyway, let's get her sorted. I have an idea how to further our ruse while keeping her safe—"

He heads down the hall at a pace I have to sprint to keep up with.

"Wait!"

He's at the door to her room before I can stop him, pushing it open. "She isn't here," he says, and a hint of alarm tinges his tone.

Shit.

"I… Maybe she went into the study—"

"Oh," Fabio says, inclining his head. "She must be in the bathroom."

Sure enough, I hear the sound at the same time he does—a rush of running water alluding to the shower being run.

"Well, let's get things into motion," Fabio says, clapping his hands, his expression stern. "You deal with the Saleris, and I'll handle Willow. And, you won't like it, but I think coordinating with Mischa can be worth the risk, if done carefully. We should stay on guard."

"Fine. I'll let you handle that as well."

"And one other thing…" He sighs, leveling me with a look that instantly sends my guard up. "You read the letters by now, I'm sure," he says carefully. "You're taking things well."

There's no mistaking the wary expression on his face for anything other than dread.

"You knew," I rasp, so thrown off that I stagger back. It's not just the shock of having that dredged up again with nothing to distract from it—Olivia was unfaithful to me. But it's the knowing, pained expression on Fabio's face that hits like a punch. "You knew Nico wasn't… That he might not have been mine."

"Don…" His eyes glisten, even as he tightens his jaw. "There is no use in tainting the past with lies and half-truths we can't verify," he says tightly. "I don't want you to let this tarnish your view of Olivia. She loved you. So damn much—"

"Do you think I killed her?"

"What?" He frowns, his brows drawn together. "Of course not! Don't be foolish."

"But someone did," I say. "I thought it was Gino for so damn long, but maybe the bastard wasn't that sick."

But I was.

"Don't do this to yourself," Fabio insists, placing his hand on my shoulder. "You have enough to focus on in the present. Now, let's get a move on."

I relent to him, letting him steer me down the hall. "Whatever you say, Fab."

But something feels off, though I can't put my finger on it. It's a lack of anger on his part—like he knows far more than just the fact that Liv was fucking Gino. Could he know for certain who killed her?

I shrug off the thought. Fab is many things, but a liar isn't one of them. Whatever he knows, if anything, he's hiding for a good damn reason.

So, as hard as it is, I push it out of my mind. For now.

"There's something else," I add, turning my attention to yet another little dilemma. "Considering you haven't led off with this little detail, I assume that you weren't given a heads-up. Mischa's wife came here yesterday. Alone."

Shock isn't a strong enough word to describe Fabio's expression. He stops in his tracks, releasing me. The color drains from his face, and he glances around as if expecting to find the woman's dead body.

"What did she want? God damn it, Donatello. Tell me you exercised some decorum—"

"I didn't beat the shit out of her, if that's what you mean," I snap. "Though if she were a man, I might have."

Color returns to Fabio's expression in the form of his cheeks turning bright red. "I take it she didn't come bearing gifts?"

"Depends on your definition. She's the one I told about my plan to see Mateo."

His eyes widen. "I didn't think to ask for specifics before, but maybe I should have. Just how do you intend to provoke him?"

I shrug. "I do have his niece."

"The girl?" Fabio lowers his voice as if afraid the girl in question might hear him, one floor below. "You really think it's a prudent move to dangle the life of a child as leverage?"

"I'm not heartless," I say. "She's merely the excuse necessary to get me an audience with Mateo. Nothing more."

"Be careful," Fabio warns. "I've had my men dig more into Gregori's death. The short story is that it seems he had a heart attack. The long story is that said heart attack was brought on by a knife, apparently. The severe nature of his wounds leads me to suspect he didn't expire entirely of natural causes."

"So, he was murdered. It isn't that shocking if you know Mateo," I say, picturing the ambitious bastard. "He's been itching to take over the reins for a while now. I guess he got tired of waiting."

"Which just makes him more dangerous," Fabio warns. "Stay on your guard."

I grimace in a way that might pass for a smile. "Don't I always?"

"In the meantime, I will make sure that Willow is protected while still furthering our ruse."

"How so?"

"You'll see," he says grimly. "Let's call it a surprise."

That doesn't sound very reassuring. If anything, this "surprise" sounds more like a punishment.

One designed with me in mind.

24

WILLOW

He haunts me. I feel his presence long after he's gone, distracting from everything else.

I barely even notice what's happening around me until I sense the caress of fabric over my skin as a gentle voice brushes my ear. "What do you think of this color, Miss?"

It's white. A blinding shade of ivory that clashes with my skin tone, making my eyes look darker and larger. Like black holes.

I blink, and the rest of my surroundings come into focus—the hotel suite, though with the main room transformed into a makeshift fitting area.

It was Fabio's idea—further enhance this fake wedding with a fake wedding gown. In reality, I think this is his way of driving home just what he thinks of this entire farce.

A dangerous play during which I shouldn't forget my role. To pretend.

"What do you think?" the seamstress prods. I can't even imagine how Fabio found her on such short notice, but she's a pretty woman just a few years older than me with brown hair and a kind smile.

Following her gaze to a full-length mirror placed before the windows, I *think* this sham looks more obvious than ever. I resemble an actress more than a prospective bride-to-be, draped in the shell of a pretty, white wedding dress.

Paired with what happened last night, I'm more confused than ever by this entire ordeal. Trying to contextualize my relationship with Donatello Vanici feels a lot like trying to nail smoke to a wall. Impossible.

And yet, I can't escape the irrational impulse to capture it by any means rather than watch it dissipate.

I hate the uncertainty being around him inspires within me. It's maddening. One minute it's like he's seeing through me, and the next, I'm the only creature in his view.

In this dress, I doubt he'd notice me at all, though. He might prefer that. Then I'd merely fit the image of the virginal martyr he wants me to be, if only because that version of me is easier for him to ignore.

But he can't overlook the reality lurking beyond his self-pitying image. He isn't a victim, and neither am I. We're opponents in a war I refuse to let him surrender. Not now.

"Miss?" The seamstress smiles awkwardly. "Should we try another style?" She inclines her head toward a nearby rack she brought with her, overflowing with fabric samples.

Viewing them in the mid-afternoon sunlight instills an inexplicable sense of dread in me. They all look pretty and artificial, perfectly befitting the sham that this wedding is purported to be. Clothed in any one of these fabrics, Donatello will be able to have his sacrifice and further cling to his tortured role as the unwilling savior in this fairy tale.

He won't look at me as he did last night.

Like I'm worth craving.

Like wanting me wasn't a mistake.

"Why don't we take a quick break," the woman suggests while removing the strips of cloth from me. "I'll see if there are other pieces of fabric you might like in my car."

She leaves, and I use her absence to pace, inspecting the various materials she left behind.

Fabio must have given her a vague idea to go off of. Something beautiful if serviceable, able to be composed quickly. Ironically, if I had to picture some nameless woman walking down the aisle to meet this current iteration of Donatello Vanici, she wouldn't be wearing something so beautiful.

Her dress would sport bloodstains and tears within the pretty lace. Her hair would stream down her shoulders as she stalked to meet him.

Though it wouldn't have always unfolded quite like that. I'm sure Olivia wore a beautiful gown with a flowing veil, her beauty exquisitely showcased. She would resemble an angel on earth, paired with his image of the devil.

Of course, Fabio must have imagined something much of the same, but the fabric I feel drawn to is of a richer hue. Scarlet. Black. I finger a bolt of crimson fabric and picture a dress garish in design that wouldn't quite fit within Fabio's careful planning.

Or Donatello's pitying game of self-destruction.

"Oh? Would you like to try a different color?" The seamstress returns, carting a rack of even more pristine fabrics. "That choice would be unconventional," she adds, coming to stand beside me, "but it's a lovely hue."

Sometimes I feel at a loss as to how to make my desires known without a voice. This time all I do is nod and know my point has been made perfectly.

If this is to be a costume, then why not make it fit my vision?

Not Fabio's, or Donatello's, or anyone else's.

25

EVGENI

The old Winthorp estate remains on the outskirts of Hell's Gambit, a sprawling hellscape of crumbling architecture and overgrown weeds. But all isn't quite as it appears—though someone has definitely gone out of their way to make it seem unremarkable.

"I had a reconnaissance team give me some background on this property," I tell the woman beside me.

I've commandeered another unmarked van from the Stepanov arsenal. Parked on a ridge overlooking the estate's west end, we have a partial view of the charred husk that once was the grand Winthorp mansion.

"Your sister inherited the property initially, but later donated it to the city. Since then, it's fallen into disrepair and quietly passed hands through a few different entities, eventually winding up in the possession of an organization that at first seems dedicated to preserving the city's unique architecture. In reality, it doesn't exist. It must be a shell company used by this brother of yours to cover his tracks."

"Clever," Briar says softly. A hint of genuine admiration taints her voice, displacing some of the usual haughtiness. It might help that she's opted for a black shirt and jeans rather than a prim ensemble, and her hair—save for a curl pinned behind her ear—is loose, draped over her shoulders like a cape. She could almost be mistaken for a normal woman and not a cunning disgraced heiress on the run.

"Very clever. I suppose you've gleaned more than that? A thorough soldier such as yourself."

I grunt in grudging acknowledgment and let the taunt slide. "It seems that, though no one has moved in to claim the property, the facilities remain powered with electricity and fresh water. A strange expense for an abandoned property."

"Very strange," she agrees with a laugh. "So, what now? We continue to gawk from the safety of this comfy vehicle?"

"The area could be booby trapped to alert its owner of any trespassers. We should be careful. Gather reconnaissance before making any definitive moves."

"You make it sound so serious."

She's smiling, and I'm more uneasy than if she were nervous.

"If you're aiming to reassure me that this isn't a trap, it isn't working the way you hope."

She pats my shoulder playfully. "I only aim to inspire utter confidence, soldier. I wouldn't dream of betraying you now." Her teeth gleam in the overcast daylight.

"Then prove it. If you believe they're here, and you know this place so well, then where? Where could they be hiding?"

"Nowhere on the upper floors," she says, inspecting the remnants of the once-grand estate.

I can easily picture her waltzing along these grounds in their heyday, her head thrown back, every bit of arrogance on display. Ironically, she seems much like the property—ravaged by the passages of time, clinging to her once-grand veneer, desperate to hold onto whatever glory remains.

"I bet the rain would have worn the roof away, and any repairs would have been noticed. No… The core of the house seems intact, but the safest bet would be in one of the underground passages. My father had a fondness for service tunnels. They made for an efficient way to move both servants and supplies throughout the estate as well as a convenient stash for enemies."

Her smile is wistful, as though the thought brings back warming childhood memories.

"My brother was particularly fond of those caverns," she says softly. "Always using them to squirrel away his toys."

"That doesn't sound like the typical playhouse," I say.

She blinks as if she forgot I was even here. "Oh, it wasn't. We had what might be deemed an unconventional childhood, though, isn't everyone's? Yours, for instance. I take it you didn't spend your time with puppies and playhouses."

"Not quite," I admit. "Now, where do these so-called catacombs begin and end?"

She uses her finger to trace a path from one end of the massive house to a few yards beyond it. "They were pretty expansive. Even after years of disuse, I'm sure they might still be secure enough to use as a temporary base, at least. There were a few entries, but I think the old service passage might be the most accessible. It has an entrance near the garden shed."

I inspect the dilapidated shack she gestures to with a nod of her head. It's on the furthest end of the property, and would definitely make for a fitting hideout.

"Useful to know. For now, we watch and wait. If anyone is here, they need to move at some point. After nightfall, we move in."

"We *wait*," she echoes nastily. "Knowing you personally, I find it hard to believe you're the same man whispered about in all those rumors."

"And I think you're exactly who I've heard you are."

"Oh?" If I didn't know any better, I'd assume she takes offense to that. "The truth is, you don't know a damn thing about me."

"Oh, I don't?"

"No," her voice deepens in a way that sets off an internal alarm. *Danger.* "Because you wouldn't have denied me if you did."

I lick my lips before replying, weighing the response on the tip of my tongue. An insult would serve to put her in her place. Instead, I toy with her, still eyeing her old family home. "And why wouldn't I?"

"Because…"

I hear her shift and whip around to face her, instantly on guard. Her hand is raised, but harmlessly lands over my chest. Slowly she bridges the gap between us, settling her weight onto my lap.

"What are you doing?" My voice lacks the anger it should have. Try as I might, I don't feel any, either. Almost amused, I watch her climb out of her seat, and I don't raise a hand to stop her.

She's surprisingly light, easily fitting in between my body and the steering wheel. Her scent lacks the hint of perfume I've become accustomed to. Instead, she smells…

Rich. Like shampoo and fresh air and a tinge of something I can't place.

"I'm bored," she declares, her sweet breath hitting me full in the face. "Can you think of a way to pass the time?"

I should push her off. Instead, I cock my head, meeting her gaze head-on. "Like what?"

"This."

Her hand hooks around my neck. A heartbeat later, her lips find mine, and I don't resist, letting her ease my mouth open with the tip of her tongue. It's as conflictingly sensual and unsettling as her last kiss.

Only this time, she uses her hands to aid her assault, running them through my hair. Down my chest. Lower.

I stiffen, hissing through my teeth as her fingers find the front of my pants, wrenching on the zipper. I grip one of her wrists. A refusal is on the tip of my tongue.

Only I never voice it.

She feels so damn good, and some selfish part of me can't deny that. As if sensing the lack of fight, she wrenches open the fly and eagerly slips her hand within the resulting gap.

In return, I snatch at her waist, feeling fabric give beneath my fingertips. Her own jeans are slightly too big on her, borrowed most likely. It's easy to tug the waistband from her hips.

But she's eager to assist, using her free hand to wrench them down.

Shit. An instinctive need to feel her takes over. The bare skin of her hips. Her thighs. Between them…

She wastes no time palming my cock in her fist, applying friction that has me hissing through clenched teeth.

Common sense can't break the lust that seems to come from nowhere. Though maybe I've been repressing it all along.

The need to kiss her recklessly. Wildly. Bite.

I can't think. I can't seem to clear my head at all until I feel her warmth swallow me like a glove.

Fucking her isn't a beautiful, perfect moment of passion.

It's messy. Brutal. I have to arch my hips and bend her over the steering wheel, taking her in a senseless rhythm she somehow manages to match.

Together, we're selfish, each greedy for our own pleasure.

And yet, when my head rears back, throat cording around a groan, I hear her mewl in return.

Her nails dig into my lower back, my teeth cinching her lip.

We're both panting when it's over, the windows fogged, the skyline slightly darker. And even as she shimmies off my lap and back into her own seat…

I don't feel an ounce of regret.

Judging from her dazed, resigned expression, she doesn't either. Her hair is a mess, tousled and ragged. Sensing my gaze, she tiredly runs a hand along the blond curls.

Glinting in the space between us, I spy a small object that I grab, inspecting it warily—a gold hairpin that seems out of place given her modest ensemble, and yet a perfect encapsulation of who she is at her core. A walking contradiction.

"Here." I reach over without permission, returning the pin to a mass of curls.

Her lips twitch in a pale imitation of her usual grin. "Only a soldier would care about order and neatness at a time like this."

I don't argue with that assessment.

I just stare forward, eyeing the darkening sky while questioning what the hell I've just done.

O nly when the sun finally goes down do I leave the van and creep toward the ruined manor house.

Supposedly, she'll wait like a good girl until I give the all clear—and even if she doesn't, I have the only set of keys with me.

Still, I can't shake this itch bitching at my concentration, irritating me as I trek through overgrown weeds to the garden shed.

I can't tell if it's my intuition warning me that I've been played—it's a trap.

Or if simply....

Something's wrong.

As I finally reach the decrepit shack, one fact becomes clear, though. Given the amount of debris and rotten wood piled in the center of the building, no one could access the tunnel entrance, let alone form a hideout here.

That uneasy feeling blossoms into full-blown paranoia. Once again, I have to question if Briar Winthorp had another aim in mind for bringing me here.

Unsurprisingly, when I return to the van, she's gone.

26

DON

This isn't the first time I've gone toe to toe with the Saleris—but it feels different. Maybe because there isn't a woman on my arm, her quiet presence unmistakable? Either way, an uncomfortable tension fills the air as I mount the rounded stairs leading to the entrance of the mansion.

Formed of white marble and tasteless architecture, Mateo Saleri, and his brother-in-law Antonio had one thing in common—their lack of class. Still, I'm surprised I've made it this far unchallenged.

Apart from watching me with their weapons in view, his guards haven't stopped me, nor has Mateo himself appeared to put a bullet through my skull yet—which only means one thing.

He isn't caught off guard. The motherfucker's been anticipating this—expecting me.

So much for Fabio's grand plan of action, and yet the closer

I come to the heart of the estate, the easier it is to sense the prevailing unease lurking beneath the façade.

Something's off. Despite the show of force, the men lining the main driveway seem stretched thin—nowhere near the numbers Evgeni reported. It's as though only a fraction of them are actually here, leaving gaping holes in their coverage. In normal times, it wouldn't stick out, but now…

Where the hell are those extra reinforcements?

They don't seem to be inside the mansion, either. Instead, mingled among the Saleris' opulence are even fewer guards, all armed to the teeth and jumpy as hell.

"You have some damn nerve," Mateo declares as I enter the spacious room he's holding court from. It overlooks the back of the estate, where a bubbling fountain spits water from the mouth of two snarling lions. "To dangle my niece's life over my head. I didn't think you still had it in you."

I match his tone, ire for ire. "I didn't think you still had the capacity to give a damn about anything beyond money. People change, it seems. Or maybe your father's death has humbled you."

He flinches, tugging at the front of his suit jacket with a trembling hand. He's gone for a white suit today, and the color appears modest compared to his usual ensembles. It seems he's been preoccupied, too distracted to focus on his typical fashion.

"Where is Kisa?" he snaps. "You were brave to come here alone to make your demands. Though I have to wonder if you even have it in you."

"To sell her?" I counter coldly. "You've heard the rumors, Mateo. I've done it before."

"And what do you want?" he scoffs. "Money? Brave man to come here on your hands and knees alone."

"I'm no fool," I warn. "It may look like I'm alone, but I'm not. You can shoot me now and see what consequences lie in store. Though, I think you've already made a recent attempt on my life, haven't you?"

His eyes flit away from me as he continues to tug at his collar. So, he was behind the hit—but considering I'm still alive, his plans have changed. Why?

Rather than dwell on the unease, I incline my head and extend a hand. "Why don't we put our differences aside in the name of the greater good?"

He spits at my feet. "Enough talk. What is your price?"

"I desire a mere conversation. I'm looking to sell my harbor. Have you heard about that?"

He has. His eyes narrow into slits, betraying his interest. "You mean the ashes? I might accept it if you're giving it away for free."

"Not quite," I say with a cold smile. "It seems I've gotten many interested buyers. I can't imagine why."

Again, his mask slips. His nostrils flare, and he grips the armrests of his chair. *Bingo.*

"Double your offer, and you can have your niece safely returned," I say.

"Oh, but when will you find the time?" Mateo snarls. "Shouldn't you be busy with your wedding preparations?"

I fight to keep my expression blank. At least now I have confirmation that Fabio's trap drew his notice as intended.

"I'm never too busy for business, Mateo," I counter. "You should know that better than anyone."

"I'll tell you what I *do* know Vanici, I'm not in the mood for a visit after all." He stands, his gaze ice. "Get out."

He doesn't have to tell me twice. Aware of a pair of armed guards watching from the shadows, I turn on my heel and start to leave.

"My offer still stands, Mateo. But keep in mind that I plan on picking a buyer by tonight. Double your offer."

I don't know if I'm relieved to make it to my car unscathed or further unsettled. I've barely made it through the gates before I have Fabio on the other line.

"Watch your accounts. I think any minute, you should be getting a signal from Mateo Saleri's accountant. Hopefully, that can lead you to the puppet master pulling his strings."

"I can't believe you met with him alone," Fabio scolds. "You should have waited for the Stepanov guards for backup."

"I bought us an hour at least," I say. The truth is that being beholden to Mischa seems just as appealing as taking a Saleri bullet to the brain. Still, I appreciate that the man kept his word. "With *mafiya* reinforcements, we can stand a chance against whatever they're planning. But we need their headquarters."

"I'm on it," Fabio says. "This could be it, Donatello. If you're right, tomorrow could serve as a defining moment. They aim to catch you off guard as expected."

"Which explains why Mateo let me walk out of his home alive," I say dryly. "Is everything else in place?"

"Yes," Fabio says. "Let's hope this works."

"It has to," I counter. "There isn't any other option."

"Well, there is one," he points out. "You could always walk away from this mess entirely and sail off into the sunset as the world falls apart."

"Nice try." I choke out a laugh. "Maybe. If I wasn't still so damn sober."

"Make sure you stay that way. You need to be in the right state of mind for your wedding, after all. It is tomorrow."

I wince at the reminder. "Fake wedding."

"That doesn't mean that the overarching situation has changed. There are plenty of issues still waiting to be resolved after this. You know that."

"I do. But frankly, Fabio, I'm just trying to stay alive."

And forget the woman who haunts my every waking moment.

I arrive at the hotel before sundown. I've barely stepped from the elevator when someone comes to block my path. Instinctively, I reach for my weapon before I even register my "attacker's" face.

Recognition stops me from drawing my gun. "Luciano—"

"Is it true?" he demands, his hands in fists. His face red, his eyes cut to slits. These past few days, I've barely interacted with the ex-Salvatore soldier—let alone enough to enrage him. In fact, him sticking around as long as he has is more of a testament to his loyalty to the lone remaining Salvatore rather than to me.

"Is what true?" I say.

"That you used Kisa as your fucking bargaining chip? What the hell is wrong with you?"

"I used her name as my way in to speak with Mateo Saleri," I clarify, pushing past him. "She won't be going anywhere. Besides, even Mateo isn't stupid enough to believe that I seriously meant to trade. The bastard was stalling. He wants me alive to bait the wedding trap we've already set. I think he and his cohort believe to catch not only me, but the *mafiya* off guard."

Which means the bastard was entertaining a meeting with his own means in mind—a thought I push to the back of my mind for now.

"What are you planning for her, anyway?"

"And what are you planning for Kisa?" I toss back. "Considering that you're her biological father."

It's a suspicion I couldn't confirm.

Until now, when he blinks as if struck, his face reddening further. "You don't know what the hell you're talking about."

"You can't look at that child the way you do and not have a tie to her. A blind man could see the truth for what it is. Why deny that?" Anger I wasn't aware of leeches into my voice, raising it. "Instead, you let her live with that bastard Antonio. He's dead. You should be eager to claim her. If nothing else, then to keep her away from the fucking Saleris—"

"You mean like you?" he counters softly.

I feel my irritation deflate, replaced by guilt. "No. Not like me. Though to my credit, the people I've failed haven't been my child by blood."

"So, what if I am her father?" Lowering his voice, he casts a wary glance at the suite up ahead. "You think I can provide for her better than Tony? He was a twisted son of a bitch, but he could give her a life I never could."

"And now he's dead," I point out. "But you don't have to worry about Kisa when it comes to me. You have my word on that. Now, where is she?"

Her location isn't a mystery for long. As I continue down the hall, I'm assaulted by a wave of childish laughter that stops me dead in my tracks just outside of the door to the suite.

All I can do is push the door open wide enough to watch and listen.

"This is how you play," Kisa explains while sitting cross-legged on the floor.

Across from her is a figure only slightly larger. Before both is an array of glass marbles.

"Like this." Kisa flicks a larger marble with her thumb and forefinger, sending it colliding into a mass of smaller ones. "Then you try to knock out more from the circle—" She breaks off, her large blue eyes moving in my direction.

Shock is to be expected. Not the fear that sends her mouth slack and has her scrambling back.

Confused, Willow turns in my direction.

"It's okay." Luciano moves forward, crouching down beside her. "Let's go back to—"

"No. Don't," I say thickly. "Just… Just let her play."

A request that seems impossible. Wide with fear, her eyes remain glued to me; she doesn't move.

Not until Willow picks up the larger marble first, using it to knock out three more. Warily, Kisa returns to the circle, her eyes darting in my direction.

I don't know how long it takes before she begins to relax, laughing openly—but I can't describe what it feels like to hear that sound again. Laughter, infectious and childish.

The sound only drives home the last time I remember seeing Willow Stepanova as carefree—juxtaposed with the last time I saw her when that joy turned to fear.

And hate.

WILLOW

I creep into the empty room that's been designated as mine though I have yet to spend a single night in here. Even as I sit on the edge of the mattress, I doubt I'll be able to get much sleep. When the door opens a second later, I know for sure that I won't.

"We've been dancing around the issue," Donatello says, his voice low.

He doesn't bother to turn on the light. Instead, he blends into the shadows, moving to stand across from me, with his back to the wall.

The windows display a pristine view of the city, speckled with neon lighting. As loud as the colors are, Hell's Gambit itself seems to fall away, becoming more distant with every second we spend occupying this space, close enough to touch.

"After tomorrow… I need to know for sure," he says, and at first, I'm not sure what he's referring to.

Oh. Then it clicks.

"Please. If you are… If you aren't," he adds thickly. "I need to know either way."

It should be a scary prospect, finding out the truth. I think I've been avoiding it, refusing an exam even after what happened at the restaurant.

A part of me doesn't want to know, not really.

Mainly out of fear. Fear for what that answer means for my future, as well as his.

And fear that no matter what the answer might be…

He'll leave me either way.

"There is one other thing…"

I jump as his lips brush my ear. While I was lost in thought, he didn't leave. He's closer, stroking down the length of my arm before entwining my fingers with his—but that isn't all. Something firm slips in between my palm and his, shockingly familiar.

"You'll need this," he says before pulling away, leaving that object in my grasp. "Just in case."

I look down at the small blade, still sharp despite everything it's been through. My heart pangs as I run my finger over the cutting edge, recalling the last time I held it.

"Don't think about that," Donatello warns, intruding upon my thoughts once again. "It can keep you safe if I can't.

Focus on that. Here—" He lumbers into the hallway, returning seconds later with an object he must have taken from his room. It's slender, catching what little light penetrates the windows—a black tie.

Crouching, he reaches for my thigh, and I stiffen, biting my lip. He barely touches me, instead looping the tie just above my right knee, securing the blade there in a way that keeps the edge from my skin.

"Keep this on you from now on."

I nod, staring down as he looks up. From this angle, he looks different. Less ravaged and worn—but not like the man I remember, either. He is a stranger I must get used to with no prior preconceptions to rely on.

A man I have to trust entirely of my own accord.

For better or for worse.

It's surreal standing before this church again. At the back of my mind, I know that this occasion is little more than an elaborate scheme. An act in an overarching play.

And yet, I feel oddly at peace with this role as I approach the steps with my head held high, and a knife strapped to my thigh—ready and willing to face my opponent on even ground. He can't make the rules here. We both hold sway with a power to end this sham before it even begins and expose it for what it was all along. Just a sick, twisted lie.

I'm ready. I can sense everyone around me, but their expressions don't penetrate this iron wall I've built around myself. No one can touch me, and when I reach the mouth of the aisle, I feel invincible.

Until I see him standing near the altar, his back to me. His posture alone betrays the true purpose of this moment. Not a heartfelt ceremony, but a battle in which he's willing to sacrifice everything to win. When he inclines his head, it's with the swiftness of a soldier sensing the approach of an opponent.

And as he spins to face me fully, I stop short. My breath catches, and I sense my palms growing damp with sweat. The air feels thicker, and the looming walls and cavernous ceiling close in, threatening to crush me in their midst.

His eyes are the only anchor I have to latch onto. Their steady, steely gaze draws me forward when my steps start to falter. There is something in the daring tilt of his chin that issues a challenge I can't resist even now.

You're here—but do you trust me?

Alarm nips at my fragile reserve of composure. When I draw close to him, he brings his mouth inches from my ear.

"Change of plans," he says. "There's a detour we need to take first. Will you come with me?"

I don't even hesitate before nodding. Then I cut my gaze to the rest of the assembled audience for our sham wedding—just a few guards dressed in plain clothes. After all, it's meant to be a secret elopement.

"It will be quick. What Fabio doesn't know won't kill him," Donatello says. "He isn't here yet. Our nuptials aren't officially scheduled for a few more hours, at least. Besides, I think this might serve us better in the long run."

I eye him warily, but when he reaches for my hand, I take it.

"Trust me," Donatello warns as his destination comes into view.

Once he parks his car, that request seems easier said than done as my entire body goes cold. I shiver, feeling my teeth chatter, but the temperature of the outside air isn't the cause of this chill.

Just horrifying memories.

I'm in a skirt and a sweater while Donatello wears his suit. Ironically, our clothing serves as an unnerving callback to the very first time I came to this property.

I've never been able to forget it.

The gray structure looks unremarkable from the outside. More like a warehouse than the opulent lair of a human trafficker.

My mind goes back to that day, seven years ago, when Donatello dragged me here out of the blue, shortly after Olivia's death. Trust is the furthest thing from my mind. Though, I had plenty of it back then...

Along with hope and unwavering faith in the man beside me.

Why on earth would he bring me here now?

"Willow?"

I jump as he snatches my hand, gripping the fingers tight enough that I have no choice but to look at him. He holds my gaze with an intensity that takes my breath away.

"Trust me. I think it's time we both got answers, don't you?"

Answers? From Nikolai himself.

My stomach turns as I eye our combined fingers. A few days ago, I would've run—before those nights in his bed and everything that's happened since. But now?

Finally, I let him guide me from the car toward the lone structure that somehow looks the same now as it did all those years ago.

The only difference is that the old man isn't waiting for us at the front of his compound.

Donatello has to knock on the front gates, loud enough that I'm sure he can be heard by anyone within a ten-mile radius.

"I know you can see me, you son of a bitch," he snarls, glaring in the direction of a square device affixed to the front of the barrier that must be a security camera. "Let us in."

"Donatello Vanici…" The voice comes from a speaker, laced with static. "To what do I owe this visit?"

Donatello eyes me sharply before hissing, "You *know* what."

Suddenly, the gates part, presumably operated by an unseen mechanism.

Still holding my hand, Donatello advances toward the main building.

But I sink inside myself with every step. The pain I feel strikes without warning. My eyes burn, and even as I try to blink back the threat of tears, they fall anyway.

He can see them, his jaw clenched.

I feel so damn pathetic, and a million insecurities swarm my mind at once. He's lying. For all I know, he intends to sell me again. I was a fool to trust him…

Far too soon, we enter through a tattered metal door that opens onto a darkened space with concrete flooring. A few cars are parked within white squares made of chalk, but the area is primarily empty.

The only potential link to what it actually contains is a lone elevator shaft that sputters open the second we approach.

There is only one level to press, and when the doors finally part—revealing the entryway of the underground den where Nikolai holds court—it's like a noose has been placed around my throat.

The smell worms into my lungs, conjuring a million terrifying images. I must stop short because suddenly Donatello is in front of me, smoothing his hands along my cheeks.

I flinch and start to shove him off, but he doesn't budge.

"Listen to me," he insists, his voice gruff. The dim lighting casts his face half in shadow, and he's a living embodiment of the creature Donatello Vanici is at his core—part darkness, part something else.

"I'm done hiding from the truth." His voice breaks. He means it. "We can face it together, whatever the hell it reveals—"

"Touching." The voice comes from behind him where a man stands, clapping sardonically. I feel my eyes widen, taken aback by how different he is to the figure from my nightmares.

This man sports a brown robe, left open to reveal the gray shirt and jeans he's wearing beneath it. He seems to favor one leg, and an ornate walking stick propped against the wall behind him takes on greater significance.

All in all, seven years haven't been kind to Nikolai or his business, it seems. The once rich burgundy wallpaper is faded, torn in places, and the emerald carpet has seen better days. And yet, the man carries himself with all of the cold, ruthless indifference I remember.

"Donatello Vanici," he says in a thickly accented voice. "To what do I owe this visit? Though, you're a little too late to the party—" He points to his left eye where a mottled patch of skin alludes to what once would have been a gruesome bruise. "I've already divulged the sad tale to someone else."

"Mischa Stepanov?" Donatello asks.

Nikolai laughs, but it's a brutal arrangement of syllables. "Who else? And I hate to cut this little reunion short, but I'm on a time crunch, and you aren't invited."

"Then repeat your little story and be quick about it," Donatello demands. "What do you remember about the time I came to you, seven years ago?"

"Ah. I was wondering when you would darken my doorstep again." Nikolai hobbles to his cane and begins to pace, slamming the wooden device against the floor in an eerie staccato. "Of course, I remember it," he says with a low chuckle. "It's rare for a man to deposit just one piece of merchandise with me and nothing else."

"If you don't want another black eye, I suggest you watch your words," Donatello snarls, taking a step.

"Of course." Nikolai waves him off with a dismissive swipe of his free hand. "Perhaps I should have kept that one." He turns his gaze to me. "She grew up pretty enough. Could have fetched far more than what I sold her for—"

"What do you remember about that day?" Donatello demands.

"You came to me with a girl and asked for a price," Nikolai says with a chilling smile. "That's it. No sordid backstory. No theatrics. Just a simple transaction between two men—"

"No." Donatello takes another menacing step forward, his fingers curling into a fist. "There must be more than that."

"I never said there wasn't, did I? You overlook one detail. A transaction between two men. I never said the other man was you, did I?"

"What?" Donatello staggers as if struck. "But I… I had to negotiate a price," he points out. "What the fuck does that even mean?"

"You said a lot of shit when you came here," Nikolai counters, inspecting him with a graying eyebrow raised. "None of it mattered. Our terms were already decided. When you came to me, you brought the girl. Someone else, however, arranged the transaction. It's conceivable that you didn't understand the nature of my business model."

Donatello shakes his head, seemingly more confused than I am. "No, that doesn't make fucking sense—"

"Then I suggest you speak to your accomplice. I've kept his secret for too damn long, even to my own detriment." Once again, he gestures to his face. "But a deal is a deal. Tell your friend our bargain is null and void from here on out. Now I hate to cut this conversation short…"

A man I didn't notice before steps forward, a gun brandished on his hip.

Donatello doesn't move. I'm sure he'll rage. Demand more answers. Attack these men as he has so many times before.

Instead, he inclines his head to me and offers his hand. "Let's go."

I don't even recognize the sound of his voice. Still, I follow him out, shaken as the daylight erases the darkness and stench of Nikolai's den.

When we return to the car, Donatello sighs. "He's lying. What the hell did he mean? I don't…"

He breaks off.

"Fabio."

At first, I assume the man must be calling him. Then his expression falls, and it hits me.

Nikolai meant that Donatello didn't arrange the transaction but that another man did.

Someone cunning enough to forge such a connection and yet smart enough to keep his hands clean.

I don't believe it at first. I'm wrong. It can't be him.

But the more I turn the concept over in my mind, the more only one name seems to fit.

Fabio.

EVGENI

$\mathcal{V}$anici's accountant isn't much in person, but he's smart. When he staggers into Mischa's study toting a stack of documents, he pauses to spit out a single location.

"I've scoured Saleri's accounts and any connected to them. There is only one place they could be," he says to preface the revelation. "Where else but hiding in plain sight?"

And I feel like a fucking fool. While Mischa heads to confront Mateo Saleri, I take a smaller contingent of men to hopefully track down this puppet master once and for all.

His location isn't as much of a shock as it is a cruel, mocking twist of fate.

Winthorp manor.

The bastard was here all along—and I led Briar Winthorp straight to him.

When I approach the remains of Winthorp manor, this time in broad daylight, I'm convinced that Vanici's accountant was wrong after all. The place looks more than deserted. Cursed—a barren landscape of silence and decay.

On the other hand, it would make for the perfect hiding place.

"You go around the back," I tell one of the four men Mischa sent with me. "I'll go in alone."

It's a stupid move, but I can't get the woman's words out of my head. I'm sure she's been here all this time, laughing with her so-called brother, gleefully planning how to lead us into another trap.

Damn her.

Preferably, she's watching now, hidden in her secret lair, convinced I won't find her. Well, she thought wrong.

Anger clouds my vision, and I go in blind, heading straight toward the main house.

I don't obey any of the tactics I cautioned Briar Winthorp to. I go in loudly, heedless of any booby traps or hidden snipers.

When I make it to a rotting back door, coated in vines, I'm sure that either no one is here, or this clever mastermind forfeited any heightened security measures.

Or…

The bastard never expected to be found.

Gun drawn, I prowl a darkened hall that reeks of mildew, imagining how it must have once appeared. Pretentious. Grand.

Nothing like the home I grew up in.

And yet, Briar spoke almost fondly of this place and the caverns she claimed lurked beneath it.

They made for an efficient way to move both servants and supplies throughout the estate…

Assuming this is a servant's wing, there should be an entrance to the lower level from here. Sure enough—past what might have once been a kitchen—I find a series of steps leading down.

Common sense warns me to make a note of this route and return with backup.

Anger, however? It spitefully drives me forward, utilizing every skill this "soldier" possesses to remain silent in the darkness. A task that seems damn near impossible as every step echoes the second I reach the lowest level.

It's dank, the air thick. There seems to be no sign of anyone who might have traversed here in recent days, perhaps years.

Until I hear it…

The noise is faint at first, driving me further down a nearly-pitch black space. It's every bit as cavernous as Briar described—until I round a corner and spy a sliver of light piercing what should be utter darkness.

Cautiously, I adjust my grip on my weapon while grabbing my cell phone with my opposite hand. With the press of a button, I alert the rest of the men, along with my location.

Then I brace my back to the wall and shift my weight enough to peer around a round doorway.

It must have been a storeroom at one point, though now a makeshift dwelling.

But instead of Mateo Saleri or his elusive puppet master.

Or even Briar Winthorp…

The only figure I find is a boy with blond hair, his blue eyes fixed on a book open on the filthy concrete floor beneath him.

I don't know what shocks me more. The fact that he seems to be alone or that with one look, there isn't any doubt in my mind who he is.

His face solves that mystery instantly.

He looks just like his mother.

My shock lasts for a heartbeat before caution overrides it. According to Briar, this boy was the keystone of her so-called brother's master plan—manipulate the Saleris, and God knows who else, with the promise of the Winthorp fortune.

And yet, for someone seemingly so important to that scheme…

This boy is alone.

I strain my hearing for a sign of anyone else nearby and come up empty. Another glance at the room he's in doesn't reveal a guard, or criminal mastermind lording over him.

Fuck it. Warily, I pocket my weapon and round the doorway, both hands raised.

He looks up, his eyes widening. It's strange witnessing those familiar features display fear so openly in comparison to his mother.

I soften my voice in response, crouching on one knee. "Are you alone? Is anyone here with you?"

Viewing him up close, I'm sure there was at one point. He's clean and neatly dressed, his blond curls combed. Though, apart from the little cot behind him and a handful of toys, this room doesn't seem designed to hold anyone else. I assume whoever's been caring for him, does so on a schedule. It's clever.

No wonder my initial search here turned up so damn little.

I stand and inspect every inch of the space, hunting for a booby trap or security measure. It isn't long before I find one, crudely affixed to the wall above the boy's makeshift bed.

A camera.

"Would you like to leave?" I ask, turning to find the boy watching me. It takes more effort than I would have thought to speak gently, absence of the irritation his mother inspires.

He shakes his head. *Shit.*

I take a step toward him, but—time crunch or not—traumatizing a child isn't an appealing option. So, I improvise.

"Your mother," I say cautiously, watching the boy's eyes widen, his head cocked. "I know where she is. Would you like to see her?"

He doesn't speak, holding my gaze for what feels like an eternity. Finally…

He extends a tiny hand.

I take it, lifting him into my arms, and I retrace my steps back to the upper level of the house. My backup is already there waiting for me, but as I scan our surroundings, I'm again struck by how deserted the place seems.

And a paranoid suspicion growing in my gut blooms in full.

This was too easy.

Too damn easy.

"He went to a party."

The tiny voice seems to come from nowhere. Alarmed, I spin in a circle, scanning the property before realizing that the speaker is in my arms. One of his tiny hands clutches my collar, and he tugs at the material as if fascinated.

"A party?" I say softly. "Who is at a party?"

"The man," he replies without taking his focus from my jacket. "He said if someone came to tell them hi. And that…" He frowns as if struggling to remember his assigned lines.

"What?" I prod.

"Oh!" The boy looks up, meeting my gaze directly. "That he'll see you soon."

DON

We return to the church and find Fabio waiting near the front of the cathedral. Rather than confront him, guns blazing, I hang back.

Dread is an unexpected reaction, all things considered. I should be ready to rip the bastard apart—especially if he had a hand in what happened.

But Fabio is the same man who held me together when I reached my lowest. Anger isn't the only emotion coursing through me. It's something beyond betrayal, beyond petty hurt.

A few weeks ago, I would be driven to drink in a desperate bid to drown it out. Now? I embrace every agonizing second. Eyeing the woman beside me, I know it's only a fraction of what she must have felt all those years ago.

A wound so deep I can't imagine how it could ever heal.

"You should go change," I tell her hoarsely. "Let me handle him."

Whatever we wear to this sham wedding no longer matters —implying as much is merely a ploy to send her away.

Her knowing glance tells me she's aware of that. And yet, she leaves without resisting, and the gratitude I feel guts me. The grim truth is that my wanting to face Fabio alone isn't brave. It's cowardly.

I can't let her see me like this, accepting that the one man I've trusted with my life could have been the very person to destroy it. Even the pain in my shoulder can't compare, and I grit my teeth, squaring my jaw with determination.

"Fabio…" Finally, I step forward, drawing the man's attention.

He seeks me out instantly. "Don!"

Rather than scold me for leaving, he approaches me in a rush. "Change of plans," he blurts, his eyes wide with excitement. "Mischa and his men have surrounded Mateo Saleri. He'll be bringing him back to the estate. We should head there now—"

"What?" It's too much whiplash to handle—to go from knowing he might have brokered the sale of a child years ago, to our present dilemma.

"That's not all," Fabio continues, oblivious. "It seems Evgeni has a lead on our mystery puppet master… Are you okay, Donatello?"

I'm not.

Standing here, it all sinks in.

Selling a girl under my protection of my own accord would be one thing. Monstrous. Sick. Unforgivable.

But having someone else do my dirty work? I can't understand it.

And Fabio…

He never mentioned his role in that scheme. He didn't want to speak of Olivia, either. He even let me think Nico was mine all this fucking time.

Why?

My skull throbs with the pressure of those conflicting truths. Groaning, I rub my temples, and I miss the moment that draws everyone's notice to the front of the room.

"Oh," Fabio says simply. His tone is too soft to be alarm at an ambush.

"What?" When I turn as well, my mind goes blank.

Willow Stepanova took my suggestion to heart, changing into the gown I assume Fabio gave her to wear for this occasion.

Only this is no average wedding dress. She's wearing red, the furthest thing from a virginal sacrament, and I can't help the broken laugh that rips from my throat.

She's so damn beautiful it hurts to face her head-on. The rest of the world looks gray in comparison, and my overwhelmed brain can't help but come to another bittersweet conclusion.

This isn't anything like the day I married Olivia. More than that. This moment feels like an unofficial severing of my ties to that past. For us both.

Safiya is gone forever, and I have no choice but to acknowledge the woman standing in her place.

And I will protect her.

No matter what.

"They have him," Fabio says, appearing by my side. His stern frown shatters the nostalgia, and the present danger returns in full force.

Absently, I choke out, "Who?"

"*Him*," he insists. He's holding his cell phone, eyeing the screen in disbelief. "It seems our little scheme worked after all. They're at the manor. We should go now."

He still hasn't sensed anything wrong between us. Fuck it, let him linger in that ignorance for a while longer. Addressing the past can wait. For now, it's time to do what I failed to accomplish seven years ago.

Protect my family.

"Don?" Fabio prods. "Time is of the essence. We should tell Willow—"

"I'll see what she wants to do." I move before he has the chance to reply, approaching her ironically near the altar. I can't resist the impulse driving me to run my finger along the scarlet neckline of her makeshift gown. It's formed of delicate lace, shrouding the peaks of her breasts in a subtle nod to her newfound maturity.

"Clever," I say thickly.

All in all, I approve. White wouldn't suit her. Just this. An angry hue, reminiscent of rage. And passion.

And violence.

"We might have a lead on the puppet master," I say, meeting her gaze. "They're at the Stepanov Manor. You can come with me or not. It's your choice."

Something in her expression wavers. For a second, I'm sure I fucked up. Another misstep by saying the wrong thing. Then, her eyes dart to Fabio, and it dawns on me just what has her so affected.

I'm not the only one willing to put off the inevitable, it seems.

Slowly she shakes her head, and I have a suspicion that returning home now amid this chaos—and the potential revelation regarding Fabio—may be the last thing on her mind. Fair enough.

I'd leave too if I could, if only to parse through these thoughts together.

Instead, I come up with another plan. "You should return to the hotel," I suggest. "You can have time to think things over."

She nods, and I savor this rare victory.

Transitioning our relationship won't be easy, but now more than ever, it seems…

Possible.

That's all I can ask for.

*M*ischa is a twisted son of a bitch—but he is damn good when it comes to what he does best—strategize a virtual war.

His men found more than Mateo. It seems they discovered his puppet master with him, ready to pull his strings as they plotted an attack on the church. On *me*, when they thought to find me isolated.

The tactician in me can grudgingly admit that it was a clever scheme—take advantage of an apparent rift and pool their resources to snuff out who they see as a primary threat in the moment. Me. Presumably, afterward, they'd transition to taking out the *mafiya*.

As it turns out, the joke's on them.

They have him tied to a chair in the lowest level of the manor, and he's far from the smug figure I first met on the

Saleris' private yacht. His tan suit is speckled with fresh crimson liquid, blood trickles down the corner of his mouth, and his glasses sit askew on the bridge of his nose. Still, he grins, flitting his gaze from me, to Fabio, to Mischa, and finally Evgeni.

"The happy family," he says in that unnerving tone.

"Who are you?" Mischa demands. "What the hell do you want?"

"Recognition," Evgeni says, stepping forward. "He's a Winthorp bastard desperate for his daddy's acknowledgment from the grave."

"And you believed that witch?" The man turns his soulless gaze on Evgeni, his lips parted into a sly smile. "Lies."

"I thought so too," Evgeni admits while I struggle to keep up with the conversation.

Are they referring to the Briar woman?

"Thanks to her, I've found your only leverage."

"A boy was discovered in the Winthorp ruins," Mischa explains, cutting his eyes to me. "Presumably, he's the son of Briar Winthorp, which makes him an heir in the line of succession."

Which explains why Mischa's eldest son was targeted in the first place.

But what about me?

"So, you wanted a fortune," I say as my first guess while approaching the man, my hands empty at my sides. "Why attack me?"

An attempt on my life was made long before the shit with Mischa began, stemming from a sniper attack the night of Willow's debutant ball.

"You?" The man laughs brokenly, spraying blood down the front of his crisp shirt. When he smiles again, scarlet liquid coats the front of his teeth. "Only a fool would rely on one bit of leverage. You asked what I wanted? I want the city, of course. All of it. And you will hand it to me on a silver platter. That is…" His lifeless eyes flit to Mischa. "If you want your daughter alive."

"She's at the hotel," I say, turning to Fabio. "Right?"

He inclines his head, reaching into his pocket. "I'll check with my contacts." He leaves the room as the man continues to chuckle.

Not even a minute later, Fabio rushes back inside. "She never made it to the hotel," he says, his eyes wide.

"No." Fear is a white-hot lance shooting through me—laced with poisonous suspicion. Fabio saw her leave. Could he have arranged to have her taken unnoticed?

I look at him, and my vision goes red.

But another man beats me to the punch—literally. In a blur of motion, Mischa lunges, a fist brandished, and the blond man doubles over, choking on presumably more blood.

Tied as he is, the entire chair rocks with the force of the blow, dangerously close to tipping over.

"Where is she, you son of a bitch?" Without even giving him the time to answer, Mischa rears back for another blow, but the bound man smirks, though his glasses now rest on the floor, feet away. In pieces.

"I have no idea what you're talking about—"

His words end in a spray of blood as Mischa's fist collides with his jaw. "Where the hell is my daughter?"

"Your daughter." The man's monotone voice turns every word into a joke. "Shouldn't you know the answer to that question?"

"You piece of shit—"

"You can waste time brutalizing me," the blond man says, still unnaturally calm. "But I'll warn you that there isn't much time before the city is treated to another explosive bit of redevelopment. You may find that your daughter could be caught in the blast, should you fail to reach her in time."

The threat lands with all the impact I'm sure the man expects—the room falls dead silent.

"Willow…" Mischa's jaw goes slack as horror threatens his stoic expression. "What the hell are you talking about? You son of a bitch—"

"Insults won't get us anywhere," Evgeni says, standing to block his employer's next move. "Where is she?"

"Might I suggest we get down to business?" the man says. Apart from his swollen bottom lip and reddening jaw, he seems unfazed. His expression could even be deemed a smile as his tongue traces his bloodied lips, cleaning them.

"You knew," I say, taking in his apparent calm. "You wanted us to find you."

And rather than aim to attack the church, he had his men waiting to take Willow instead. It's a level of intelligence I can't underestimate. In fact, the only man capable of rivaling it may be the figure standing beside me who disguised his own hand in a treacherous scheme for seven years.

"This was your plan all along," I say, meeting the man's stare directly. "What do you want?"

He makes an amused grunt in his throat. "I want control of the *mafiya* territory, of course. As well as the harbor office. Have your men stand down, make the necessary arrangements, and your daughter will be returned safe and sound. As a bonus, you can even have the traitorous little Winthorp whore, free of charge."

"You took her," Evgeni says with a harsh laugh.

"I am a fan of tying up loose ends," the bastard says, still smirking.

"What's stopping me from killing you?" Mischa demands. Judging from his stance, he seems more than eager to do just that.

I'm the last person in the world keen to stop him, but I approach him anyway. "Let's try and get him to talk," I suggest, flexing my fingers. "By any means—"

"There isn't time for torture," the man explains in that eerie monotone. "Kill me, and your daughter dies. I shouldn't have to state that so bluntly. If my associates do not hear from me by midnight, our discussion will be moot, regardless."

"A few hours is plenty of time to make you talk," Mischa says murderously.

"Wait." Fabio stands near the doorway, cell phone in hand. "There might be another way." He inclines his head, beckoning me into the hall.

I only hesitate a second before following him, aware of Mischa begrudgingly on my heels.

"He wants us to panic and fight," Fabio explains, his gaze still on his cell phone screen. "But I've decided to retrace his steps instead. He mentioned the explosion. My gut tells me I might know where he's keeping Willow."

I can't help the suspicion that rises within me, hardening my voice. "And you want us to trust you?"

Fabio blinks. "Have I ever given you a reason not to?"

I grit my teeth rather than answer that question, not that he seems to expect a response.

"If you can trust me, I think I can give us a rough location to search. The downside is there are several potential properties. If I lead you in the wrong direction, there might not be time to salvage that mistake."

"We don't have any other options," I admit. "Where?"

"A clever hiding spot, if correct," Fabio says with a hint of grudging admiration. "I probably would have picked a similar locale myself were I a psychopath."

"Which is?" Mischa interjects.

"The site of his last crime, of course," Fabio replies. "Now hurry. There isn't much time."

I don't need to be told twice.

"I'll drive," Evgeni calls from the doorway. He must have overheard the entire conversation because he surges into the hall, racing ahead of me.

"I'll see if I can get more information from him," Mischa says ominously. "You go."

Even with everything hanging in the balance, I hesitate. Trusting Fabio again could be the biggest fucking mistake of my life.

But I can't even think of what will happen if he's wrong.

He can't be.

WILLOW

The first coherent realization my mind can form is that I taste blood, and my head is throbbing.

But why? Pain sears through my head when I try to recall anything else. The last thing I remember is leaving the church…

Then nothing. I don't know where I am, or even how long I've been here.

One thing I am sure of is that I'm not alone. I can hear someone else's heavy breathing, along with a quiet, persistent ticking noise. A clock?

"I suggest you don't resist," a woman says dryly. Her voice comes from nearby, echoing throughout what must be a cavernous space. "I've tried. They've gotten smart and used a thicker rope. We'd need a knife to cut it."

What? I recognize her voice though my skull aches as I try to place it with a name. Someone like Ellen but colder, speaking with none of her gentle cadence. *Briar?*

I can't see if I'm right. My eyelids flutter, but it's pitch dark wherever we are. Not only that, but the air smells like rust and wet metal. Not the church, I suspect. Somewhere more confined.

"I assume we're underground," the woman says as if reading my mind. "And I'm sure you hear that infernal sound. What is that?"

A hint of fear taints her otherwise toneless speech.

"I suggest we find a way of getting free, first. Hello? Do you understand anything I've said? Though… That's right, you're the mute one, aren't you? Serves me right. Jonathan is quite the sadist. Even if I told you everything and you did escape, you wouldn't be able to tell anyone, would you?"

Irritation flares as that statement plays on a million different insecurities—the same ones Donatello aggravated before he finally acknowledged that I am not a child. I'm so sick of being underestimated. By him, and by this stranger—but I ignore her in favor of getting my bearings.

I'm seated upright with my hands bound behind me and my feet on a firm surface that must be the floor. My mouth is free, and I don't feel a blindfold shrouding my vision— which means the darkness is a side effect of wherever we are.

Underground, the woman said.

It's cold. I can hear the faint drip of running water, and the only place that comes to mind is a sewer system of some kind. Or perhaps the harbor. Could that be where we are?

"I won't sugar coat it," the woman continues with a heavy sigh. "Unless we can find some way of breaking these binds, we might both wind up dead."

She lamented not having a knife. But I do. I can still feel its weight against my right thigh, securely tied with a strip of silk—not that it does me any good with my hands bound. I test the binds, unnerved to find that Briar was right in her assessment. They're strong.

But if living with Donatello Vanici has taught me anything, it's that strength is relative. There is always a weak point. In this case, at least, my legs are free.

I kick out my heels against what feels like a solid, gritty floor. Whatever I'm tied to doesn't budge, however. It feels too firm, like a ledge, not a chair. Still, I can feel the mass on my thigh shift with the movement. When I lift my leg and slam it down, the knife slides just an inch.

"Are you stomping in morse code?" the woman asks. "Pay me no mind. Carry on."

I do, repeatedly slamming my heel against the floor until the tie begins to loosen. Looser…

Sweat drips down my neck with the effort, my knee burning with exertion. Then, finally, the blade falls free with a clatter.

Now to find a way to grab it.

I strain my binds again, finding them just as immovable as before. Then an idea strikes me. Force won't help.

It didn't serve me against Donatello. No…

Instead, I utilize patience, turning my focus to extracting just one wrist. Slowly I can feel the tension give way, tightening over my left wrist, but allowing just enough give for me to wrench on the right. Slowly. Slowly…

My shoulder screams with pain at the unnatural angle, but I keep going until finally, I tug my hand free.

My heart races as I lean forward and feel along what seems like damp concrete until my fingertips brush over a familiar leather handle. I grab it and contort myself to attack the ropes, still restricting my left hand.

They give way, and I stand, staggering to find my balance in the dark.

"What's happening?" the woman demands. "Are you freed?"

I follow the sound of her voice, feeling out until my fingers strike a warm, flesh-like surface.

"Is that you?" I feel the woman flinch out of my reach, only to cautiously place herself within my range again. "Help get me free!"

I brush over what I'm sure is her arm and work the blade through the mass of ropes coiled at her wrist.

"Finally!"

Clattering noises echo wildly, forming a deafening clatter. Footsteps? The woman's, I assume, because I suddenly feel warm breath on my shoulder.

"Now, to find a way out…"

Her disjointed footsteps continue, coming to an abrupt stop.

"There's something here," she says. "A box… Damn. I think this is where that noise is coming from."

Her fear is so visceral I feel a cold sweat instantly slick the back of my neck.

Tick. Tick. Tick. That soft metronome seems louder by the second. There aren't many objects I know of capable of making such a noise.

"This must be a bomb. Get back," Briar warns, and I sway as she slams into me in her rush to move. "I was partly joking before—" Her voice shakes. "But I might not have been wrong after all. If we can't get out of here, we're dead. We need to find an exit. Now! Try getting on your hands and knees so that you don't trip over any more explosives."

I obey the suggestion, wincing as my hands and bare knees come in contact with the ice-cold floor. It's slightly damp, and several potential explanations come to mind—none of them reassuring. Choking back the disgust, I move cautiously, feeling out for any nearby structures.

It isn't long before my arm brushes a solid, metallic area that rings hollow as I tap my knuckles against it. A pipe? It's several feet tall, and its contours feel familiar to the surface I woke up tethered to. Behind it, my fingers strike what feels like concrete. A wall?

Inching back, I discover a few yards of empty space before I finally contact another firm barrier.

"We're in a room of some kind," Briar remarks, sounding close by. "There are pipes, and—wait! I think this is a door. But... Damn! It's locked."

I hear a thud against a metallic surface, and I pivot, crawling toward it.

"It's made of bars... Like a jail cell door. I can't get it to budge. I think it's chained." She howls in frustration. "There is a padlock here on the outside. Can you feel that?"

I reach between the metal bars and immediately strike a bumpy mass of what could be chains. They must be looped around the outside of the door, secured by the padlock. Sure enough, I strain my wrist further through the bars and brush against a dangling, round object.

"We need to find a way to open it," Briar says. "Give me your knife."

Warm fingers swipe blindly at my forearm, but I hesitate, gripping the handle of the knife tighter. I've been clutching it all this time, and relinquishing it to a woman I barely know isn't appealing.

"Come on," she snaps. "We have to try something. Or would you prefer to blow up?"

Sure enough, that quiet, steady ticking noise relentlessly counts down the seconds.

"Please."

Finally, I hand the blade over, but a second later, the woman scoffs and shoves it toward me. "It's too big. I need something smaller. Damn. Do you have a hairpin? No… I think I have something," she says. "Thank God for macho soldiers."

Rather than explain, she falls silent, and the ever-present sound fills the void, as if counting the seconds down.

Tick.

Tick.

"Fuck, this is harder than it looks," Briar hisses.

Tick.

"Damn it!"

Impatient, I reach out until I find her shoulder.

"What?" she snaps. "You want to try? Wait… Here—" she shifts, urging me closer. "See if you can help me. Hold it steady."

I don't follow the logic, but I let her snatch a lock of my hair and use it to guide me closer to the bars. They feel ice-cold, with barely enough space to fit a hand between them. The lock faces away from us, making it hard to reach easily. I manage to grip its scratchy, presumably rusted, surface as the woman once again attempts to open it.

"Come on… Come on!"

Tick.

Tick.

"Shit. I… I think I've got it!"

Suddenly, the lock gives way, and I paw at the chains, freeing them. When we push on the bars, the door itself easily gives way with an eerie creak.

"I think this might be a way out," the woman says as we enter a passageway and feel a wave of fresh air rush past, displacing some of the suffocating stillness. "We don't have a choice but to try. Let's go," she says, feeling for my hand. "Who knows how long we have?"

31

DON

Fabio managed to pinpoint one location, though it doesn't look promising when we arrive.

As he stated, it's a spot near where the initial explosion rocketed through the city, but there's nothing in view, certainly not somewhere large enough to hold two women.

"This can't be it," I say to Evgeni. "Fuck, we need to check the next property—"

"Wait. Look!"

He points to a spot in the distance that seems little more than a shifting bit of debris strewn over the earth.

Until a human-shaped figure crawls from beneath them.

I don't think before taking off, reaching the area in an instant.

By the time I reach them, it's clearer to make out the shape of a woman's body, small and lithe. Someone else scrambles from the wreckage behind her, her face streaked with grime.

"I suggest we get out of here," she says in between pants. "There's a bomb down there. We need to go! Now!"

I grab the woman nearest me while Evgeni rushes forward to take the other.

Then we run blindly for the car. As the quiet murmur of the city hums in the background, our frantic scramble toward the van must appear comical to anyone watching.

Until a monstrous sound rattles the silence. It's like something slams into my back, pushing me forward. Only by sheer force of will do I remain on my feet, steadying Willow against me.

When we finally reach the vehicle, it's a mad rush to climb inside while Evgeni takes the wheel.

"We need to regroup," he shouts, slamming on the gas, propelling the vehicle into reverse before quickly changing direction. "Here—" he tosses a cell phone onto my lap. "Call Mischa."

I reluctantly dial the number he rattles off, unsurprised as a gruff voice answers.

"You found them?"

"Yes," I reply. "But barely. Apparently, he wasn't kidding about an explosion."

"I haven't gotten much out of him," Mischa admits coldly. "But what I have learned, I'll relay when you bring my daughter home."

I don't argue. Given that Evgeni has the wheel, I couldn't change our course if I wanted to. Still, I put all thoughts of Mischa and anyone else from my mind and turn to the only person who matters in this moment.

She's beside me, her hair matted and streaked with mud. A foul smell clings to her, emanating from the muck coating her extremities.

I grab one hand, scanning the rest of her pale limbs for any hint of an injury. "Are you alright?"

She meets my gaze and nods, but one look at her face contradicts that assurance.

"You're hurt." I swipe at a cut on her forehead with the pad of my thumb. It's bleeding, though it isn't deep. Thank God.

Still, when she doesn't flinch at the contact, I use the pretext of searching for more injuries to touch her, feeling along that delicate jawline.

A wave of guilt washes over me, rousing a dread I can't shake. How the hell can I expect to protect her, let alone anyone else? She'll never be safe with me.

I've barely let the thought fester when I feel a faint touch ghost across my cheek as if to argue against that thought.

Confused, I look down at the pale fingers pressing there, and I sigh.

"You're safe now," I say thickly, capturing her hand in one of mine. "You're safe."

If I go the rest of my life without seeing the inside of Stepanov Manor again, it will be too soon. This time, though, Mischa isn't the figure waiting to greet me.

I turn back to Willow, willing to stave off the inevitable for a little while longer. My fingers are still in her hair, smoothing the strands from her face.

Fabio can wait. As we exit the van, I pull her against me, tempted to return to the hotel and avoid facing Mischa as well.

But if I'm reluctant to have this conversation, so is she. I can see the confusion in her eyes as her gaze flits in Fabio's direction.

Unwilling to be ignored, he takes the initiative to approach us, his hands clasped behind his back.

"Thank God, you're okay," he says with genuine relief. Once again, I'm reminded of just how unassuming he can seem.

Until he has a knife pointed at your back in a way you never saw coming. Deep down, am I truly surprised? His calculating nature was always an asset to Fabio, but I'm only starting to understand that I was always in his crosshairs. While he gleefully used his manipulation tactics to help advance my interests, he also used them on me all this fucking time.

To make sure I didn't remember. That I blamed myself and wallowed in pain so deep, I would have done anything to end it. Anything.

The sad part is I don't even know if I have the right to be angry with him. After all, I made his job ten times easier by running from the truth myself.

"They should go to the hospital," Evgeni says, coming up behind me, his arm slung around a woman. She's so alarmingly pale that, at first, I don't recognize her.

Then she eyes me, her chin haughtily in the air. "I didn't know you had it in you to be so civil, soldier," she says hoarsely. Despite the audible weakness in her voice, her mocking tone is unmistakable.

"I'll put a team together as an escort," Evgeni says.

By my side, I sense Willow stiffen, but he's right.

"I'll meet you there," I tell her, easing my arm from around her waist. "Then I'll tell you everything."

She wants to argue; I can see it in her eyes. For whatever reason, she doesn't, relenting to follow Evgeni back to the van.

As I watch her go, it hits me—she trusted me at my word.

"Is something wrong?" Fabio questions as I turn back to him.

There isn't a pretty way to broach this topic. Even his fancy words can't soften the blow.

"You knew," I tell him coldly.

He stops short, his eyes widen.

"About Olivia. About her affair—but it's more than that." I add, not caring who can hear as my voice echoes loudly. "You've always known from the fucking start."

He can't even face me. He turns, eyeing a ridge of trees in the distance. "Don…"

"You knew about Liv." I sound like a child, repeating it so tonelessly, but I can't seem to find a better way to put it. "You knew she was fucking Gino—"

"Of course, I knew," Fabio croaks as the color drains from his face. "I was the one she told when she was planning to leave you for him."

I flinch. A million different memories come flooding back. *Olivia…*

"Did you kill her?"

Rather than gloat, he groans. "How can you even ask that? Of course, I didn't kill my sister!"

"But you know what happened, don't you? I went to have a little chat with my old friend Nikolai—"

If possible, he turns even paler.

"Our friend, as it turns out—because you were the one who arranged the sale. Didn't you? Tell me!"

In all the time I've known Fabio Botelli, I've never seen him break. It's the only word to describe it. He visibly deflates, and only sheer force of will seems to keep him standing. "Yes," he rasps. "I'm the reason you sold Safiya. I arranged it. I had you take her there. I even named the price."

A pain I've never known claws through my chest, ripping apart whatever sliver of my heart remained intact after all these years. Amid the destruction, all I can croak is one word. "Why?"

"Because I hated you."

He lets that statement hang, as tears flood his eyes. "For what happened to Olivia. God, I hated you. For so long… I couldn't see past it. God, I hated you and anyone connected to you, who I held responsible. Even a child."

I've never heard him talk like this. Gone is the trademark calm and poise. His voice wavers, his cheeks wet with shed tears. The sight awakens a possibility I would have never considered until now. The Fabio I knew was incapable of violence. But this stranger?

"Did you kill her?" I ask again, curling my hands into fists. "Olivia. Did you kill her?"

"No," he croaks. "But I felt responsible anyway. So damn responsible. She was there that day because of *me*. I'm the one who told her to stay with you. To end that stupid affair for good and pray to God that you never discovered it. Olivia was a lovesick fool, but I knew you were a better option than that bastard Gino, who couldn't even love his firstborn. You would protect her. Or so I thought."

"Then who did?"

"I spent years trying to figure it out before I settled on the only logical answer. Gino Mangenello preyed on my sister. He never loved her. He used her as bait to lure you out. It's not poetic, but there it is."

"Why didn't you tell me?"

He shrugs. "That I hated you enough to use a child as a tool in my revenge? How could I face you and admit that? And looking back... You were a dead man walking. I believe you don't remember." His eyes glisten, and he sways, bracing his hand against the wall. "I could have told you to jump off a bridge, and you would have. I don't know when I realized that you weren't responsible. Maybe I always knew, deep down," he admits, looking down. "But it was too late. I learned that Safiya had already been sold, and I... How could I come clean about what I'd done? I tried to make amends in my own way, first through Vincenzo, by protecting him. I know he isn't my son through blood, but he might as well be. I did everything in my power to keep him safe, and even at your darkest moment, you did the same. That's when I realized... Don, it took me years to see that, but you have to believe me. You and Vincenzo, you are my family. You're all I have left."

"I don't have a choice," I croak. "You've been there for me when no one else was. But," I add, "I want you to tell Mischa the truth. And Willow."

He winces, but nods. "Of course, I will."

"And…" I draw in a ragged breath and force myself to meet his gaze. "If you were able to stand by my actions for nearly a decade, I should be able to return the favor."

Forgiveness won't be easy, but nothing in my life has been. Whether I like it or not, Fabio earned his place in my family.

And it's only with his help that I can salvage what little of it remains.

32

EVGENI

Willow's safety is my paramount concern. Once she's safely ensconced within a hospital room, however, by her side isn't where I find myself heading.

Ironically, my destination is the next private room down, where two figures sit on a narrow hospital bed. The smaller of the duo is asleep, his small body curled on his side, his head near his mother's lap.

I thought he would look like her. Blond with piercing blue eyes and cherub cheeks.

If anything, he's her in her truest form, untainted or jaded by the Winthorp legacy. His hair is a little more golden, his eyes slightly darker. When viewed together, she almost looks normal in comparison.

"Thank you." It hurts her to say those two words, but she does anyway. "Considering that I'm not in chains… I think you have something to do with that."

"Something," I say gruffly. "Your little friend won't be so lucky."

Though sympathy is the last thing I feel. Still, his fate will be fitting enough.

"Mischa hasn't killed him," I add. "But I've heard him mention the name of a prominent human trafficker, so who knows where he might end up."

"Is that a threat?" she asks, an eyebrow raised, but I shake my head.

The truth is that I believe the Stepanovs are too busy dealing with their changing reality to give a damn as to Briar Winthorp.

"I'm only here, to learn where you'll go now."

Not that it matters. She's just as dangerous as Mateo Saleri and anyone associated with him. A smart man would put her in chains, rather than risk letting her go.

But I doubt even captivity would hold her for long.

"Where?" She laughs, but the sound isn't as mocking as I expect. Paired with the wary glance she casts the room, I think it might even be a sign of genuine confusion. "Where is there to go?"

Her nose wrinkles, and she smooths her hand along the sleeping boy's head, seemingly out of instinct. "Ellen... I thought she'd gloat," she says with a scoff. "But no. Always the bleeding heart, she had to prove she's the better woman. The better sister. The better mother—"

"What did she say?"

She frowns. "She offered me the manor. My home… The Winthorp house." She clears her throat and shrugs. "A pity offering, of course."

"And yet, it's a place to go," I point out. "So stay, and stop running from your past. Face it and demand a future here. You're bold enough."

She purses her lips, withdrawing her hand from her son. "A future alone?"

I don't answer. Whatever happened between us should smartly be written off as a mistake, never to happen again. I know that.

But I don't leave, either.

33

WILLOW

*D*espite the ordeal at the harbor, I feel fine. Physically at least. If anything, I submit to an examination at the hospital if only to buy myself some privacy. A chance to breathe.

Instead, Mischa and Ellen arrived soon after, and I nearly had to force them to leave.

"We won't be far," Mischa warned, stroking his fingers through my hair. "We will always be here."

At his shoulder, Ellen flashed a worn smile. "Of course, we will. For now, we'll let you rest, but we'll be back soon. Perhaps with some of that jam, you like?"

I watch them go, feeling oddly relieved. And confused. After everything that's happened, no one could blame them for wanting to wash their hands of me for good.

The fact that they haven't sends a pang through my chest, and I'm more grateful to them both than ever.

Yet, even as they leave, one figure remains, lurking beyond the room until finally given clearance to enter.

"Are you alright?" he asks.

I know he must have gotten a report already from one of my doctors or a nurse, but still, he demands an answer from me.

I nod, but something pangs in my chest as if to contradict that.

I'm not okay.

The superficial bruises and scrapes barely register against another exam running in tandem.

Does he know the results of that test?

Looking at his face, I can't tell.

He chooses not to say as much, either way. Instead, he takes a seat near the window and faces me. "There is something you should know," he says grimly.

✦

A narrow hospital bathroom should be the last place I hope to seek refuge in. Still, I stand before a wide mirror and watch the woman starring back.

It terrifies me to realize that I don't recognize her. Not those dark, hollow eyes or the grime smeared over my skin.

It could be shock. Hearing the truth from Donatello doesn't provide the relief I thought it would. There is no closure to be found in the layers of conflicting emotions washing over me.

Fabio knew of Olivia's affair. He convinced her to stay, but she wound up dead regardless.

And, suspecting Donatello, he used me as a pawn in his revenge.

I should hate him—seethe in rage and fury. In all honesty, I think I feel more exhausted instead. After seven years, the truth doesn't tie up everything with a neat bow and a happy ending.

It's confusing and complicated.

Do I blame Fabio?

Yes. But even Donatello seemed to harbor some tiny semblance of forgiveness toward him. Could I find the space in my soul for the same?

Rather than come to a conclusion now, I spy a shower and eagerly strip my clothing, turning the water as hot as I can stand it. Methodically, I erase all traces of that underground prison, scrubbing until my skin is red in the aftermath.

When I emerge and face the mirror again, I wipe away a swath of steam and find a shadow of myself beneath it. The same Willow, just slightly older. It's unreal how much someone can change in just a few short weeks.

And depending on the results determined by a doctor, I may stand to undergo even more drastic changes. Am I even ready for that?

I look down, inspecting my stomach, running my fingers over the ridge of flesh. It feels the same it always has. I can't imagine the prospect of another life potentially growing beneath the pale flesh.

I don't know how long I stand here—long enough that most of the steam has dissipated, and someone feels driven to come find me. They knock first, easing the door open when I don't reply.

"Willow?" He breaks off with a sharp intake of air.

I'm still naked, freezing to the point my teeth chatter. When I look back, he's gone, only to return with a towel taken from the room. He comes up behind me, easing the material around my shoulders.

The picture we make is an odd one, I can admit that. He towers over me, and the artificial light enhances the shadows etched into his features, and the dark circles beneath his eyes. Somehow, I know without him having to say it out loud that he's learned the definitive answer to the question looming between us.

Still, he takes his time drying me off, securing the towel with a knot that rests against my collar bone. Then he grips the edge of the sink on either side of me, bringing his mouth to my ear.

"It would have been easier for you if that test was negative," Donatello says softly, and the pain in his voice… I don't deny for a second that it's genuine. "You could have moved on with your life without me. You still can."

He's as single-minded as ever, but it doesn't irritate me this time. He's right.

And I feel driven to respond to his unspoken question the only way I can.

My finger shakes as I raise it, finding one of the few remaining patches of steam. Slowly and carefully, I form a series of letters, every bit as jagged as the ones etched onto his chest.

As he reads over my shoulder, I feel my cheeks flame.

But he doesn't laugh. He eyes those words in a way that makes my heart ache. Suddenly, his weight feels heavier, as if he's using my body to stabilize his.

I could move on with my life, but hopefully, these words resonate within him more loudly than if I spoke them aloud.

I choose you.

At least this time, it's my choice. The truth is, I haven't had a life without him, not only because of the trauma he caused. I'm broken in that I've always mourned him in some way. Always.

But ignoring him or leaving won't change a damn thing.

This isn't about us anymore.

"Fine. You've made your choice," he says thickly, even as he stands to his full height. His breaths echo, unsteady and broken. Finally, I feel his hands palm my hips, barely touching. "I have no choice but to honor it. I'll be here. No more relying on Fabio. No more lying to Vin."

I still don't know if I can trust him, but therein lies the reality I have no choice but to face.

I can't rely on the past. I only have his present actions and words to go off of.

It won't be easy or perfect, but it's a future I can imagine, imperfect and beautiful.

EPILOGUE

DON

a baby changes nothing.

It shouldn't anyway. A new life can't heal two broken people on opposing ends. Such healing can only begin internally; the effort of so much fucking hard work, it seems impossible at times.

No way can there be a light at the end of this dark, winding tunnel.

But then you see it. A light that comes in the form of a smiling face, conveying such innocence it doesn't seem possible to exist.

It's a second chance.

This house, far from the shadow of Hell's Gambit, is merely a symbol of that fresh start. Or so I hope.

"You going to just stare, or are you going to help, old man?" someone remarks from behind me.

I feel my lips quirk into a grin as I turn to find Vin, a cardboard box in his arms. Looking at him, no one would guess that just over a year ago, he had a brush with death.

Of course, he wasn't surprised when he learned the truth—like his mother, he'd already discovered it for himself. He only needed to hear it from me.

And much like with Fab…

It seems that the ties that bind family go deeper than even an apparent betrayal.

As long as I promised from here on out—no more lies.

It's been strange watching him, and Willow connect again, in very different roles. At their core, they're the same as they've always been. And yet…

Vin's changed as much as she has, throwing himself into his studies. The rare times he pulls himself away is when I see a hint of his old self again. Carefree, he scampers up the front steps, nudging open the front door with his hip.

"Wait for me!" A blur of black and pink brushes past me, scampering after him.

"Don't go far, Kisa," Luciano warns, carrying a box of his own.

"Don't worry, Daddy! I'll be with Vin." Her cheerful tone marks a world of difference from the scared girl who used to cower at the sight of me.

Having her real father in her life might have helped in that aspect.

"You should watch that one," I feel compelled to say to Luciano. "In a few years, she may make a run at being my daughter-in-law."

"Funny," Luciano says without an ounce of humor. "Remind me why I decided to stick around your ass again?"

Because I'm rebuilding my own empire, but this time I'm making another crack at doing things on the straight and narrow. Mostly.

"For the pay, of course," I tell him.

With an amused grunt, he continues toward the house. "I'll expect a raise."

"Get a move on, Don," Vin calls back, sticking his head through the doorway. "Or we won't be done before you start sprouting more gray hairs."

"Laugh all you want," I call after him. "Once you graduate from that fancy doctor school, I'm sure your hair will be gray soon enough."

He doesn't reply, presumably deeper inside.

Only slightly larger, and made of brick, this cottage doesn't resemble Havienna in the slightest. There is none of the wild harm that old house held. This home is different, nestled on the outskirts of Stepanov Manor—as close as a compromise with Mischa that we could come to.

I still wake up every damn morning not believing that she married me—in that red dress with Mischa's grudging approval.

Months later, I'm still getting used to it.

And every day tests that part of my soul I swore couldn't care for anyone beyond a select few again. I once told Willow exactly that—I could never love her the way she deserves.

Maybe I still can't. She deserves far more than me, and always will.

But I can't deny that the battered, neglected shell of a heart in my chest beats stronger as I sense two figures come up beside me. One is slender, her blond hair loose, her youth more apparent than ever. In this instance, it's a strength, boding that she'll be more than able to keep up with the figure in her arms, nestled within a blanket.

If I imagined how our child would look, no image would come close to the reality.

A perfect creature with dark eyes and hair like spun gold.

She's every bit as beautiful as her mother, and I know in my soul I don't deserve them. My *tigre* and a little cub with an equally probing stare... Adelina, meaning royalty in our native tongue, a fitting name for a princess.

But I'll protect them both until the day I die. That, I can
promise.

AFTERWORD

You have finished Donatello and Willow's story. Do you want to see where it all began? Check out the War of Roses Trilogy!

XV: Fifteen: War of Roses Trilogy Book One

Kidnapped, Ellen must do whatever it takes to survive her cruel mafia captor, Mischa. Will he break her— or will she outsmart him?

WHEN HATE BECOMES OBSESSION...

Mistaken for her beautiful half-sister, Ellen Winthorp is taken captive by a madman who declares that she will be his "fifteen": the fifteenth victim of a vicious mafia blood feud. Armed with only her instincts, Ellen must resist her captor for as long as she can—which is easier said than done the more she's exposed to the complex man beneath the beast.

Because Mischa Stepanov isn't a mindless monster—he's a wolf, and she's the unwitting doe caught in his midst.

Unraveling the torment of his past may be her only hope of salvation...

Or the secrets uncovered may destroy them both.

CHAPTER 1 OF XV: WAR OF ROSES TRILOGY BOOK 1

Noise…
Chaos…
Briar…

The first thing I'm aware of is that I'm blindfolded—a fact that could be a blessing in disguise as my thoughts blur and jumble together. Only one coherent question escapes the fray: *Where am I?*

No answer comes to me immediately. My straining ears can make out only a few words muttered nearby in unfamiliar voices. Deep, *masculine* voices.

Various smells irritate my nostrils as well: sweat, body odor, male. *All* male. God, *where am I?*

I try flexing my shoulders only to wince. My hands are impossible to move, tied behind my back with something rough. Rope?

Oh, God.

Familiar terror gnaws at my belly as moisture gathers in my armpits and sweeps across my palms. At least, now, I have an inkling of my fate. I'm trapped in another one of his games. My nostrils flare with renewed purpose: seeking out *his* scent.

He must have hired lackeys this time; foreign body odor drowns out the stench of his cologne. I can't smell him.

But you can survive this. I fall back on the mantra that has gotten me through every day for sixteen years. *You can survive, Ellen. Focus, Ellen. Breathe, Ellen.*

Ten hours—that's how long I endured last time. My resolve had nearly splintered by the end. I'd almost given in. Almost.

But even psychological wounds eventually heal and leave tougher scar tissue behind. I can last another ten hours with Robert. My brain makes that distinction as the barrage of scents dissipates, revealing one that overpowers the rest: a man's. I taste the nuances in his stench rather than smell them—he's *that* potent, composed of a multitude of different things.

Cigar smoke.

Vodka.

One scent in particular makes my heart stop. Salty and sweet, it's almost as familiar as the flowery perfume wafting from my skin now. *Blood?*

Robert never smokes. He doesn't drink. Whenever he hurts me, he always washes his hands before and after. It is our routine, and he is nothing if not predictable.

No. This is someone new. Someone taller, whose shadow completely blots out what little detail plays across my blindfold. His footsteps are steady. Heavy.

"This her?"

I sense the outline of his fingers before the callused edge of one grazes my forehead.

"You made sure?"

His voice is deep. Almost *too* deep to be intelligible: a series of grated, rumbling notes. There's an accent tucked among them—something thick. Eastern European? Briar had a maid from there once. Sonja.

Sonja liked to read Jane Eyre. She liked scribbling love notes to Robert Sr.'s men before fucking them in the broom closet late at night when she thought no one was looking. Sonja liked a lot of things before Robert took a liking to her.

But another figure from my memory possessed this accent as well. Even though his words were hissed in a whisper, I still remember. *Breathe!*

"Bring her."

Those two words snap me back to the present. Unfamiliar hands grab my shoulders, cinching the soft silk of my blouse. *Briar's* blouse. She dressed me in it lovingly, remarking on how the color complemented my eyes. Our eyes, the same shade of light blue.

"Move!"

A tug on my shoulders hauls me upright and unseen hands shove me forward. Every sound echoes. Four footsteps, including mine. The biggest man takes the lead, I suspect, his gait rhythmic against creaking floorboards.

In contrast, the men holding me dig their nails into my skin and scurry toward an unknown destination. A rusty squeal seconds later conjures the image of an old door opening, and the footsteps trail off.

"Move!"

Something rams into my side and I stagger for balance until my cheek strikes a hard surface. It's warm. *Human.*

"Get her on the bed."

Those harsh hands return to my shoulders to fulfill the command.

"Sit her on the edge…like that. Cut her hands free."

A metallic hiss sends a shiver down my spine—then *pain!* Fire courses through my fingertips as circulation returns to them. I long to flex each one, but I know better. Instead, I keep them close, settling them onto my lap.

These men kept my skirt on, at least. Her skirt. The hem comes down past my knees, and I've never been so grateful for four inches of satin. It will buy me more time.

Ten hours. I've already lasted ten minutes. *You can do this,* the courageous part of my soul whispers. But then that voice dies in the wake of two more words uttered in that guttural cadence.

"Leave us."

The two smaller men scatter in the direction we entered—but it's all wrong. No. No. I don't smell Robert, and he'd never leave me alone with another man. Not his lackey. Not even his own father.

Most alarming of all, this man certainly is no Winthorp. His voice isn't familiar and this house doesn't smell like any property on the familial grounds.

They took me from the motorcade…

Fire sears through my skull as memories return in snatches. The clearest one is of her face. *Briar.* So beautiful, dominated by that pure, sweet smile. "I want you there," she insisted. "We're sisters, after all."

Sisters. I cherished how that word sounded in her soft cadence, tucking that moment inside myself like one of the trinkets hidden in my secret cache. Love was more precious than a button or rock I'd stolen away. Those four words meant everything. *I want you there.*

But the memory of that moment serves as a weak antidote to the terror paralyzing me now. More bits and pieces come back.

I was in the car—the beautiful limousine for once, instead of one of the servant vans that took up the rear. For part of the way, I was even sitting beside her while she braided my hair. "We look alike now," she wistfully remarked, beaming at our reflections in the polished windows.

We look alike. The phrase haunts me. As if I could ever look like Briar, with her lighter ringlets and her creamy skin. The only feature we truly share is our eyes. Our mother's eyes. Large, round, and blue. In every other respect, she takes after her father, with a beautiful aristocratic nose and a graceful neck. Every Winthorp possesses the same subtle characteristics—markings of the blood, they like to claim. Good blood. Blue blood.

I take after my father, whoever he is.

Briar loves to tout our tentative resemblance anyway—especially to her benefit. *I* am the one the maid saw sneaking out back two summers ago. *I* am the one who scurried out of the room of that visiting businessman one winter.

And now…

We look alike.

"Take off the blindfold." That voice…

I swallow hard, uneasy. Robert has found a new monster to play with. Someone who shares his flair for the dramatic. *But where is he?* My tormentor always relishes this part of the game. How he enjoys savoring my fear as I try to piece together where I am. Admittedly, it wasn't this hard before; he never strays too far from the property.

His favorite lairs are the boathouse, or the deserted crypt, or the east wing. I could always hear the bluebirds chirping throughout the grounds, no matter which corner of the estate he deemed my chosen cell.

My ears strain, searching for that faint, familiar song. This time of year, they're nearly deafening, able to be heard in even the farthest reaches of Winthorp Manor.

Two seconds. Three.

I hear nothing.

"Take off the blindfold."

The harsh rasp of syllables steals my breath away. I know anger on Robert. On Robert Sr. Even on Briar. They stutter. They shout. They scream.

None of them ever exude their impatience to the point where I can sense it in the air. Or taste it: copper on my tongue. This man isn't a Winthorp.

The realization coaxes my body into action. My sore fingers finally contort, trembling after what must have been hours of captivity. Whoever tied my blindfold snagged bits of my hair in the process and every tug on the knot at the base of my neck rips tiny strands loose from my scalp—comparable to my pathetic hopes being ripped from underneath me one by one.

I don't hear the bluebirds.

I can't smell Robert's favorite cologne.

When I finally get the knot loosened enough to uncover my eyes…

I see hell.

Mother used to say it was beautiful, forsaking the teachings of the local priest. "Hell is a rose," she used to murmur, her gaze turned inward, wistful and distant. "A flawless one, with all the life sucked out of it. The thorns have become knives. Its leaves have swallowed up the stalk. It's grotesque. It's deadly. But never forget that, underneath the violence, it's still beautiful."

He is beautiful. Or he was once. Blond hair draws my attention first—a sun-kissed gold in places, darkened with age in others. It's been clawed back from his face into a ponytail longer than mine was before Briar trimmed it. His eyes are that dangerous color between blood and brown. Like a flame, they catch the light filtering in through a sloppily boarded-up window beside him. His face is angular. Chiseled. Stone. Every feature is sculpted to convey just one emotion: determination. The way an owl might watch the mice scurrying underfoot in the stables. Or the way Robert used to look at me.

The way the devil looks, I presume, as if he has all the time in the world. More than ten hours.

An eternity to torture me.

~ Continue Reading XV ~

A WORD FROM THE AUTHOR

Hey there!

Thank you so much for reading! If you enjoyed the story, please leave a review and recommend the book to any friend you think would love this twisted world. You'd have my eternal gratitude. Even a short sentence goes a long way!

Then, come join the rest of us dark romance lovers in my Facebook Group where you can get snippets, sneak peeks of upcoming books and even help vote on aspects of future novels.

Come to the dark side:
https://www.facebook.com/groups/lanasbeautifulmonsters/

WANT MORE STUFF TO READ?
Join my newsletter and get a **free book**! Plus, you get to stay updated with any new releases, random giveaways and exclusive sneak peeks!
https://www.lanaskybooks.com/newsletter

Other Novels: https://lanaskybooks.com/

Lana Sky is a reclusive writer in the United States who spends most of her time daydreaming about complex male characters and parenting her Cockapoo Joey. She writes dark, twisted romance across several genres. Her titles include everything from mafia romance to vampires.

facebook.com/AuthorLanaSky

twitter.com/lanasky101

amazon.com/author/lanasky

pinterest.com/lanasky101

goodreads.com/lanasky

instagram.com/lanasky101

bookbub.com/authors/lana-sky

tiktok.com/@author_lana_sky

www.ingramcontent.com/pod-product-compliance
Lightning Source LLC
Chambersburg PA
CBHW060757210726

48292CB00013B/204